The TRUST

M.H. ECCLESTON

HEAD
ZEUS

An Aries Book

This paperback edition first published in the UK in 2022 by Head of Zeus Ltd,
part of Bloomsbury Publishing Plc

9 7 5 3 1 2 4 6 8

A CIP catalogue record for this book is available from the
British Library.

ISBN (PB): 9781803280363
ISBN (E): 9781803280349

Cover design © Ben Prior

Typeset by Siliconchips Services Ltd UK

Printed and bound in Great Britain by
CPI Group (UK) Ltd, Croydon CR0 4YY

Head of Zeus
First Floor East
5–8 Hardwick Street
London EC1R 4RG

WWW.HEADOFZEUS.COM

For Ellie, Charlie, Jake and Daisy.

I

Astrid turned the Mini into a wide avenue of beech trees and Sherborne Hall slid into view. It was a huge red-brick mansion – three storeys, a steep roof accessorised with turrets, battlements and rows of gargoyles. A bright copper lightning conductor winked at her through rambling ivy. The house was a Georgian fop – overdressed and ageing badly, but still trying to get attention.

As she pulled in alongside the wooden gatehouse, she realised she knew almost nothing about the English Trust. Their brown oak leaf road signs were all over the countryside – but up until now she'd never visited one of their properties. Her mother was a fan though. She'd once said, 'The English Trust represents all that's decent about England.' Before adding something about their 'spotless bathrooms'. Maybe she should keep that in the back pocket in case the interview stalled.

A man who looked like he'd been sewn into his tweed jacket eventually came out of the hut and pointed her towards the side of the house. Astrid crunched up the gravel path under the stony glare of the gargoyles until she came to a door marked 'staff'. Before she could knock, a young assistant swung the door open and introduced herself as Emily. Then took her to the head office at a pace that suggested they didn't want to be late.

Cressida Giles sat behind a broad mahogany desk. She was in her mid-forties, blonde hair cut perfectly straight just above her shoulders. A slash of magenta lipstick complemented her navy blue tailored suit. 'Soo...' She pushed her Alice band back on her high forehead and smiled broadly. 'Thanks so much for coming in, Astrid.'

'No problem.'

'Okay.' Cressida scanned the laptop screen in front of her. 'Let's print your CV out. See what you've been up to.'

A printer in the corner whirred into action. The printer and the laptop were the only modern things in the room. All the furniture was late Georgian, presumably borrowed from elsewhere in the house. Around the walls were a few old portraits in heavy frames. Nothing she could put an artist's name to, though.

Cressida went over to the printer and returned with two sheets of paper. She ran her nail down the CV, stopping now and then to study Astrid's face. 'Fine Art at Edinburgh... internship at the Brera in Milan.' She tilted her head to one side as if she could somehow check the facts by looking at her. 'Eight years as a conservator at the National Gallery.'

'It's all up to date,' said Astrid.

'Very impressive.' Cressida beamed. 'And we can check your references?'

Astrid remembered that Simon was still one of the references. 'Yes, of course.' They never checked references, right?

'Super-duper.' She pushed the CV to one side. 'So, let me

just run through some stats about our fabulous English Trust. You probably know them.'

'Yes, but I don't mind hearing them again.'

'Right then.' Cressida bounced to the edge of her seat. 'The Trust owns over five hundred stately homes, castles, monuments, stuff like that. It has nearly six million members. Over sixty-five thousand volunteers. That's a lot of people, but as I like saying…' Cressida knitted her fingers together and pretended to be unable to pull them apart. 'We are one big family.' She unclasped her hands and waggled a finger in the air. 'And I am just thrilled to have been given the job here as Head of Heritage Marketing.'

Astrid had never met someone with so much positive energy. It was hard to match. 'Well done,' she said, half raising her fist.

'So, Astrid…' Cressida fixed her with a stare. 'What's the most important thing about heritage marketing?'

'Um… heritage?'

'No, it's visitor numbers – footfall, as we say in the trade.' This was clearly the speech part of the interview and Cressida was going to enjoy it. 'As you know, the Trust is 125 years old.'

'Yup, I knew that.'

'And it's time for it to adapt – for *everyone*.' Cressida stressed the word 'everyone' as if Astrid should repeat it.

'Everyone,' said Astrid.

'Exactly. Head office want visitor numbers up at Sherborne Hall, and I'm going to deliver.' She stood up and pointed straight at Astrid. 'And here's how I'm going to do it, Astrid.'

There was a knock on the door and a woman dressed in

a Victorian cook's outfit bustled in. 'Sorry to interrupt,' she said cheerily.

'Oh, hi Denise.' Cressida sat down again.

'Just to let you know… An Italian gentleman on one of the tours was in the pantry and took a bite out of a wax kipper.'

'Oh, dear.' Cressida grimaced.

'He's fine now. I just wanted to let you know.'

'Well, thanks for keeping me in the loop.'

Denise retreated round the door.

'That's Denise, one of our volunteers. She's lovely. Anyway, where were we?'

'You're going to deliver visitor numbers.'

'Thank you, Astrid. Basically, we have to attract a wider demographic with more events and activities. Often, they're tie-ins with brands. And of course, not everyone's happy with that. You probably heard about the pushback for our Cadbury's Egg Hunt.'

'You know, I don't think I did.'

'Okay, well a lot of the members thought it was too commercial. Not what the Trust should be doing.' Cressida opened the top drawer in the desk and brought out a stack of letters. 'Here we go.' She started to read from a small magnolia note. '*My wife and I have now cancelled our membership after fifty-three years. If we wanted to visit a theme park we would have gone to Disney World.*'

She carried on to the next letter in the pile. 'This is more to the point: *The fiery coals of hell await those responsible. Yours sincerely. Reverend Lionel Armitage.*'

'I guess people don't like change.'

'Exactly, Astrid.' She tapped her temple. 'Blue-sky

thinking. It scares people.' She put the letters back in the drawer. 'Ah ha...' Out came a stiff shiny piece of paper. 'Here it is – the Trust's "core values". I'm supposed to read them to you. Are you ready?'

'Fire away.'

'Alright.' She cleared her throat. 'It's – inspire people. Love places. Thinking long term and...' She squinted at the sheet. 'Mmm... sorry, the laminator is running a bit hot. It's melted that bit. I think we've probably covered it though.' She tucked the fact sheet into the drawer and slammed it shut. The door creaked open and Denise poked her head round the frame.

'Sorry, I forgot to ask. Do you want me to fill out the usual incident forms?'

'If you would, Denise. Thanks.'

'And the offending kipper. What would you like me do with that?'

'I'll leave that decision to you.'

Denise's head ducked out of view.

Cressida rolled her shoulders back. 'When I came here three months ago I sent an email saying I had an "open door policy". Don't even knock – just come on in.'

'Well, that backfired.'

'I think it might have.'

Astrid shifted in her chair. She had been there nearly five minutes and there had been no mention of the job. 'So, Cressida, why exactly do you need an art conservator?'

'You know.' Cressida glanced at the door. 'Why don't we walk and talk?'

★

They took a side entrance that led out into a walled garden. A herringbone-brick path wound through triangular beds bordered by a low hedge of lavender. Neat rows of seedlings poked up from the soil. Hand-painted labels promised carrots, dwarf beans and parsnips. There wasn't a weed in sight.

As they walked, Cressida talked excitedly. The kitchen garden, she explained, was just a very small part of a 350-acre estate that had been in the Sherborne family since the mid-seventeenth century. Recently the current Lady Sherborne, widowed for two decades now, had reluctantly decided to downsize. She'd agreed to sell more than half of the hall to the Trust as long as she could continue living in the East Wing. The Trust had also struck a deal to buy a selection of paintings from the family collection.

Finally, as they cut through an archway in a yew hedge and out to the gardens, Astrid's role in all this became clear. The best dozen or so of these paintings were going to form the centrepiece for an exhibition called 'The Treasures of Sherborne Hall', which Cressida had every confidence would be one of the 'blockbusters' of the Trust calendar. They just needed a conservator to come in and get the paintings looking their best. A bit of cleaning to brighten them up. Astrid had barely said a word. Which was fine – her CV, according to Cressida, 'spoke for itself' and the job was hers if she wanted it.

'Wow, yes please,' she said extending her hand for an awkward fist bump. Not the sort of thing she usually did, but this was worth celebrating. She'd seen off the competition in twenty minutes. Or had nobody else applied?

'Fantastic,' said Cressida, rubbing her knuckles. 'Now,

I know it's Friday, but would you mind popping in and making a start tomorrow? I'm really keen to get the ball rolling.'

'Well, I have a basic conservator's kit with me so yes, that's fine.'

'Wonderful. And congratulations on the appointment.'

There was a screech of wheels on the gravel drive in front of the house. An old Land Rover ground to a halt, sending up a plume of dust. An elderly woman with a bright, floral headscarf was leaning out of the driver's window and shouting something at a mother. The woman quickly clapped her hands over the ears of the child by her side. The Land Rover roared off through the gravel, sending visitors jumping onto the verge.

'Who was that?' said Astrid.

'That,' said Cressida, 'was Lady Sherborne.'

'Interesting.' Astrid watched the Land Rover skid round the side of the house.

'Oh, there was one thing I forgot to ask you,' said Cressida. 'What's brought you all the way out here?'

Astrid paused. 'It's complicated.'

2

Wednesday, 48 hours earlier

Astrid stood at the floor-to-ceiling window of her apartment and admired the view. It was, as always, breath-taking. A low bank of cloud hung over the city. The Thames, muddy brown from a week of spring rain, swept out to the estuary in the east. Ribbons of cars and vans flowed over the bridges – a living landscape, framed in gunmetal grey aluminium. Like everything in the flat, the windows had been planned to the last detail. No corners had been cut. It had stretched their budget to the limit but, as she'd told Simon, they might as well make it perfect.

The decor had been inspired by a hotel suite in Milan – everything from the dark walnut floor to the Art Deco side tables. She'd added a few touches of her own. Like the geometric print cushions she'd seen in *Elle Decoration*, and the gilded starburst mirror she'd picked up in Portobello market. The only contribution Simon had made was a canvas he'd given her as a wedding present four years ago. It was plain white with all the milestones in their relationship in bold black print. *The Ivy* – their first date. *Cyprus* – their first week away. *Harry's Bar, Venice* – where he'd proposed. A bit tacky really, for him. But it reminded her of so many romantic times together, she'd grown to like it.

Her phone rang in her pocket, snapping her out of her daydream. It was a landline number – an area code she didn't recognise. She hit *'Decline call'* and slipped the phone back into her pocket. Who even used a landline these days?

She checked her watch. There were a bunch of work emails to deal with. A pile of letters in the hall to go through. But they could wait. Tonight was just for her. Simon wouldn't be back until tomorrow night and she had the whole evening planned out.

First, she'd have an hour on the exercise bike in the private gym. She'd probably have the place to herself. Most of the apartments were owned by foreign buyers who rarely visited. Her sister had once told her that, given the housing crisis, it was a disgrace. 'They're just glass and steel safety deposit boxes to these people.'

'Clare,' she'd replied, 'these apartments are works of art. That's what people are really buying.'

After the gym she'd grab an apple and kale recovery smoothie from the juice bar and take a shower down there. No point adding wear and tear to your own bathroom fittings. Then she'd order something to eat – a new South Korean street food restaurant round the corner was getting rave reviews. A bottle of Premier Cru Montrachet in the wine cooler was screaming to be opened.

But there was something she was looking forward to more than the gym. More than the food or wine. Her guilty secret. At 7.30 p.m., she'd turn on the TV, stretch out on the sofa and watch the latest episode of *Dogs Need Homes*. This was her favourite show, even though it was on the kind of channel she'd never admit watching. She'd already checked the listings. *'Tonight – Pam from Norfolk bonds with a pug called Toby over short walks and shortbread.'* She would love to have a dog, but Simon was allergic to them. Just thinking about them made him itch. So *DNH*, as fans of the show called it, was as close as she'd get.

She went to the bathroom to get a painkiller. She'd been getting mild headaches recently, which she'd put down to the air conditioning. It seemed to be running drier than usual. Francois at reception had promised to 'escalate' her complaint to building management, so she'd find out soon enough.

There was a fresh pack of Nurofen in the medicine cabinet. She prised out a tablet, filled a clean glass with water and sluiced it down. Then she studied herself in the mirror. She could do with a trim. Sharpen up her blonde bob. Other than that, she looked okay. A bit tired maybe? There was a short break to Cyprus coming up to celebrate their fourth anniversary. They'd been working too hard recently. A bit of sun would do them both good.

She walked back towards the door, the underfloor heating warming the soles of her feet. Then she stopped. Something had caught her eye – a shimmer of gold on the edge of the plughole. She stepped round the glass partition. Yes, there was something there. Standing directly above the plughole she could clearly make it out. It was a length of chain. She went back to the medicine cabinet, found a pair of tweezers and returned to the shower. Getting down on all fours, she pinched the end and carefully lifted it out. It was a bracelet. And it wasn't hers.

Astrid suddenly felt like she was going to throw up. She crouched on the marble tiles, fighting back the waves of nausea. After a few minutes she stood up again and waited for the room to stop spinning. Simon would never cheat on her. Would he? Not *her* Simon.

By the time she got to the kitchen the idea of him in the shower with another woman had begun to sink in. The more she tried to fight it, the more the images flooded her. A soaking embrace, the bracelet slipping from a trembling hand. No, there had to be an explanation. Four years of marriage. Why would he just throw that away?

She took the bracelet and laid it gently on the marble countertop. Her hands began to shake. She breathed in slowly through her nose. Exhaled quietly. It was something she'd learnt in her hot yoga class. Count down from ten. Release the negative energy.

When her hands stopped trembling, she went to the cupboard in the hall to get her old work case. It was made of black leather and was the size of a packing box. A bit scuffed here and there from years of toting it between jobs. She set it down on the desk and flipped open the brass clasps.

The upper part folded out to reveal two trays. They were filled with little glass bottles of solvents, varnishes and paints. Each had a small hand-written label stuck to the side. The main body of the case was divided into sections for cotton wool, disposable gloves, scalpels and other tools. She fished out a magnifying glass and hovered it over the bracelet. There was a stamp on the underside. It said 950 – which indicated it was 24 karats. Or so it claimed.

She reached into the case again and brought out a small matt black tile. Taking the bracelet, she rubbed the chain hard against the tile until a smear of gold twinkled on the surface. Next, she chose a solvent with $14kt$ written on the label and carefully poured out a few drops over the gold streak. Slowly, minute flecks of gold drifted up into the liquid – like a tiny snow globe. Right – the bracelet was less than 14 karats. She went through the same routine with a solution marked $10kt$. This time the liquid remained clear. The bracelet was gold then, somewhere between 10 and 14 karats. Cheap. A fraud. So, who did it belong to and when had they left it at the flat?

Astrid began to pack up her work case, her mind narrowing down the possible explanations, a sharp icicle of dread forming in her chest. Okay – it was now Wednesday. The last time she'd used the shower was when she missed the gym on Monday. She'd have definitely seen the bracelet if it had been there then.

The cleaners came in on Friday morning, so it couldn't be them. And they'd had no guests to stay at the flat since they moved in last year. She only had a couple of close friends and they lived in London.

Clare lived in Slough and never strayed inside the M25. Her mother wouldn't be seen dead in cheap jewellery, and her father was still holed up in his villa in Spain knocking back the cheap Rioja.

So that could only mean Simon had invited someone back to the flat. The icicle was growing. Her heart quickened.

He'd been away on business since Tuesday afternoon, so they – whoever they were – must have come over on Monday between 8 a.m. when she left the flat, and 6.30 p.m. when she got back from work. In that time, this person had taken a shower. And probably not on her own. Oh, God – had they been in her bed? More images, worse ones, crowded her mind. No, she had to do something. Stop thinking – do something. That's it. There was still a chance this would make sense.

She snapped the work case shut and began a thorough search of the apartment, starting with the kitchen. There was nothing she couldn't account for in the fridge. The dishwasher contained only three dirty wine glasses, which she knew she'd used. The Nespresso machine was spotless. Neither of them drank coffee. It had been a wedding gift they'd hung on to because it matched the black and chrome KitchenAid, which was also untouched.

In the bedroom she searched under the bed for discarded clothes. Nothing. Thankfully the sheets had been freshly cleaned and returned that morning by the laundry service – which spared her the indignity of having to closely inspect them. In the cupboard she went through the pockets of Simon's suits. Again, there was nothing suspicious. A sweep of the living room didn't turn up any clues.

There was nothing in the hall either, except a pile of unopened mail in the top drawer of the bureau. Simon liked to open all their mail himself, but he'd obviously not got round to it for a week or two. On the top of the stack was a postcard – a glossy picture of a sandy beach. Below were the words *Greetings from Spain*. It was from her father, just keeping her up to date with his 'news'. There had been problems with the roof of his villa. A trip to a 'local meerkat'. Market? It had to be.

There was something about her uncle Henry but she couldn't make it out. Her father's writing had become increasingly spidery, trailing off to a crescent stain of red wine. The rest of the mail appeared to be bills so she left them in the drawer.

As she pushed the sofa back against the wall and tidied the cushions, she realised the chance of finding any evidence had gone. But she knew enough. She would have to accept it now. He had cheated on her. The thought of him with another woman was unbearable. Revolting. As she collected a towel from the bathroom, she avoided looking at the shower. She slammed the door as she went to the bedroom to get her sports gear.

The gym was empty. She chose an exercise bike in the corner and dialled in the video setting to 'moderate hills'. After half an hour of hard pedalling, her anger had been joined by something else: disappointment. That was it. Bitter disappointment. He had let her down. This hadn't been part of their five-year plan, and it certainly wasn't part of their one-year plan. The question was – would she end it because of his affair?

Up until now they'd been happy. Blissfully happy. They loved the same things: art, food, travel. And they loved each other – they had done since the first night they'd met in a crowded bar in Bloomsbury, when he whispered in her ear that she was the most beautiful woman he'd ever seen. The life they had, this apartment, their careers – they'd worked so hard for everything. Together. He'd told her she belonged to him.

The video showed the track rising ahead of her. 'Come on, Astrid,' she muttered, churning the pedals harder.

One last push over the brow of the hill and she'd decided what she was going to do. She'd confront Simon when he got back tomorrow. He'd apologise, explain it was a moment of madness and beg her to forgive him. And this other woman, if she was still around, would be sent packing. Then, after their anniversary trip to Cyprus, they'd slowly get back to normal. This might be the wake-up call they needed. Alright, challenge accepted. This was going to make their marriage stronger than ever.

Clare would no doubt be shocked that she hadn't thrown Simon out. 'How could you forgive him? If I caught Warren in the shower with someone else…' But Clare didn't need to know. Nobody did. She might tell Gina, the only person she could ever confide in. That was it, though. The video screen froze – *34 minutes 15 seconds*, a new personal best.

At 7.30 p.m., on the dot, Astrid settled in to watch *Dogs Need Homes*. She huddled in the corner of the sofa, a wool throw pulled up to her chin. A large glass of wine in her hand. She didn't know if she had the emotional energy to get through the show. But why should Simon spoil it for her?

Five minutes before the end there was a montage of Pam and Toby's day together – Pam throwing a ball badly, Toby rolling down a sand dune. Then there was the big reveal.

Would Pam pick Toby as her Pet for Life? Astrid gripped the corner of the throw. Yes... Pam would do the right thing. She had to.

'Of course I will,' sighed Pam.

Toby barrelled towards his new owner, an expression of sheer joy across his sandy jowls. Pam scooped him up in her arms... and Astrid began to sob. Tears ran down her cheeks. Wine sloshed from her glass onto the sofa. A good five minutes of uncontrollable ugly crying.

The sofa cushion buzzed beside her. She wiped her eyes with the back of her hand. It was that landline number again. Definitely a sales call. 'Uggh... !' She threw the phone across the room, then stumbled to the kitchen to refill her glass.

3

Thursday, Day 2

Astrid usually took the tube to work. Waterloo Station was just round the corner, then it was two stops under the Thames to Charing Cross. This morning she decided to walk. She didn't feel like being underground today.

The people flowed in both directions over the footbridge. Two speeds. The commuters from Waterloo leant into the wind and pressed north. The tourists drifted aimlessly south. Below her, a sightseeing boat surged upstream. In the sky far to the east, a plane was coming in to land at London City Airport. A train rattled along the tracks beside the footbridge. Everything was moving. London was waking up. Stretching its muscles. This was what she needed today. To be lost among strangers and the hum of the city.

She carried on to Trafalgar Square, past the great bronze lions guarding the base of Nelson's Column. Ahead of her, the National Gallery loomed over the square. She weaved her way through knots of tourists and up the sandstone steps, relieved that her decision to stick with her marriage was as strong as the night before. Simon would be back this evening to explain himself. She was almost looking forward to his grovelling apology. Then they could get on with their life together. The gold bracelet was in her handbag. She'd stop on the footbridge on the way home and throw it into the river. It would be symbolic. A fresh start.

The Art Conservation Department looked like an upscale chemistry lab. It was well lit with bright white walls. A thick silver foil tube ran along the ceiling and split into fingers that hovered over five stainless steel tables. On a board on the far wall hung a range of tools from tiny screwdrivers to bolt cutters. And there were paintings everywhere, leaning against the walls or propped up on easels. Portraits, landscapes, still lifes, battle scenes. A nude coyly turning away from the window.

Astrid hung her coat on one of the pegs by the door. Seated at a desk in the corner was a young man staring at a computer. He had a mop of jet-black hair that bobbed to a tinny beat that leaked from his headphones. She was right next to him before he noticed her.

'Hey, Astrid.' He spun round in his chair and flipped off his headphones. 'How's it going?'

'All good… thanks Muraki.'

'Simon still away?'

Astrid was usually suspicious when colleagues asked about Simon. Being married to the head of conservation at the gallery made people distant. Or they tried too hard. They'd casually say, 'Oh, we must go for a drink.' Then add,

'And bring Simon if you like,' as if it was an afterthought. Muraki was too good at his job to care about networking.

'He's back this evening. Anyway…' She pointed at the computer screen. It was divided up by jagged bands of colour. 'Is that the Titian sample?'

'Yeah. That's it.'

Astrid studied the image. She took a pencil from the table and ran the point along a seam of white on the screen. 'You see that? There's no carbon underneath.'

'Amazing, isn't it?' said Muraki. 'No sketching – straight onto the canvas.'

'I know… genius.' She got up and turned to go.

'Hey,' Muraki called after her.

She turned back.

'I saw that actress you remind me of in a film last night.'

'Really? What's her name?'

'The thing is…' Muraki rocked back in his chair. 'I kinda fell asleep before the credits.'

'Seriously?'

'But you know her. She's really cool and gorgeous.'

'Is that right?'

'Like Grace Kelly.'

'Ooh, Grace Kelly.' She did a twirl. 'I can with live with that.'

'Yeah, but you're bit older.'

'A bit older? Muraki… you know Simon is doing your appraisal this month? It would just take one word from me and you'd be toast,' she said, trying to keep a straight face.

'Yeah, yeah. But I'm brilliant, right? So, I'm bulletproof, baby.' He giggled, then did a full spin of his chair.

'You know, Muraki, are you sure you didn't come here on some "bring your kid to work" scheme, and your parents forgot to pick you up?'

Muraki smirked, then swivelled back to his screen. 'See you later, loser.'

'See you later.'

Astrid spent the rest of the morning cleaning a self-portrait by William Dobson. Using cotton buds and solvents she slowly drew out the original colours. She imagined the artist standing there, studying himself in the mirror. Was he pleased with what he saw? Probably not – he'd hardly flattered himself. His hair was unruly. His nose was large and mottled, like the rest of his skin.

Tracing over each brushstroke she felt the quickness of his hands – his impatience to get the painting finished. But he'd spent a lot of time on his eyes. They were dark emerald – glossy from the tiniest brushstrokes. There was a pinhead detail of white that gave them the slightest twinkle.

Astrid loved days like this. Quiet days, when the only noise was the purr of the silver ducts drawing in air. She could lose herself in the work – slowly watch a painting come to life as if she had nothing to do with it. And today, it meant she could forget about Simon for a while. She wiped carefully around Dobson's left pupil with the cotton bud and his mood changed. He seemed to be smiling now even though she hadn't started on his mouth yet. She felt a flutter of joy. She'd made someone smile again after four hundred years.

★

At 12.20 she set the portrait aside and headed up to the National Gallery's private dining rooms on the third floor. She'd booked a table for two at 12.30 – lunch with Gina, and she couldn't wait. She hadn't seen her since she'd left the department to start work at a swanky art dealer's on the King's Road. The date had been in the diary for a couple of weeks, and it hadn't moved. With her other friends plans would usually be postponed. People were busy. Some of them, she suspected, would hang on until the last minute in case something better came along. Not Gina. She could rely on Gina.

At the entrance, the maître d', a slim man with dark gelled-back hair, was checking the reservations book. He heard Astrid's heels on the parquet floor and straightened up, like an otter who's just heard the clatter of a keeper's bucket.

'Ah, Astrid. How lovely to see you.' It was the kind of greeting you might get if you'd been missing at sea for weeks and all hope had been lost. 'Please… follow me.' He swept off ahead of her towards a table by the huge window that ran the length of the restaurant.

He drew back her chair. 'Will your husband be joining you?'

'Not today.'

'Excellent.' He reached out and picked up the wine glass opposite her.

'No, sorry.' She held up her hand. 'My friend will be coming along soon.'

'Of course.' He returned the glass. 'And what's her name?'

'Gina Russo.'

'Excellent. I'll get you some iced water and I'll send Ms Russo over when she arrives.'

'Thank you.'

Astrid pinched the top of a napkin, shook it open and flattened it out on her lap. She turned the knife and fork in the light – they were spotless. The wine glass too. She sank back in the leather chair and gazed out over Trafalgar Square.

In her mind she picked up Nelson's Column as if it were a chess piece and moved it through the streets. Back down Whitehall and past the thicket of spires of the Houses of Parliament. Then over Westminster Bridge, being careful to miss her own riverside development of course. Then off to South London, which fused with a layer of smog on the horizon.

'Astrid!'

'Gina!' Gina leant down to hug her before she could get up from her seat, smothering her with her woollen shawl. Astrid untangled herself. 'You made it.'

'Of course.' She eased herself round the edge of the table. The maître d' was already standing there, ready to slide her chair forwards. 'I'm so sorry I'm late. I couldn't get an Uber.' She sat down and brushed a tangle of hair from her face. Her hair was honey-coloured and curly. Apart from that, they looked remarkably similar. Same height: five foot six. Same light blue eyes and olive skin. People always mistook them for sisters, and Astrid never corrected them.

'Ladies. Some water?' The maître d' started filling their glasses from a pewter jug without waiting for an answer. He timed it perfectly so that a bundle of ice cubes and a single slice of lemon sluiced out into each glass. 'I'll be back to take your order when you're ready.'

'I might need a bit of time,' said Astrid.

'Of course.' The maître d' backed away.

'Yes.' Astrid leant forwards. 'Simon always orders for me.'

'Does he?' Gina shifted in her chair. 'That's sweet of him.'

'Isn't it. He knows exactly what I'll like. Anyway—' she reached out and gripped Gina's hands '—it's so good to see you.'

'You too.'

'Now, I want to hear all your news. How are things at the art dealer's?'

'It's awful. They're only interested in sales. They've got hold of this car boot sale Rembrandt and they've given me two weeks to restore it because they're short of cash.'

'A Rembrandt? And they're trusting you?'

'Yeah.' Gina giggled. 'There's some big buyer in Singapore who wants it now. So they're always leaning over my shoulder, asking me when I'll be finished.'

'You should quit. Come back to the gallery.'

'Don't worry, I can deal with them.'

They laughed, immediately falling back into the easy pattern of each other's company. 'Should we get a proper drink?' said Astrid.

'That's a terrible idea…'

'Let's do it then.'

'Cocktails?'

'Definitely.'

The maître d' returned with the water jug and topped up

their glasses. He waited to catch a gap in their conversation. 'Are you ready to order?'

'I suppose we should,' said Gina, picking up the menu. 'You ready, Astrid?'

'You know, I think I'm going to have something meaty. Simon has been insisting we go vegetarian to save the planet.'

'Really?'

'It's killing me. I could eat my shoes with the right sauce. Just make sure you don't tell him; he'd be mad at me.'

'I promise.'

The maître d' picked out three options from the menu, explaining in some detail how the chef would prepare them. Astrid chose the third, chicken Monte Carlo, which sounded creamy and indulgent.

'Wonderful choice,' he said, taking her menu. 'And if you have your member's card I can run up a tab.'

'Of course.' She brought her bag up to the table and started rummaging around – taking a few things out and putting them on the table. A small make-up bag. Her keys. The clear zip-lock bag with the bracelet from the shower.

Gina reached over and picked up the bag. 'Where did you get that?'

'Sorry?'

'It's my bracelet.'

4

Astrid sat on a bench by the lake in St James Park – still not sure how she'd got there. She remembered grabbing the bracelet back and getting up from the table. Had she said anything to Gina then? Other than mumbling something about needing to get some fresh air? Then she was in the corridor, back to the wall, hoping her legs wouldn't give way. As if a raging current was trying to pull her under.

She remembered stumbling through the gallery. Getting stuck behind a knot of schoolkids with the same blue backpacks. Then out into the sunshine.

She checked the time – it was almost two o'clock. There was no point in going back to the lab. But she couldn't sit here any longer, the same thoughts on repeat. Simon and Gina. Why did it have to be her? Her only real friend. She had only just processed the fact he'd been having an affair. She'd dealt with that, hadn't she? But this? This was unforgivable.

Astrid wiped her tears with her sleeve. After a minute she choked off her sobs. She couldn't cry any more. Not after last night. Simon and Gina… the tears came again. A couple glanced at her as they walked past. They gripped each other's hands and hurried on. As if her misery was contagious.

A man in a hi-visibility yellow vest was emptying a nearby bin. He stopped and stared at her. Great – she'd become a public sculpture. 'Jilted Woman in Park – Do Not Touch.'

Her phone buzzed in her bag. It was the same number as yesterday. She took a deep breath and composed herself, her finger hovering over *'Call accept'*. 'Alright then,' she growled. 'You asked for it.'

She pressed the button. 'Whatever you're selling, I'm not interested. Take me off your database and never call me again. Do you understand?'

There was a pause – then a man's voice. 'Sorry... am I speaking to Astrid Kisner?'

'Yes.'

'My name is Anthony Dutton from Dutton and Parker Solicitors. Did you receive the documents I posted to you?'

'Oh... sorry.' Astrid sat up. 'I haven't caught up with my mail. Can you tell me what this is about?'

There was another pause. 'Mrs Kisner. I think you probably need to read those documents straight away.'

Back at her flat, Astrid went over to the bureau and took out the stack of mail. The first two were bills she'd already paid online. She tore them in half and dropped them in the wastepaper basket. The next was the booking details for her trip to Cyprus, along with two airline tickets. Her anniversary. Four years. They hadn't even managed four years. She ripped the tickets up and stuffed them in with the bills.

The next piece of mail was clearly more important. The envelope was good quality paper, light cream with the address written by hand. A proper fountain pen too – the full stops were heavy dots.

She opened it up and checked the address bar in the top corner – *Dutton and Parker Solicitors. Poole. Dorset. DH14 8XG.*

Then she scanned the key details. It appeared that these solicitors had been trying to contact her for a while regarding her uncle Henry's death. She sighed, a barb of sadness piercing through the pain of Simon's betrayal. When she was a child, he'd been one of her favourite people. Her family had stayed with him in Dorset for a few summers. He was a landscape painter, and a good one. Over those holidays he taught her everything he knew. How to mix colours. Choose brushes. Capture a storm or sunrise on a canvas. Those summers painting with him in his garden were some of the happiest times of her life. He was the reason she was an art conservator now.

But he'd fallen out with her father for some reason and she never saw him again. Like most of her family's disputes, it was never explained. This must have been why her father had written the postcard. The news about Uncle Henry was hidden in the scribbles.

She sat down on the edge of the sofa and read the letter more thoroughly. It said that they'd also written to her last month and were now concerned about settling her uncle's estate. Could she please fill in the previous forms as soon as possible?

Sure enough, among the rest of the mail was another cream envelope. This letter made it crystal clear. She, *'Astrid Kisner (nee Astrid Swift)'*, was the sole benefactor in her uncle's will. After all taxes and fees were taken into consideration this amounted to his primary residence, *'Curlew's Rest, Hanbury, Dorset'*. Dutton and Parker would be her *'obedient servants in settling the probate and transferring the deeds'*. The letter was signed with a flourish by *A. Dutton*.

Nothing for Clare. Well, they'd never been close. But her father? That was strange. She read the final section again, to make sure. Yes, Uncle Henry had given her his house which, as she remembered from her childhood, was huge. It was a handsome stone building overlooking the river, five bedrooms at least. Not too far from London either. That would make it worth even more.

Astrid stuffed the papers into her handbag, her mind made up. Simon would be back in a few hours so she would have to leave for Dorset straight away. She'd take possession of the house and stay there until it was sold. Then she'd buy Simon out of his share of the apartment. They'd both sunk nearly all their life savings into the place and there was still a hefty joint mortgage. He couldn't afford it on his own, so he'd have to sell his share to her. Then she could come back to London and find a new job.

She felt a stab of guilt. Uncle Henry, a kind and brilliant man, had died, and all she could think about was her inheritance. But, she reasoned, today was not a normal day. This windfall meant that she had somewhere else to go now. There was no need to spend another night at the apartment. Tiptoeing around, thinking about what they did – and where. Scrubbing down the shower. Uncle Henry also had a wicked sense of humour. And this was pretty funny. A suitable revenge for a slimeball husband.

Astrid checked her watch. It was two-thirty. She tapped

the solicitors' number into the phone and wandered towards the bedroom, already working out which clothes she was going to take. The call clicked through.

'Hullo. Anthony Dutton.'

'Hi, it's Astrid Kisner. Look, I'm sorry I shouted at you before. You caught me at a bad time.'

'Don't worry about it, Mrs Kisner. Have you read your mail?'

'I have, yes. And if it's alright with you, could I come down and sort things out this afternoon?'

'This afternoon? Let me just check…' There was a muffled clunk of a drawer being opened. A rustle of papers. 'Yes, that will be fine. Pop down before five-thirty and we can get everything sorted out.'

She rang off and set up a new contact on her phone for 'A. Dutton – Henry's Solicitors'.

Then she pulled down her suitcase from the top of the wardrobe. It was the one she used for holidays longer than a weekend but shorter than a week. It had a hard black shell and small wheels at the corners. She packed quickly, rifling through the rails and drawers and putting together a dozen outfits. They included a couple of classy pieces – a grey Armani trouser suit and her favourite black Chloe midi dress. Too much? No. She was about to be the owner of a country house. She'd have to look the part.

Shoes – workday Mary Janes, Asics trainers, and a smart pair of court shoes for the evening. The rest included a mix of more relaxed work clothes. Tailored shirts, trousers and a couple of cashmere jumpers.

Finally, she reached to the back of the wardrobe and brought out a yellow paper bag. Inside was her latest forbidden purchase: a silk, pale blue Stella McCartney cocktail dress – half price in the Selfridges sale. Simon still wouldn't approve. Too 'revealing', something like that. So she'd bought the dress on her credit card. There was no way it could appear on the joint debit account.

The case was almost full. Just enough room for her laptop, charger and some other bits and pieces. Definitely her Chanel No. 5 eau de parfum. 'A good fragrance is a woman's secret weapon,' as her mother used to say.

She also took her work case from the kitchen. It was too precious to her to leave behind. In all, it took around fifteen minutes to get everything together. Nearly an hour knocked off her packing record.

In the living room she found a notepad from the bureau. Her pen hovered over the top sheet. Keep it simple, Astrid. Nothing hysterical.

'I hope it was worth it, Simon.' She paused. *'And you can take this as my resignation.'* She took the bracelet from her handbag and laid it next to the note. Then she put her wedding ring alongside it.

She swung her Mulberry handbag over her shoulder and surveyed the room. The next time she came back the place would be hers. All of it. The furnishings could be changed. The sofa, the rugs, the side tables, the canvas with the montage of their 'special places'. How sad that seemed. *Harry's Bar, Venice. Hyde Park Boating Lake. Amsterdam.* He could take Gina to all of them now.

She went to the bathroom, and for the next five minutes she very carefully cleaned the toilet with Simon's toothbrush.

5

The drive out of London was easier than she'd expected. She was on the road by three, and hitting clear motorways twenty minutes later. Now and then the satnav interrupted the *Afternoon Concert* on Radio 3 on the car stereo.

'Continue on the M3,' it commanded. 'Merge onto the M27…'

Not that these roads meant anything to her. This was the first time she'd driven this way since those childhood holidays. How strange that she was coming back decades later, single and unemployed. That was going to take a while to get used to. Being fabulously wealthy would help, though. She turned up the heating to twenty-two degrees and eased into the outside lane.

The office of Dutton and Parker was in a small town on the outskirts of Poole. It was above a Chinese restaurant in a parade of shops, half of which were closed down. Their windows were clouded up with a white removable paint, so you couldn't see inside. She pushed open the door and took the narrow flight of stairs up to the first floor.

A portly man appeared above the last step, eclipsing what little light was filtering down.

'Is that you, Mrs Kisner?'

'That's me.'

'Come on up,' he said, then disappeared into his office along a short landing.

She found him seated behind his desk. He took out a handkerchief from the pocket of his pinstripe jacket, dabbed at a bead of sweat at his temple and smiled – happy, it seemed, that he'd struck the right mood of lawyerly authority. 'Please…' He swept a hand in front of him. 'Take a seat.'

'Thank you.' Astrid settled into the swivel chair opposite him and glanced round the room. Everything had seen better days. The red carpet was threadbare around the doorway. The filing cabinets were scratched and dented. The only thing that looked new was a framed law diploma, which was directly over his bald head.

'Welcome to Dutton and Parker. I'm Anthony Dutton – the Dutton bit.'

'And where's the Parker bit?'

'There isn't one.' He laughed. 'Two names make it sound more important. Don't you think?'

'Well, you had me fooled.'

'Right.' He heaved himself out of the chair and went over to a shelf filled with identical box files. 'Here we go.' He prised a file out with a pink finger and put it down on the desk next to a handful of fortune cookies. He caught her staring at them.

'Do you want one?'

'No, I'm fine. Thanks.'

'Righty oh.' He took out a wad of papers from the file.

'I'm sorry to have been the one to tell you about your uncle's passing,' he said solemnly. 'Were there no other relatives who could have informed you?'

'My father might have.'

'Sorry?'

'He sent me a postcard that might have mentioned it. His writing is so bad it's hard to tell.'

'Got it.' He crushed a fortune cookie in the heel of his hand, picked out the folded paper and scrunched it up without reading it. Then he threw a couple of pieces into his mouth from an inch out. 'Anyhoo. It was a heart attack, apparently. Your uncle was out rambling and...' he snapped his fingers '...that was that.'

'Not too bad a way to go, then.'

'Indeed. A farmer found him in a field with a smile on his face. That's what I was told.'

'That's comforting, I guess.'

There was a sound of muffled shouting from downstairs, followed by the clacking of a ladle against a pan. He looked up at the clock on the wall. It was almost five-thirty. 'Do you have your passport with you?'

She reached into her bag for her passport and slalomed it around the fortune cookie crumbs. He opened the front page and examined the photo, glancing up at her a couple of times. 'Yes, that's definitely you.' He handed the passport back, then signed a few of the papers on the desk. When it was done, he slipped them into a transparent folder and slid them over. 'There you go. All done and dusted.'

'So how much do I owe you?'

'Nothing – your uncle set aside some money to pay for legal affairs.'

'Right. Well, I'll head off.'

She packed the folder into her handbag and got up. He followed her down the stairs and out into the street. A man came to the door of the Chinese restaurant and waved to him. Dutton gave him a little thumbs up and turned back to Astrid. 'Oh, there's one more thing then.' He pulled out a set of keys from his pocket. They were attached to a ball of cork about the size of a small apple. 'Your keys,' he said, dropping them into her palm. 'Now is there anything else I can help you with?'

'Actually, I'm going to be selling the place. Maybe you could handle the paperwork.'

'More than happy to.' He winked. 'Dutton and Parker at your service.'

'Just Dutton.'

'Mmm... yes. Very good.'

She watched him slowly wander into the restaurant. The sunlight angled over the tiles of the building and there was a warmth in the air that felt like it planned to stay. Astrid tossed the keys up in her palm. The house was hers. 'Thanks, Uncle Henry,' she said under her breath.

She checked the paperwork and typed 'Windmill Lane, Hanbury' into her phone. It quickly picked out a wide arc some way off the coast. Another clear run, first along B roads that cut through a number of small towns, then a dive back towards the sea down a narrow winding lane with high hedgerows that glittered with acid-green leaves. After a few miles the road opened out to a wide floodplain. Black and white cows as fat as bumblebees grazed between tussocks of grass.

It had taken her less than two hours to get here, not including the detour to the solicitor's.

That had to be a big selling point. Two hours from London. Perfect for a family looking for a weekend retreat in the country. Excellent local amenities. A scenic coastal setting. By the time she pulled up in the small car park at the end of the road, she'd practically written the estate agent bumf.

According to a wooden signpost, Windmill Lane carried on beyond a metal gate. It was locked. Fine. She could easily copy a key from a neighbour. For now, she just wanted to get into the house and have a bit of time to nose around before it got dark. She took her bag from the passenger seat, then went round to the boot and wrestled the suitcase out. Flipping up the handle she dragged it through a gap between the gate and the hedgerow. The lane ahead was rutted and muddy – impossible for anything but a four-wheel drive. Best keep that off the sales pitch.

The lane soon reached the river and followed it upstream. She carried on, the little wheels of the suitcase leaving a snaking tramline in the dirt. After a hundred yards the path opened out to a scruffy boatyard. There were a dozen old sailing boats propped up with wooden sleepers. Another handful on a concrete ramp that sloped gently into the water. Set back from the water's edge was a long shed with a rusty tin roof. The name *Archer and Sons* was painted on an old wooden rudder that hung over the double doors. A man was bent over a boat grinding a sander along its side, too engrossed in his work to notice her.

The lane stuck close to the river, which was lined with

chest-high bulrushes. Every so often there was a battered wooden jetty with a boat moored up against it. The going was even muddier now. At times puddles ran from one side of the path to the other so she had to pick up her suitcase and jump across.

Eventually the lane was barred by another gate. There was a thin bridleway on the other side and a signpost that said 'Hanbury 1/2 Mile'. She checked her phone – there was still no signal. A small cloud of midges had been following her since she left the car. She wafted them away and headed back to the boatyard.

The man was still working on the boat. He was wearing a pair of trousers with pockets on the outside and a navy blue jumper with holes at each elbow.

'Excuse me?'

He didn't look up, even though she was just behind him. She clapped her hands together. 'Excuse me.' He switched off the sander, which juddered to a halt.

He was about forty, with brown hair that was slightly wavy and bleached by the sun at the ends. His face was tanned, with a five-day stubble that had collected some sawdust at his chin. A thin silver chain hung over the neckline of his jumper. She grimaced. A chain on the *outside* of a jumper? How tacky.

He grinned back at her, the corner of his mouth catching up with a smear of grease on his cheek. Then he looked her up and down, and laughed so hard he started coughing. Astrid couldn't remember the last time a complete stranger had openly laughed at her. Maybe never.

'What's so funny?'

'Yeah, sorry.' He snapped out of it. Then he pointed at her shoes and burst into laughter again. 'Oh God... the shoes.'

Looking down, she realised that her brand-new white trainers were caked in mud. 'Oh, no.' She scraped a shoe against a tuft of long grass but it only smeared the mud higher up the side. Astrid felt the blood rush to her cheeks. 'Right so... um...' she spluttered, '*Curlew's Rest*. Do you know it?'

'Yeah.'

'Do you want to tell me where it is then?'

'Are you the new owner? We can't have any old person snooping around.'

Astrid brought out the keys on the cork ball and jangled them in front of him. 'Happy now?'

'Okay.' He took off his work gloves and set them down on the edge of the boat. His hands were large and rough. The thumbnail on his right hand was purple at the tip. 'It's right at the end of the lane.'

'No it's not.'

He smacked his lips. 'Umm... yes it is, love.'

'Love? What?' The midges were back. She swiped at the air in front of her.

'Four miles per hour.'

'Sorry?'

'If you walk more than four miles an hour then the midges can't catch up with you. Or stand still and see if they get bored with you.'

'How fascinating – thank you. Now, let me repeat myself – Curlew's Rest is not at the end of the lane.'

'You must have missed it.'

'Missed it?' The midges shimmered off towards the field. 'Interesting. Anyway… I didn't miss it because I'm not an idiot. Also, it's hard to miss a house.'

'You're quite observant, are you?'

'I am actually. In fact, not that it's any of your business, but I'm an art conservator, so I have a good eye for detail.'

'Amazing,' he drawled. 'Well… go on then.' He stood upright. Hands on hips as if he was in a police line-up. 'What would you say about me?'

'Alright, if you insist.' She drew in a long breath. 'You're clearly not doing well for yourself. You're probably the least intelligent of the Archer sons. The one who didn't have the brains to move away.'

He puffed out his chest and grinned. 'Anything else?'

'Yes, you drink at work to forget you're stuck in this backwater junkyard. That's why you hit your thumb with a hammer.'

'You're wrong.'

'Oh, am I?'

'Yeah… it was a spanner.' He laughed. 'Right. It's my turn.'

'Well, I suppose that's only fair.' Astrid squared up to him.

'You're one of those people who think they're so important they don't have to work on their personality… which sucks, by the way. You're so uptight you could win a contest crushing walnuts with your butt cheeks. Even the midges can't stand to be near you.' He pointed at her shoes. 'And you've never spent any time in the country. I mean, have you not heard of wellies?'

'That it?'

'No. You're rude – damn rude. Who claps their hands to get someone's attention? Might work in the kind of restaurants you go to, but not here, love.'

'Are you finished?' She was beginning to think she should have spent longer criticising him.

'One more thing then. You don't know anything about the properties of cork.'

'Cork?'

He reached out and took the keys from her hands. 'Cooork.' He swung the cork ball in front of her face, like he was trying to hypnotise a cat.

She grabbed the keys.

'What's the main property of cork then?' he said.

'It floats.'

'Exactly. So if you drop your keys overboard you can get them back.'

'Overboard?' Her knees felt a bit wobbly. She could hardly look at his grinning face.

'That's right. *Curlew's Rest* is a boat.'

6

Until now, Astrid hadn't taken much notice of the boats on the river. As she walked back down the lane, she frantically searched for the names on the side of each of them. The first was not much bigger than a rowing boat. It was called *Finnegans Wake*. She breathed a sigh of relief. The next was a red and blue canal boat called *Aphrodite*. Then a converted tug boat with the words *Miss Conduct* daubed in white paint on its side. After that came a boat with a cabin and a couple of masts. It was stained green down its side so she could barely make out the name. There it was – *Long Time No Sea*.

She carried on, not noticing that the little wheels of the suitcase had jammed with mud, so they were dragging through the puddles.

Finally, she came to the end of the lane where the rushes were so high she couldn't see over them. She stopped and searched the reeds. Almost hidden from view was a gap with a thin gangway. She picked up her suitcase and pushed through the undergrowth, her heartbeat quickening. This had to be it.

After a dozen steps the gangway met the water and turned left, running alongside a wooden boat. It floated high in the water, its prow rising gently to meet the current, which chuckled down its flanks. Like a fat turtle on its back, enjoying the sunshine.

It was larger than the other boats, over thirty feet long maybe, but it was in no better shape. The varnish on its planks was peeling off in flakes. The windows in the upper cabin were coated in dust. Wrapped around the mast was a faded red sail. Wherever she looked she saw signs of weather damage. Then she saw the name. Hanging below the roof of the cabin was the blade of an oar. Painted on it were the words *Curlew's Rest*.

The wind picked up and rattled the tops of the reeds. The boat rocked slightly and chuckled again. Brilliant – now a boat was laughing at her. She put the suitcase down on the gangplank. She checked her watch – it was nearly seven-thirty. Simon would be back at the flat and would have found the note. There was no going back to London now. Best to stick it out here for the night until she could come up with a new plan. Over the years, lots of people had told her to relax – just go with the flow. But what if you didn't want to go where the flow was taking you? Like now. This was exactly the reason you always needed a plan.

She heaved the suitcase over the rail of the boat and quickly stepped across the gap. A shoal of small fish darted away from her shadow and sunk to the riverbed, glittering in the darkness. The deck shifted under her feet, sending a wobble up to her knees. The rail was too low to hang on to so she quickly sat down next to an old lobster pot that smelt of fish.

There were two sets of steps in front of her. A narrow climb up to the cabin and a short flight down to a wooden door. She lifted her bag onto her lap, shuffled forwards on her bottom and swung her legs over the drop. At least nobody walking along the path could see her.

There was a padlock on the door, which took a few minutes of fiddling with before it clicked up. She shouldered the door and a faint musty smell – old books and salt – drifted up from the gloom. Inside she found a light switch and the room was flooded with yellowish light.

She slumped down on the bottom step, but not because the boat was moving. The sight ahead of her had drained all her energy. Even the greatest estate agent would have a tough time selling this. There was a tiny sink and draining board under a porthole. Bolted to the floor on the other side was a battered table surrounded by a U-shaped bench. Between them, they took up much of the floor space. 'Cosy? Homely?' They could try that. 'Cramped' would be more honest.

The whole room was about a third of the size of her kitchen, except her kitchen didn't have a bed in it. Right at the back was a platform of slatted planks with a mattress on top. Next to it were shelves of books hemmed in by a section of netting. She got up and walked across to the bench. The floor was covered by a worn Persian rug.

She sat down and gazed around her – trying to take it in. There was no grand house in the country. This was it – a tatty old boat on a river she didn't even know the name of. 'Not your best work, Astrid,' she whispered. And now she was talking to herself. There was only one thing for it. Some decent food, and a very large and very potent glass of New World wine.

★

Astrid followed the path upstream in the last of the fading light until she reached a stone humpback bridge. The town of Hanbury was on the other side. It was not much more than a row of cottages overlooking a cobbled wharf. There were a couple of shops – a newsagent's, and a hairdresser's called *Curl Up and Dye*. Both were closed. The only light came from a window in the tallest building at the end of the row.

She wandered over and peered up at the sign hanging over the door. It was a painting of a fisherman in a top hat over the words *The Angler's Arms*. Propped up outside was a chalkboard advertising *Fine Ales and Food. Free Wi-Fi*. Astrid set her shoulders back. Food, wine, and free Wi-Fi. Maybe today wouldn't be a complete and utter disaster after all.

Inside she took the door marked 'Snug' and found herself alone in a warm wood-panelled room. A handful of tables were arranged on the stone slab floor. There was fishing paraphernalia everywhere. On the walls were framed sets of flies, metal lures and bits of rope tied in different knots. Bamboo rods and reels dangled under every beam. A stuffed fish in a glass case hung over the fireplace. It was olive-coloured with a pointed, toothy snout. A glassy eye gazed out on the instruments of its downfall.

'What do you want?' An elderly woman shuffled out from a side door and stood behind the brass bar. She had silver hair in tight curls and a pale face that had lost a long battle with gravity – like a small landslide on a chalk cliff.

'Oh, hi there.' Astrid strode over to the bar.

'Well then?' said the woman wearily.

'Let me see.' Astrid scanned the bar. There was no sign of a wine cooler.

The woman wiped her hands on the front of a floral apron and picked up a pint glass from under a row of beer pumps.

'No, sorry... I'd like a glass of wine.'

'Would you now,' sighed the woman. 'Alright, we have a house red and a house white.'

'Where's the red from?' said Astrid as calmly as she could.

'I think it's Australia. I'll check the wine box.'

'Wine box? Hang on... I'll...'

Too late. The landlady was already in the corner pushing a bony thumb on the plastic tap of the wine box. She teetered back with the glass. 'That it then?'

'Can I look at the menu?'

'Of course you can.' She took a black folder from a stack behind the bar and handed one over. 'But you won't be getting any food tonight.'

'Really?'

The landlady squinted at a clock on the wall that was made out of a brass diver's helmet. It was four minutes past eight. 'Kitchen shut at eight.'

'What? Is there nothing I can have?'

'Well...' The woman sucked in some air through thin lips. 'There's half a pork pie at the back of the fridge, but honestly, I'm not sure how long it's been there. So on your head be it.'

'I might not risk it, thanks.'

'There's crisps.'

'What kind?'

'Potato kind.'

'Lovely. Well, a couple of bags of crisps it is, I guess.'

The landlady shuffled off and plucked out a couple of bags from a wicker basket. She slid them over. 'And before you ask, the Wi-Fi code is Freeloader44, with a capital F.'

Astrid paid up, gathered her crisps and glass of wine, and went over to a table by the fireplace that had a church pew at either side. She sat down, took off her Burberry blazer and hung it neatly on the back of the pew.

The wine was every bit as bad as she'd expected. But it was warm and it quickly melted her bad mood. She hadn't had any text messages from Simon since she left London. He usually sent a few every day, when he was away on business. Just checking where she was, and if she was okay. Which was very considerate of him. So, he'd obviously decided to compose a long email. Maybe it was an apology. He'd realised what he'd lost and ditched Gina.

She logged on to the Wi-Fi on her phone and waited for her emails to load up. She could feel her heartbeat quickening. The big pike peered down at her from its case. A little gold plaque said it had been caught in 1964 in the River Frome.

Nothing on the phone.

The fish weighed 36 lbs.

Nothing.

Was that big for a pike?

Another gulp of wine. Nothing.

Presumably they don't stuff the little ones?

Brrrr. Her emails began to pop up on the screen.

She sifted down the list with a trembling finger. There was

one from Muraki titled 'Hope you're okay?' How sweet – she'd deal with that later. Something from HR that looked official. Half a dozen bits of junk, then a single message from Simon at 18.34 that said, *'Re: Your Note.'* She tapped the screen and inhaled deeply.

Astrid – I'm so sorry.

She drained the glass. It was a good start.

But if we're honest with ourselves I think we know that things haven't been working for some time. In fact, I'm sure one day we'll look back on this and realise it was for the best. In the meantime, let's try and approach this as maturely as we can and find the right solutions for both of us. Gina is very upset and is hoping you and she will be able to reconnect in the future. I have passed on your resignation to HR, which will avoid any drama spilling into the office. Let's touch base when you're feeling calmer. I hope you are well, wherever you are tonight. Simon.

The anger burnt on her cheeks. It wasn't true. Their relationship had been working, until he'd decided to jump on her best friend. Whose idea had it been anyway? His or hers? Did it even matter? They'd both betrayed her. The thought of them together, right now, in *their* flat, made her want to scream out loud.

Breathe in. Count down from ten, nine… arrrrgh. How dare Gina claim to be upset? She wasn't the one who was on her own now. In a boat. She felt a tear form at the corner of her eye. She quickly wiped it away with her sleeve.

'You alright, love?'

Astrid looked up. Standing there was a woman, mid-thirties with a cheery open face and glossy hair that tumbled to her shoulders. On one side were a couple of multi-coloured braids. She was wearing a shapeless blue sweatshirt with a logo that said '*Shell Bay Café*'.

'Sorry?'

'Hay fever, right? This time of year is a bugger, isn't it? I've got a tablet if you need one.' She glanced at Astrid's empty glass. 'Unless you're planning to get stuck in tonight. Or you're driving, of course.' She looked round over her shoulder conspiratorially, even though nobody else was there. 'Although… the local copper drinks in here and he doesn't mind as long as you go under ten miles an hour.' She glanced at Astrid's empty glass. 'Fancy another?'

'I'm fine thank you,' said Astrid.

'Oh, go on – red, is it?' She picked up Astrid's glass and turned to the bar without waiting for an answer.

Astrid checked the door. The last thing she wanted right now was company. Could she make a run for it? Say she was going to the bathroom and not come back? She watched the landlady wrestle the silver bag out of the wine box and wring the last of the dregs out into her glass. It would mean leaving her blazer behind but it might be worth it. Chances are though, this was the only place for miles with decent Wi-Fi.

Too late – the woman was heading back across the bar holding a glass of wine and a pint of honey-coloured beer. She put the drinks down on the table. 'Budge up.' She squeezed into the pew next to her, trapping the blazer before Astrid had time to rescue it. 'Cheers my dears.' She clinked Astrid's glass. Then held out her hand. 'Name's Kath.'

Astrid took her hand. 'Astrid Kisner.'

'Yeah, I know. You're Henry Swift's niece. You've moved into his old houseboat.'

'News travels fast.'

'Sure does.' Kath took a gulp of her pint and wiped the streak of foam off the top of her lip with the back of her sleeve. 'Sorry for your loss, by the way.'

'Thank you. Although I really only knew him as a child.'

'I didn't really know him either. Saw him out walking now and then, but he kept to himself.' She drained her pint. 'Anyhoo. What do you think of Hanbury?'

'Well... the service is a bit of a shock,' she said, nodding over at the woman behind the bar who was cleaning a glass with a damp tea towel.

'Dolly? Oh, she's a sweetheart really. You just have to be a regular for a few years before she likes you.'

'To be honest, I wasn't planning to stay that long. I'm just going to arrange the sale and head back to London. My husband is there now.'

'Rrright,' drawled Kath. 'Husband.'

Astrid straightened up. 'What's that supposed to mean?'

'Well, there's a mark on your finger where there used to be a wedding ring.' Kath tapped the side of her nose. 'I don't miss much.'

'No, no. It's at the jeweller's. The stone needed resetting.'

'Course.' Kath leant forward and rummaged a crisp out of Astrid's packet on the table. Astrid stared at the blazer on the back of the pew. It was rumpled and flattened at the collar. Was there time to grab it? Just sprint across the room to the door? Kath leant back on the coat again. Or just sacrifice it? No, she didn't have any money now. Not enough for new jackets or to buy Simon out of the flat.

'In my experience, though,' said Kath, 'there's no point going back to a relationship once it's gone wrong. It's like when you take sour milk out of the fridge.'

'Milk?'

'Yeah, when the milk's gone off. You put it back in the fridge for some reason. And then it tastes even worse the next time you try it.'

'You've actually done that?'

'Many times.'

'Right. Well, it's an interesting analogy. But as I say, I'm happily married.' There was no way she was going to open up to the village gossip.

'I know. None of my business anyway.'

A shadow filled the frosted glass panel of the door. It swung open and a broad man in a tatty tweed coat entered with a small white dog on a lead. Two ruddy cheeks perched above a white moustache that swept down to a large beard. He moved in a rocking motion, as much sideways as forwards. As if two invisible removal men were shifting a wardrobe. He wandered over, his bald head almost touching the beams. Kath clapped her hands. 'Here he is. Homeless Santa.'

He roared with laughter. 'There she is. Seaweed.' He unclipped the little dog, which snuffled around the stone floor.

Astrid looked to Kath. 'Seaweed?'

Kath shook her head. 'It's nothing.'

The man heaved himself into the chair opposite. 'We call

her Seaweed because even the tide won't take her out.' He roared with laughter again.

'You bugger.' Kath giggled, then turned to Astrid. 'Not true, by the way. I've just got high standards.' She turned to the man, who was still sniggering. 'I'd like you to meet Hanbury's newest resident – Astrid.'

'Hi.' Astrid held out her hand.

'I better not. I've been filling the Defender with chip oil.' He gripped his belt and hitched up his trousers. 'I'm Grub… and it's Astrid right? You inherited Henry's old houseboat?'

'Apparently so.'

'She's come down from London,' said Kath.

'London, eh? You know what we call people from London round here?'

'Go on.'

'Filth.'

'Filth?'

'Yeah, it stands for "failed in London, try Hanbury".'

'Oh, right,' said Astrid uncertainly.

'Don't worry – only a bit of fun. Right.' He looked at their empty glasses. 'Same again.'

'No, honestly.' Astrid put her palm over the top of her glass. 'I should really…'

Grub put his fingers in the corners of his mouth and whistled over to the bar. Dolly drifted out from a side door like a figure in a cuckoo clock. 'Pint of Badger's and the same again for the ladies,' he shouted.

The little dog came over and sat at Astrid's feet. It tipped its head to one side and made a soft whining sound.

'Oh, go on then,' said Grub, helping it up onto the pew. The dog circled around a couple of times then lay down, its head resting on Astrid's knee. She cautiously stroked the top of its head, which had a tuft of fur between the ears.

'Looks like someone loves you,' said Grub.

The dog closed its eyes and she could feel the warmth of its chin through the material of her dress. 'I'm glad someone does,' she said.

7

Thursday night, Friday morning

Even after three large wines, Astrid couldn't get to sleep. She lay in the box bed under a patchwork quilt she'd found in a wooden chest, trying to forget her evening in the pub. She'd never met people like this. They reminded her of characters out of a Mike Leigh film she'd seen as part of a season at the BFI. They were just so unfiltered. Kath had revealed the most personal details of her life, and expected her to do the same. Conversations were kept up full volume across the bar. They roared with laughter at their own jokes, which included vocabulary that should have been left behind in the Seventies. At one point Grub referred to a woman he knew as a 'bit of crumpet'. She'd told him it was highly inappropriate, but he said 'good one!' and laughed even harder.

Light from the moon streamed in through the curtains on the portholes. She pulled the quilt over her head – it smelt faintly of tobacco – then realised her feet were sticking out at the other end. She brought her knees up. If only she was back in her apartment, between the Egyptian cotton sheets. The darkness embracing her. The smell of her sandalwood and vanilla diffuser. The gentle sound of Simon's breathing. It was truly over, wasn't it?

Outside, the reeds rustled in the breeze. Or was something moving through them? She curled up tighter. An owl called from some distant wood. Another replied from the other side of the river. They kept on going. Back and forth. Could owls really have that much to discuss? Just two or three hours' sleep – that's all she needed. But then what would happen if she was fast asleep and the boat started sinking? Or the rope tying it up gave way and she was swept out to sea? She could be floating about in the Atlantic for weeks before they found her.

She drifted in and out of sleep for the rest of the night, until a boat passed alongside. Its wake rocked the cabin, sending the row of tin mugs jangling on their hooks. Outside the window was a slow *humphing* sound. She peeped out of the porthole to see a line of fat cows by the fence, tearing up mouthfuls of grass. It was 7.20 a.m. She was exhausted. But there was no point staying in bed. The sun was up now and there were things to do – a new plan had taken shape.

Somewhere in that fevered mess of a night a thought had struck her – and it was a good one. The boat might be worth a bit of money. It was sturdy enough – a classic even. All she had to do was renovate it and a rich yachty type would snap it up. Then she could get a short-term rental back in London while she wrangled with Simon about selling the flat. Only thing was, she didn't have much cash at the moment. All her life savings had been ploughed into the apartment. In fact, she should probably try and pick up some freelance work while she was here. There were bound to be a few country houses out here with art collections in need of sprucing up.

She got out of bed and planted her feet squarely on the rug. Maybe it was the hangover, but the boat felt steadier. She located the shower and the toilet. They were both in a closet no bigger than a wardrobe. The shower water wasn't much warmer than the wine in the pub. Even cranking the white plastic dial right round produced little more than a tepid drizzle. She'd forgotten to bring her wash bag so she had to use a small square of soap perched on a ledge. In a couple of minutes it was worn down to the size of an after-dinner mint. Thankfully she'd brought her own towel. She dried herself, carefully avoiding her elbows touching the walls, which were speckled with black mould. She winced as her knee almost made contact with the toilet lid. Then she got out and dressed quickly, straight from her suitcase. Maybe there was a private gym she could join. She didn't want to go through that showering experience every day.

She headed up the towpath towards Hanbury, her laptop bag swinging by her side. In the daylight the town was prettier than she'd expected. The houses were made of a cream-coloured stone that almost glowed. There were elegant slates or new thatch on the roofs. On every windowsill were planters full of sulphurous daffodils and multi-coloured tulips. Astrid checked a local map and was pleased to find there was a library not too far away. Chances were they'd have Wi-Fi so she could catch up with her emails and look for work. And it meant she didn't have to go back to the *Angler's Arms* and risk bumping into Kath and Grub.

The library was at the end of a narrow alleyway that ran up from the wharf. It was a white breeze-block building bristling with handrails. A long access ramp wound up to the front door. It was just after nine and already busy. The only free table was next to a well-stocked section marked 'Large Print'. On the cover of the 'book of the month' was a highwayman in a shirt opened to the waist. He was in a clinch with a startled milkmaid.

Astrid sat down and hitched onto the free Wi-Fi. It was a good signal and her emails quickly poured in. Top of her inbox was one from Simon sent at 2.12 a.m. A sleepless night, wracked with guilt from his previous email? Maybe not. It was entitled *Hi*, and simply said: *'Do you know where the dishwasher tablets are?'* Just ignore that one then.

Next was something windy and full of jargon from HR. The thrust of it was that she'd effectively cancelled her contract by walking out of her job. So there would be no further salary after this month. Now she really did need to find some work.

She logged into *The Restorer* – a website and chat room for art conservators. She'd usually drop in once a week for news and advice. This was the first time she'd been to the jobs section. For Dorset, which she was now sure she was in, there wasn't much. A couple of listings from private collectors looking for valuations. Plus a short-term vacancy at a English Trust property called Sherborne Hall. There was no more information than that. Except a note saying the lucky candidate would have to be 'highly qualified and available as soon as possible'. She checked the date of the ad. It had been up there for a couple of weeks, so she'd probably missed the boat. Still, worth a shot. She filled in the form, attached her CV and snapped the laptop shut to a few muffled 'tuts' from behind newspapers.

She headed back through the town to the newsagent's, which seemed to also be a chemist. A queue of about a dozen people waited patiently as the man at the front was given a lengthy explanation about how to administer worming cream for his cat. Astrid picked out some basic soap and shampoo and searched the aisle for a decent moisturiser. She never wore much make-up, instead spending the money on La Mer. Obviously they wouldn't have that. But there wasn't even anything by Clinique or Neal's Yard.

'You should try this.' Astrid turned to face a young woman with dyed blue hair and nose piercings, who was holding out a heavy green tub. 'It's Gardener's Hand Butter.'

'Ah, no, I was looking for a face cream.'

The assistant studied the label. 'Yeah, reckon you could risk it,' she said.

'Great.' Astrid reluctantly took the tub. The assistant was so friendly, it was hard to say no. The assistant also picked out a purple nail varnish. 'I wear it myself.' She beamed – which meant Astrid had to buy that as well, even though it was hideous.

She waited in the queue, which was flanked by envelopes and packing materials on one side and magazines and newspapers on the other. She picked up a copy of *The Purbeck Times* – there might be some information on local gyms – and shuffled to the head of the queue.

In one of the alleyways she found a camping store. There she bought a sleeping bag and an inflatable pillow – it would have to do for now. Plus a pair of hiking shoes. They were a bit drab and heavy-duty, but at least there would be nothing she didn't mind treading in.

On her way to the bridge her phone vibrated. She slipped it out, pleased to see a couple of bars. A mental note – signal hotspot, three paces south of the stone cross in the middle of the wharf.

It was a new email from *Cressida Giles – Head of Marketing at Sherborne Hall*. That was quick. Apparently, Cressida would like to meet her 'before close of play today, if that was possible'. She toyed with the idea of not replying for a while. They obviously hadn't found anyone after a couple of weeks so must be desperate. But then, so was she. This was no time to play games. She sent a reply saying she'd be there shortly.

8

On the drive back to the boat after the interview, Astrid mulled over this turn of events. This was working out nicely. The job would look like a planned sabbatical, rather than a black hole in her CV. The pay wasn't too bad either. She hated to haggle over money, so had been grateful when Cressida came up with a weekly rate that was almost the same as what she'd been earning in London.

She eased the car round a sharp bend and slowed down. In a deep gouge in the ridge were the ruins of a castle. Most of it had fallen away in great chunks. As if a giant had swiped it up and crumbled it in their fist. There was something familiar about this castle.

The Mini surged over a steep drop in the road and the memory was dislodged. She was twelve years old and in the passenger seat of a different car, bare feet up on the walnut dashboard. Her uncle was at the wheel – the window open, a warm breeze ruffling his linen shirt, which had coloured dashes of paint at the sleeve.

Memories are supposed to be misty. That's how it works in films. But she could see him clearly – his tanned face, the easy smile. Hear his laugh as if he were sitting next to her. He'd just wound up a joke that she didn't quite understand, but had laughed along with anyway. Her father stifled a giggle in the back seat. Next to him, her mother crossed her arms. 'How vulgar,' she sniffed.

The road rose again and the memory was gone – sinking back into the silt. This was the first time she'd really thought about her uncle since moving down here. How he'd been so much fun to be around as a kid. So why had he fallen out with her father? And how had he ended up living on a boat instead of that big country house, wherever that was?

The river level had dropped and the boat was sitting lower against the boardwalk. She stepped over the rail. Then she stopped in her tracks. The door to the cabin was half open. She checked to see if her keys were still in her pocket – they were. And she was certain she'd locked the door after she left. Someone had broken in. Someone was rattling around in there right now.

She looked around on the deck for something to use as a weapon. There was nothing except a pile of driftwood. The largest piece felt far too light to do any damage. But she wasn't backing down. She tiptoed down the steps and pushed open the door with the piece of wood.

A cheery face turned to greet her. 'Ahoy there, matey!' Kath was standing by the cooker working a spatula under something in a frying pan.

'Oh, it's you,' she said, tucking the wood behind the door. In all the time that she'd lived in London, nobody had come round uninvited. Let alone broken in and started cooking.

'How did you get in?' said Astrid, sitting down at the table.

'There was a spare key under one of the herb pots.'

'Good to know.'

'Thought I'd drop in and see how you're doing.' Kath reached for a couple of plates from an overhead cupboard and brought them to the table. She set one in front of her, the other opposite it. 'Then I got thinking about an early dinner and ended up buying far too much. So...' She laid out a knife and fork by the plates. 'I thought I'd cook some for you and if you turned up then great. If not then I'd finish it myself. It's a win-win frankly.'

'Makes sense.' Astrid checked the cutlery as Kath turned back to the cooker. She returned with the frying pan and slid two semi-circular parcels covered in bright orange breadcrumbs onto each plate.

'Are they empanadas?'

'Emper... what? No. You never had crispy pancakes before?'

Astrid shook her head.

'You sure?'

'I think I would have remembered.' She stared at the parcels. 'How can something edible be so orange, and not be... an orange?'

'You're gonna love 'em. They're mint!' Kath went to the cooker and flipped open the glass door. She brought out a tray of chips, which she shovelled onto the plates. 'And look at these beauties. Like bars of Pharaoh's gold.' The final addition was a dollop of chalky green goo, which from the open tin on the side would appear to be *Mushy Peas*. 'Bon apple tea!' she said theatrically.

'I think it's *bon appétit*. It's French.'

'Oh... is that right? Okay, get stuck in,' said Kath.

Astrid watched Kath dig into the food, each forkful loaded with equal amounts of chips, peas and pancake. She gingerly sliced off a corner of one of her own pancakes and chewed down. It was filled with some kind of creamy mushroom sauce that congealed around mysterious cubes of meat. And it was just about the tastiest thing she'd ever eaten. Having had nothing but a couple of bags of crisps in nearly twenty-four hours, and with all the stress, this was exactly what she needed. They ate without talking, Kath humming between mouthfuls. When they were both finished, Kath ran her finger round her plate and licked it. Astrid lined the knife and fork in the centre of her plate.

'You know, Kath, that was excellent. Thanks.'

'My pleasure.' She pushed the plate to one side.

'So, Kath, I forgot to ask you last night. What is it that you do?'

'Do?'

'For work?'

'Oh right. Well, anything really. Dog walking. Fruit picking. At the weekend I work in my brother's café on the beach.' She twirled a multi-coloured braid that fell from behind her ear. 'And I do these braids at the music festivals. I could do one for you, if you like?'

'That's very kind. But I couldn't.'

'Don't worry – it's free.'

'Maybe later, thanks.'

Astrid got up and cleared the plates. The window was open behind the sink, and the cabin was nice and cool again.

Kath had tucked herself into the corner, her feet up on the bench. 'You sure you have to go back to London? You're just what we need around here – a bit of glamour.'

'Glamour? Really? Um… you know, I'd love to stay but I just need to get this boat refurbished and then get home.'

'That right?'

'Yes, I'm going to do it myself.'

'Oooh…' Kath sucked in air between her teeth. 'It'll need a big overhaul. New engine maybe.'

'You think so?'

'Yeah. I've been around boats all my life. This one needs a bit of work – if you want to get any money out of it.'

Astrid put the plates and cutlery in the plastic bowl in the sink. There was no point even checking if there was a dishwasher. She ran the hot tap and a whining sound travelled down the side of the boat. Then there was a thumping of pipes, as if something was chasing a tiny ghost behind the panels.

'See. Your plumbing's buggered.'

She turned off the tap. 'So, do you know who could do the work?'

'Cobb could do it.'

'Cobb?'

'Runs the boatyard round the corner.'

Astrid frowned. 'Cobb? So that's his name? No, that oaf isn't touching the boat.'

Kath slapped the top of the table with her palm. The tin mugs rattled. 'Oaf?' She laughed. 'Seriously? Cobb's catch of the day round here, lady. Plenty of people been sniffing around that tree.'

'Lovely image – thanks.'

'He's not interested though. Just been through a bitter break-up. It was horrible – his ex-wife took his van.'

'That is sad – but I'm not giving him any work. The way

he spoke to me. You weren't there, Kath. There's no way I'm dealing with him.'

'So where are you going to go then?'

'Another boatyard.'

'Astrid, you can't exactly sail off to Poole can you?'

'Can't I?'

'Course not. The boat's not in good enough nick. So it's him or nothing.'

'Then it's nothing, then.' Astrid knew she was being stubborn, but she couldn't help it. Something about that man had really got under her skin. She brought the shopping bags onto the table and quickly changed the subject. 'Oh, by the way... I just got a job for a couple of months today.'

'Wow. Who with?'

'It's at the English Trust. An art conservation project at Sherborne Hall.'

'Oh, yeah... the English Trust,' she said dismissively.

'What? Surely you don't have a problem with the English Trust.'

'I do indeed. They're too big for their boots, if you ask me. They own everything round here. It's like the mafia with cream teas.'

Astrid looked at her sceptically. 'Really? The mafia?'

'Oooh...' Kath whistled. 'You don't know the half of it. I read that there's a billion pounds just sloshing around in the Trust's current account.'

'Where did you read that?'

'Internet.'

'Right.'

Astrid began unpacking the camping gear. She placed the sleeping bag on the bed with the inflatable pillow for later.

Kath began rummaging through the other bag. 'Garrrdeners' Body Butter,' she drawled. 'That looks fab. Go on – try it.' She slid the tub over to Astrid who opened it and scooped out a dollop.

'It's very thick,' she said, working it into her hands.

'Ooh… and this is gorgeous.' Kath brought out the purple nail varnish and held it up to the light. 'What a lush shade.'

'I didn't mean to buy that.'

'Tell you what,' said Kath, gripping Astrid's hands and pulling them towards her on the table. 'I'll do your nails. Get you looking all fabulous. Then you can go and speak to Cobb. Right?'

The boatyard was deserted. The only noise was the clicking of wire rigging against the boats' masts. Astrid made her way to the shed, muttering to herself. Of course, Kath had been right – he was the only person who could do the work. She shuddered. If she was going to apologise to him, she might as well get it over with now.

In front of the entrance was an oily puddle. Circles of green and royal blue swirled on its surface like peacock tail feathers. She stepped across it and peered inside. Cobb was at a bench welding a piece of metal that was clamped in a vice. The white sparks danced in the glass panel of his helmet.

'Hullo…' He carried on welding. 'Cobb?'

He put down the welding torch, took off his helmet and came over. 'What do you want?'

He was taller that she'd remembered. Good posture for someone who seemed to spend their life hunched over things. Same jumper though. That silver chain still hanging over the neckline.

'I'd like to apologise,' she said, thrusting out her hand. 'I think we got off to a bad start.'

He took her hand, which immediately slipped out of his grip.

'Sorry, it's this butter stuff...'

'Butter?' He wiped his hands on his trousers. 'Who puts butter on their hands?'

'No, it's more of a cream,' she mumbled.

He stared at her, confused. 'Cream?'

'Look... just forget it.'

'Okay... so what do you want then?'

'Want? Oh, right. It's about the boat. I'm going to sell it and I need someone to do it up.'

'You're leaving – that's a shame.'

'Is it?'

'Yeah, I had a bet with someone in the pub you'd last at least a month.'

'Very funny.' Then she remembered something she'd been told at a training seminar for 'future managers'. A trick to get people to do what you wanted. All you had to do was appeal to their vanity. For Cobb, it was obviously his repair skills. She ran her hand along the rail of nearby boat. 'Mmm... lovely work.' She nodded sagely. 'You're clearly a craftsman, Cobb.'

'I haven't started on that one.' The annoying grin was back.

'Look.' She was close to shouting. 'Can you do it or not?'

'It's hard to say.' He strode past her towards the water's edge.

She hurried after him and caught up with him by the concrete slipway.

'Just take it in,' he said, gazing out over the estuary.

The tide was out and low islands had revealed themselves. The blackened ribs of a sunken boat poked out from the mud. Small white birds skittered through the shallows. 'Not bad for a backwater. Don't you think?'

'Yes, lovely,' she said flatly.

He sat down on an upturned rowing boat, took off his gloves and let them fall to the ground. 'I know that boat inside out. Worked on it with my father twenty years ago. Before your uncle bought it. You know what type it is?'

'No idea.'

'It's a Hillyard – nine-tonner. Made in Littlehampton. Good steady boats – safe but a bit slow. You know the joke about them, right?'

'Of course not.'

'You won't drown but you might starve.' He slapped the side of the rowing boat and laughed loudly.

'I don't get it.' She waited for him to stop, then folded her arms. 'Do you think it will be expensive?'

'Depends.' He smacked his lips.

'On what?'

'Well. Do you want me to flush out the bilge hold?'

'Possibly.'

'Run a new fuel line?'

'Okay.'

'You want me to refurb the engine? New rudder port?'

She held up her hands in front of her. 'Listen. You know full well that I have no idea what you're talking about.'

'Just trying to be helpful.'

'No you're not. You're enjoying every minute of this.'

He rocked back and laughed again. 'You're right – I am really enjoying myself.'

'Ugh… you vile man.' She turned round and set off back across the yard.

He waited until she was a few yards away, and called after her. 'Astrid!'

She stopped and faced him. 'What?'

'I'll have a look at the boat sometime. Might be able to sort it out for you.'

'Right. I mean, thanks.'

'No problem.' He picked up his gloves and headed back inside.

Astrid watched him go. He strode back to the shed whistling to himself. Okay, so he clearly felt he'd won that one. Fine. If he kept to his word though, she'd still got him to do what she wanted. A new job and a new boat. The plan was definitely coming together. It was just a shame there was nobody to celebrate the news with. Kath had left to do 'some stuff' as she'd said. The library shut at five-thirty, over an hour ago, so there would be no *Dogs Need Homes* on catch-up to watch. A quiet evening on her own it was then.

She rummaged around in the cupboard for something to make a light meal. She was already hungry again – it must be all that fresh air. There were a couple of items that might do: a tin of baked beans mixed with small sausages, and a packet of *Smash* – an instant potato powder that, according to the instructions, only needed boiling water. Simon wouldn't approve. 'Fresh and organic', that was his rule. It was Friday evening. Which restaurant would he be going to tonight? With *her*, presumably?

No, forget it. She needed a night off from thinking about him. A stiff drink would help with that. She searched the back of the cupboard and found a half-full bottle of brandy. She took a tin mug from the rack and sloshed some in, then knocked it straight back.

Even with a bit of fiddling around with the cooker, the whole meal was prepared in less than ten minutes. It was eaten even quicker. The combination was much tastier than expected. She pushed the empty plate in front of her, stood up and played the part of an overattentive waiter. 'And how was your *Smash* this evening, madame?'

She sighed dramatically. 'Divine. The best I've ever had.'

She dumped the plate into the sink. 'And would you care for some more cheap brandy?'

'Well, I shouldn't really... but there again, I am a bit sad and talking to myself again, so why not?' She poured another measure into the tin mug and took it over to the bed.

She scanned the books behind the netting. It was an odd mixture – crime novels with embossed gold titles, anthologies of poetry, some local history, nature reference books and tide charts for every one of the last twenty years. She picked up *The Purbeck Times* and clambered into the sleeping bag without changing. There was a story on a section of cliff that had fallen into the sea. The picture below the text showed a wooden stile with a warning sign stuck on it. '*Successful church roof appeal*' was accompanied by a picture of a vicar holding a giant cheque.

Soon the fresh air and brandy caught up with her and the words began to blur. The vicar circled around with his big cheque. 'Where do you cash those giant cheques? At giant banks? Urrr…' She tossed the paper to the floor. Closed her eyes. The boat rocked gently. The reeds rustled. The owls called across the river, and she was asleep.

9

Saturday, Day 4

The next day, Astrid set out to Sherborne Hall feeling brighter than she had done for a while. Thanks to the brandy, she'd managed to get a good night's sleep. The sleeping bag had proved to be quite comfortable and even the shower, once she'd worked out the exact position of the dial between hot and cold, had been quite pleasant.

She headed up the path from the car park at Sherborne Hall, her work case in her hand. It felt strange to be setting out with it on a freelance job again, after all the years under contract at the National Gallery. Emily met her at the staff entrance with a taut smile. Her hair was up in a neat ponytail, not a strand out of place. She handed over a lanyard on a green ribbon, which she informed her should be worn at all times. 'It's protocol,' she said, gravely. It appeared that much of Cressida's marketing speak had rubbed off on Emily. Astrid rolled up the lanyard and put it in her pocket.

The house was every bit as magnificent on the inside as it

was on the outside. Each room echoed through generations of luxury. On the walls were huge tapestries or old portraits of past Sherborne families. The women in opulent dresses. The men in hunting gear, glassy-eyed spaniels at their feet. There were souvenirs from every corner of the world. Cabinets with delicate shell inlays, four-poster beds and Chinese vases. The plundered treasures of countless Grand Tours.

They reached the second floor via a wide marble stairway then turned into a long gallery that looked out over the formal gardens. Astrid hung back to inspect a large blue and white bowl. It had been painted with scenes of pagodas and geishas drifting through bamboo glades.

'Now this,' said a clipped voice, 'would originally have been used to keep goldfish.' A man got up from a seat in the shadows. He was wearing a jade green fleece that hung loosely over his slight frame. She noticed that underneath he was wearing a pressed white shirt and a red and blue striped tie – regimental, possibly.

'It's estimated to be early Qing Dynasty. Early 1690s.'

Astrid smiled at the man. She'd place him in his early seventies. 'Yes.' She leant forward and studied the bowl. 'The underglaze of cobalt blue... you're probably right.'

'I'm impressed.' The man beamed, his grey moustache riding up at the corner of his mouth. 'A fellow expert.'

'No, no. I only know a little bit about porcelain. I'm an art conservator. I just started today.'

'Oh, well done. Military history is my speciality – I'm a former second lieutenant. Based at Allenby Barracks.'

'Is that right?'

Emily stalked over. 'Harold,' she said firmly.

'Yes?'

'Astrid is staff.'

'Of course.' He sat back down on his chair with a creak – Astrid couldn't work out if it was from the antique chair or his knees.

'It was lovely to meet you, Harold,' she said.

'You too. And if you ever want to know anything about the house, come and find me.'

'I will,' she said, hurrying after Emily.

At the end of the room Emily unhooked a low red velvet rope and they pushed through a door marked *'Private'* into a long corridor.

'So is Harold a volunteer?' said Astrid.

'Yes, I think there's about half a dozen of them. History buffs, retirees mostly. Some of them fall asleep in the warmer rooms. Kids think they're animatronics and poke them.'

'That's a shame.'

'I know. But it shows you why you have to have your staff badge on display. Or the volunteers will pounce on you. Cressida says it's like garlic to them.'

'Oh, right.' Astrid dug the lanyard out of her pocket and slipped it over her neck.

'Excellent. And don't forget, that badge gives you access to all English Trust properties and a fifteen per cent discount in the gift shop and the Orangery Café.'

'Got it.'

They finally reached a door at the end of the corridor. Emily worked the larger of two keys into a big, heavy mortise lock. 'Cressida wants me to tell you the doors must be locked when you're not there.' She handed over the keys then brought out a white envelope from her jacket. 'And this is the list of the artwork.'

'Thank you.' Astrid took the envelope.

'Right, then I'll leave you to it,' she said, turning on her heels, her ponytail making an audible swish.

Astrid pushed open the door to a bright, airy room. It was illuminated by a long window made up of small diamond-shaped glass panels. She put her work case down on a broad wooden table, which was the only piece of furniture in the room, and went over to the window. From high up the layout of the gardens began to make sense. The paths between the flowerbeds and borders all led to some feature – a statue, a fountain or cypress tree. The design flowed and tilted, ushering visitors in one direction then the next. It was a garden and a game. A puzzle where the people in it didn't realise they were playing.

There was another door by the far wall. The second key fitted and she found herself in a smaller, darker room that smelt of damp wool. There were no windows, only a bare bulb hanging in the middle of the ceiling. There were paintings propped up against the walls, five or six deep. Most were in heavy gilt frames. A bunch of rolled-up canvases had been carefully placed in the corner. Astrid felt a rush of excitement. The same thrill, she imagined, an explorer might have on breaking through into some long-lost tomb.

For the next few hours, she brought out around half the paintings into the main room. She laid them out on the table and ticked them off on the list Emily had given her. Then she found her digital camera in the work case and photographed them, front and back. First a wide shot – then, using a hand-held strip lamp, more detailed pictures. Each time she checked for damage – noting down the repair work she'd have to do and extra materials and equipment she'd have to order.

There were a handful of works by well-known painters. The rest seemed to be landscapes by local artists she hadn't heard of, or stock Venetian scenes that were unsigned. Overall the collection was in good shape. The watercolours, which made up about a third of them, hadn't aged well. The colours had muddied, making summer days overcast and calm seas look ominous. The oil paintings were brighter and most of the varnishes had held up. Some had a sheen of grease or soot from a fireplace, but that could be easily cleaned. There was a lot to do, but if she could focus on half a dozen of the best pieces, throw in a handful of local scenes, then the Trust would have its exhibition.

She'd been so absorbed in her work she hadn't noticed it was just past four o'clock. Time for a late lunch – if she could find her way out. There were so many doors leading off the corridor and they all looked the same. Eventually she stepped out into the sunshine and followed the signs to the Orangery Café.

As she walked alongside a tall yew hedge she noticed footprints on the path. She stopped for a closer look. They were wet marks left by a trainer or boot. Adult size, no clear tread. That was strange. The sun was out and there were no signs of any puddles nearby. She followed the footprints in the direction they'd come from. Soon they turned through an arch in the hedge. There was a chain across the gap with a sign hanging from it – 'No Entry'. She lifted it off its hook, walked through and put it back in place.

The path wound through the woods for a while, then rose to meet a mossy dome in a clearing. It was about six foot high with a small wooden door that was ajar. A hand-painted sign next to it said: *'Icehouse – Warning. Steep stairs'*. She stepped inside and took a deep breath. The air felt cooler, five degrees less than outside maybe.

She followed the footsteps down a flight of stone stairs that curled to her right. After a dozen steps it levelled out to a ledge with an iron railing that blocked the way. Beyond it was another drop to a wide well. She stood by the railings and peered into the gloom. The base of the well was ten feet below her. In the centre was a bundle of clothes. She leant out further, waiting for her eyes to adjust. Her heart beat faster. Someone was wearing the clothes – and they weren't moving.

She slipped her handbag over her shoulder and carefully climbed down an iron ladder on the other side of the railings. The base of the well was full of grey ice, with an inch of water sitting above it. She edged forwards, her feet tingling as the cold water soaked into her shoes. She stood over the dead body – there was no doubt in her mind that that's what she was looking at. The pasty skin tone, the eyes – a man's, maybe early sixties – were open and unblinking. The position of the body as well, an ankle at an impossible angle, the neck twisted, arms outspread – a snow angel, left behind when the thaw came. She checked her watch – it was 4.29 p.m.

Astrid had never seen a dead body before. Of course, she'd seen thousands in paintings. The grisly Italian masters, with their saints and martyrs. The soft alabaster skin and rivulets of crimson. Maybe that's why she wasn't that shocked now. She'd pored over so much human flesh on canvas. She felt sad for whoever this was, but to her own surprise, there was no sense of panic. She was completely calm. And if she were honest with herself, excited.

Right here in front of her was a real-life mystery. Since she was a kid she'd always loved mysteries. Maybe that was partly why she'd got into art restoration. The job was all about peeling back layers to see things more clearly. Exposing the truth.

So, who was this? How had they ended up here? And was it an accident? These were questions she was sure she could answer, with a bit of work and time. And if the local police were anything like the people she'd met so far, they were going to make a hash of things. She might as well do it properly. Five minutes with the body. That's all she needed. What difference would it make?

Astrid scanned the chamber. It was constructed of reddish bricks with a grey mortar. The position of the body was directly below the railings. That must be where he'd fallen from. Or been pushed? Someone had come down the ladder to check on him. That would explain the set of wet footprints leading back up the stairs and along the path.

She knelt down by the body. There wasn't time to go back to the art storeroom for her work case. Luckily, she had a pair of plastic gloves in her pocket from earlier. She put them on and pressed two fingers under the jawline at the neck. Just to make sure. The skin was cold.

She took out her phone, turned on the torch feature and ran it over the length of the body. He was wearing tan brogues, maroon cords and a dark wool jacket. His hands were slim, with clean nails. On the inside of the cuffs of his jacket were cloudy white marks. She reached inside her handbag for something to take a sample.

She found an old receipt in her purse and began plucking at the fibres on the jacket cuff, dropping the larger grains of white material into the middle. Then she folded the receipt in a square and slipped it back into her purse. Inside the pocket of the man's jacket she found a thin wallet. There was no money in it, just a few credit cards. The name on all of them said 'G. DeVine.'

She listened for any noise back up the stairs. It was silent. Still – better be quick. Crouching over a dead body on your first day of work wasn't the best look. She set up the flash option on the phone and took a few close-ups of the body. Then the same number of long shots to show the body's position in the room. Done. She checked her watch again – 4.34. Five minutes. She was out of the icehouse and back onto the main path in another three. She reached for her phone to take photos of the footprints on the path. But they had gone. It took her a moment to realise that they must have evaporated in the warm sunshine. She cursed under her breath. That was a valuable clue, gone.

Astrid headed back to the house. It was probably a good idea to report the body to Cressida straight away – she could take it from there. There was nobody around so she took a shortcut across the lawn, despite a small sign advising her not to. Halfway across, something caught her eye. A figure was standing by a window on the top floor, watching her. It was hard to tell though. The sun was shining in her eyes. She stopped, brought her hand up to her forehead to shade her eyes. And now there was nothing. The person had melted back into the darkness. If that's what it was.

*

Cressida paced behind her desk. She clapped her hands to the sides of her head and made an expression that reminded Astrid of Edvard Munch's *The Scream*. 'Noo...' she moaned. 'This is terrible.'

Astrid was sitting at the other side of the desk. 'It's not good.'

'Not good? It's a disaster.' She slipped into her chair and stared at Astrid. 'We're just about to go into high season. That's our peak footfall.'

'I don't think anyone is going to blame the Trust though.'

Cressida brightened. 'Do you think so?'

'Of course. It's probably a tragic accident.'

'But even an accident, that's still not great.' Cressida set off on a small circle of the room. By the time she came back to her chair, her good mood had disappeared again. 'No, no. The Trust doesn't *do* accidents. Accidents happen at those DIY places and out-of-town supermarkets.' She shook her head. 'I've seen the focus group data for words associated with the Trust. It's things like "cosy" and "welcoming". Not "tragic" and "death".'

Astrid watched Cressida slump forward, the energy draining from her. Clearly, as far as Cressida was concerned, the reputation of Sherborne Hall, her precious job even, was on the line. 'Listen, Cressida,' she said, 'I think it's going to be okay. I mean, there is a warning sign in the icehouse.'

'Is there?'

'I'm pretty sure, yes. It says not to lean over the balcony. Which means—'

'Which means,' Cressida said, clapping her hands, 'the Trust can't be held responsible. If a visitor ignores the signage and starts clambering over railings, that's not our fault.' Cressida smiled. 'Thanks, Astrid.'

'No problem.' Astrid glanced at the clock on the wall. 'Well, it's nearly five. If you don't mind, I'll head off.'

'Yes, yes... and I'll give the police your address, in case they need to speak to you.'

'Of course.' Astrid got up and pushed the chair back to the desk. 'Oh, and can you tell them it's a boat. It's hard to find.'

'You live on a boat?'

'Yes... it's a long story.'

10

Sunday, Day 5

Sunday at the apartment would generally be the same. A late breakfast with Simon – coffee, smoked salmon and bagels, Danish pastries from Borough Market. Then out to a gallery or museum. A walk in a park or along the river, back for a session in the gym then out for the evening. Sometimes they'd meet friends, usually his. Or it would be just the two of them – happy to have the chance to catch up. Talking about the week's gossip in the department or the art they'd seen. However Simon dressed up this affair, he'd thrown away something amazing. And now she was facing a Sunday on her own. The first for years, and it made her feel hollow. Especially as this was the weekend of her surprise trip to Cyprus.

She wolfed down the last slice of pizza from the night before. She'd found it tucked away in the freezer cabinet of a nearby garage and heated it up under the grill. 'Happy anniversary, Astrid,' she said, wiping her hands on a tea towel.

At the apartment she'd probably spend a bit of time picking out an outfit. Doing her hair. Here in the boat, there didn't seem any point. Cold pizza for breakfast, throw on some leisure gear – it didn't seem to matter, somehow. Anyway, there was the icehouse mystery to investigate. In fact, it would be the perfect distraction from thinking about her failed marriage and her cheating scumbag of a husband.

Cressida clearly wanted to brush off the whole thing as an unfortunate accident. But after sleeping on it, Astrid now wasn't sure. The metal rail was waist-high – tall enough to stop anyone toppling over. You'd have to lean right out. Or someone would have to give you a good shove from behind.

Astrid searched her work case and brought out a metal spoon and a small glass bottle of hydrochloric acid and the sample – that's all she needed. She unfolded the receipt and carefully tipped the white dust into the bowl of the spoon. Next was the acid – five per cent should do it. A small bead of clear liquid dropped from the pipette in the stopper onto the sample and a second later the liquid fizzed and turned grey. It was chalk. Simple blackboard chalk.

Astrid swung open the cabin door and clambered up to the deck. The morning was as bright as a newly minted coin. The sun had burnt the mist off the water and the sky was azure blue. She spotted an old mountain bike tucked away behind some plant pots. Alright then, a long cycle ride it was. It would be a chance to think over a few things. She picked up the bike, lifted it over the rail and wheeled it along the boardwalk. Her mind tracked ahead. How had the chalk got onto DeVine's jacket? Was it there before or after he fell? There didn't seem to be anything chalky in the icehouse. The first thing to do then was find out who G. DeVine was.

As she reached the path, she remembered Kath saying she worked at a beach café at the weekend. Maybe she'd know? She seemed to know everyone round here. That night in the Angler's Arms she was wearing a sweatshirt with *'Shell Beach Café'* written on the front. It was sorted then, a leisurely cycle downhill to the coast in the morning. A bit more snooping around in the afternoon.

She straddled the bike and pushed off. It wobbled into the verge. Another try and she was soon lodged in the reeds on the other side. The last time she'd ridden a bike was when she was a kid. Apparently, the saying wasn't true – it *was* something you could forget how to do.

She wheeled the bike past the boatyard, just in case Cobb was around, and tried again. The bikes at the gym were fixed to the floor and didn't have gears to worry about. How did bike gears work again? She squeezed randomly at the controls. The pedals whirred round at high speed, the bike barely moving forward. Then they almost jammed, her legs straining to turn them over. Eventually she found a setting somewhere between the two and decided to not touch the gears again. That should cover most gradients, and she could get off and walk up any steep hills.

The path stuck with the river until it fanned out into the estuary. Then the trail veered off through a pine forest. Slowly it came back to her. The handlebars became steadier and she picked up speed. Dodging tree roots that ran like veins across the path. The tyres *brudddering* over fat pine cones. It was all a lot less relaxing than she'd imagined. On the gym bike you just watched the video screen. Here you had to keep checking the path in front of the wheels, and when you looked up the scenery was rushing towards you. Maybe she'd invest in a helmet.

Ten minutes later she emerged on open heath land. The track had changed. It was mostly rutted peat or white sand dotted with chunks of flint. She got off the bike and let it fall in the heather, which hummed with bees. The landscape slid away below her to the sea. It was criss-crossed with paths that knitted together copses of trees, grassy bogs and clouds of yellow gorse. Out beyond the heath was a vast bay broken up by wooded islands and swirling channels. In the distance a ferry set out across the neck of the bay. Another ferry, three times its size, ploughed through its wake on its way out to sea. At the other side of the channel a white building clung to the rocks. The perfect position for a hotel, if that's what it was.

She inhaled deeply. The air was scented with pine sap and the sweet coconut smell of the gorse. So far she hadn't managed to do much thinking about the case, as she'd now decided to call it. She'd been concentrating far too hard on not falling off. But the trip had been worth it for this.

She climbed back on the bike and followed a ridge to a crossroads. There was a wooden post with half a dozen signs pointing in different directions. *Agglestone Rock*, *East Creech*, *Worth Matravers*... the sort of place names you might find in Middle Earth. At the bottom was a sign for *Shell Beach* that aimed down the hill. She freewheeled onwards, and eventually ended in a gloomy gulley that led down to the sea. Either side were high banks of ferns, some with glistening olive tongues. Others were just bursting to life – their green knuckles unfurling from mounds of dead leaves.

The *Shell Beach Café* was at the bottom of the path, on the edge of the sand. It wasn't much more than a wooden shack made of weathered wooden boards with a sailcloth awning. It leant slightly out to sea. As if it had been washed up on a storm tide and was yearning to set out over the waves again. At the front was a metal board with pictures of ice creams and lollies. There were tubs full of plastic spades, little colourful windmills that fluttered in the breeze, and fishing nets on bamboo canes. Kath was there, elbows on the counter, engrossed in a magazine.

'Hi there.'

Kath looked up. 'Hey – it's you!'

'I thought I'd find you here.' She propped the bike by the side of the café.

Kathy dipped down below the counter and came up holding a can of orange Fanta and a red and blue chocolate bar with the word *Chomp* along the side. 'There you go. On the house.'

'That's kind, thanks.' She took them both as Kath raked down a tin shutter over the serving hatch.

Behind Astrid came a low 'awww...'

A doughy boy was standing there. He was only wearing a pair of swimming shorts that were covered in wet sand. 'It's shut,' he said.

'You want this?' Astrid held out the Chomp.

He curled his lower lip. 'You got a Twirl?'

'Do I look like Willy Wonka?'

The kid looked her up and down. 'A little bit.' He took the Chomp and padded off towards the beach.

Kathy appeared from the side door of the café. 'Come on. Let's get out of here.'

They walked together past a row of pastel-coloured beach huts and along the top of the dunes. It didn't take long before the crowds thinned out. Most people, it seemed, had hit the sand and decided not to bother going any further. A hundred yards from the café and there were only a handful of people on the beach. They sat down in a hollow in the dunes and Astrid opened her can of Fanta, which said 'not for sale individually' on the side. It tasted tangy and sweet, and after the long cycle ride was just what she wanted. 'Were you busy this morning, Kath?'

'Could be busier. There's another café round the corner. It's English Trust. Everyone goes there.'

'Is that right?'

'Yeah, and it's way more expensive. I don't get it. People will pay five quid for a bag of fudge because it's got a flippin' oak leaf on it.'

'Very odd.'

'They're squeezing the life out of the little guy if you ask me. It's not right.' She flipped off her sandals. 'You should have a word with them when you're down there.'

'I'll see what I can do, Kath.' Astrid took off her shoes and worked her feet into the sand. It trickled between her toes like warm water. How had she forgotten how good that felt? Or this beach? She must have visited it with her uncle. Maybe it would come to her.

'Oh, Kath...' She might as well get it out of the way. 'Do you know anyone called G. DeVine?'

'Let me see. Err... yeah – that must be Gerald DeVine. He runs an antique shop in town. Don't really know him though. Why do you want to know?'

Astrid had hoped Kath wouldn't ask. She still hadn't been honest about Simon and it didn't seem right to add another lie to the pile. She knew how much being lied to hurt. But there again, she did need to buy some time to investigate before it got around the village. 'Oh, I found his wallet at Sherborne Hall. I need to get it back to him.'

'Got it. He owns DeVine's Antiques. Near the church. You might catch him this afternoon if you're quick.'

'Thanks, I might head over later then.' She gazed out at the sea. The wind was chasing ripples into the shallows. 'So, Kath, this brother who owns the café. Are you close to him?'

'Yeah – he's good. I've got four brothers. Tons of uncles and aunts. Big, big family.'

'That must be nice?'

'It's alright. Except everyone knows your screw-ups and won't let you forget them. Oh, Kathy...' She put on an accent that was even broader than her own. 'Remember that time you set fire to the bins at school. Or, that time with the cow and the cider. Yeah, yeah...' She chuckled to herself, the memory clearly coming back. 'Anyways – what about you?'

'I have a small family. It's all a bit frosty to be honest.'

'Go on.'

'My father used to be an art dealer. I really like him, but he retired to Spain so I don't see him these days. He sits around drinking wine and watching regimental marching bands on black and white VHS tapes. He fell out with my uncle ages ago. Don't know why. That's why he wasn't in the will.' She would never share this much personal information with a stranger. But Kath didn't seem like she would judge anyone. 'My mother lives in Northumberland in a big house in the country. Only talks to dogs – thinks they know what she's saying. And some "little people" who come in to look after the house.'

'Little people? Like Munchkins?'

'No, local handymen who come in and fix the house. Plumbers, gardeners… that's what she calls them – "her little people". Anyway, I have a sister but we're not really in touch. She sided with Dad when he left my mother… although we all know it was the "ghastly Jennifer's" fault. That's his second wife. She ran off a while ago.'

'Right, well there you go.' Kath smiled. 'At least you've got your husband.'

Astrid pushed her heels out in the sand. A tiny landslide of sand slipped down the dune. It dragged a part of her with it. 'Yes. At least I've got my husband.'

They talked a bit longer. More than Astrid had with anyone for a while. Then Kath got up and brushed the sand off her jeans. 'Better get back. In case my brother shows up.'

Kath led the way through the dunes. Astrid hung back, dodging the sharp grass that poked through the sandy path. When they got to the café, Astrid knocked the sand out of her shoes and put them back on. Kath went in the side door and a moment later the shutter raked up. Down on the beach a few people heard the sound and wandered their way. The doughy boy rolled off an inflatable alligator and dodged ahead of them.

'Thanks, Kath. See you later.'

'You too.'

It took twice as long to get back. It was mostly uphill and the sun was beating down. Plus, she had to stop now and then to check the signposts. Even in broad daylight the rolling heath was disorientating. She arrived at the boat just before five, nipped in for a glass of water, then carried on into town on foot.

DeVine's Antiques was down an alley near a car park in front of the church. The door was shut. The lights were off. She peered into the bay window that took up much of the width of the shop. Inside was a clutter of dark brown furniture and grandfather clocks. There were a few paintings on easels, mostly farming scenes. Nothing that looked too valuable – like everything else in the shop. On a table was a collection of bric-a-brac – copper candle snuffers, porcelain dogs, stone ginger beer bottles – the sort of stuff you might pick up in the closing-down sale of a faded seaside hotel. On the window ledge was a row of dusty crystal sherry glasses. A price tag tied to one of the stems said £3, which felt optimistic.

Astrid noticed a fly on the corner of the window that was tethered by a wisp of cobweb. It fizzed and spun, drawing the strand tighter. The light in the shop came on. There were footsteps from the other side of the door, a key shifting in the lock. She stepped back into the alley. One thing for sure, it wasn't going to be Gerald DeVine.

A man emerged and turned to lock the door behind him, mid-twenties at the most. He had cropped sandy hair that was shorn in a perfect straight line at the back of his neck. His movements were quick and precise – as if he were hurrying to get to something more important. Door shut. Key in pocket. Turn on heels. 'Who are you?' he said without emotion.

'Who are you?' she threw back at him.

He ignored her. 'Are you on holiday?'

'No, I'm here on business.'

'What kind of business?'

'None-of-your-business.'

He stood his ground. There was no room to squeeze past him. 'You mind letting me through?'

'Not yet. I'm Sergeant Harper. Dorset Crime Division.'

Her heart sank a little. Although she wasn't sure why. After all, she hadn't done anything wrong. 'Isn't this the bit where you bring out a wallet with a gold badge on it?'

'If that would cheer you up.' He dipped into his jacket pocket and pulled out a leather wallet. Sure enough, there was a gold shield inside it.

'Well, there you go. I've always wondered about that,' she said. 'Okay – I'm Astrid Kisner. I work as an art conservator at Sherborne Hall.'

'Astrid Kisner?'

'That's right.'

'Good – that saves me a trip. I need to get a statement from you.'

Harper led her towards a bench just inside the church graveyard. They were the only people there – alive at least. There was a small field of weathered headstones in front of the church. Over time some had tilted and sunk. Others were laid flat, face up in the uncut grass. They reached the bench and Harper sat down. He had his notebook open before she'd sat down next to him.

'So, you're an art conservator.' There was a flicker of a smile. 'I'm not sure if I know what that is?'

'I restore paintings. Clean them. Repair them. That kind of thing.'

'What a fascinating job.' The smile dissolved. It seemed like the 'good cop' part of the interview was now over. 'When you found the body, did you make a note of the time?'

'It was 4.29.'

'So... 4.29.' Harper wrote it down, a gold signet ring glinting on his little finger. It was the only thing on him that was showy. Everything he was wearing was clean and tidy. The dark trousers with the sharp crease, the matt-black boots. If you're not smart, at least look smart. That's what they say, don't they?

'Not many people would check the time.'

'Is that right?'

'Yes – most people who find a dead body are shocked. They'd run for help.'

Astrid shifted on the bench. 'Well, I thought it might be important later.'

'Did you?' He wrote on his notepad again. Astrid peered over to see what he'd written, but his handwriting was too small and spidery. He had other questions, and she was ready for all of them. She paused before calmly answering. No, she hadn't seen anyone leaving or near the icehouse before she found the body. No, she hadn't touched or removed anything. Yes, she had gone straight to report the matter to Cressida.

He snapped his notebook shut and stood up. 'There's

one more question.' He pursed his lips, as if a thought had surprised him.

Really? Anyone who'd seen a few TV detective shows would know that the trick question was coming up next. Astrid suspected Harper had watched more than most.

'Did you know the deceased?'

'No.'

'But you were at his shop – DeVine's Antiques. So how did you know the dead man was Gerald DeVine?'

The shadow of the church spire had ever so slowly scythed round to the bench. There was a chill in the air now.

'Local gossip. It travels quickly around here.'

'But I'm the only one who knows his name, from items on his person. And I've not been gossiping.' Harper clasped his hands together in front of him and smirked.

Astrid rarely felt this annoyed with herself. How could she have made this mistake? Of course, nobody would have known the man was DeVine unless they'd rifled through his pockets.

'Astrid, is there anything else you've forgotten to tell me?'

'I've told you everything I know.'

'Then I should remind you, it's an offence to interfere with a crime scene.'

'That's what you think this was? A crime, not an accident?' She held back a smirk of her own.

'Well, that is a possibility.' He rubbed his chin. Another mannerism he'd no doubt practised in the mirror. 'So what motive would there be to kill a friendly local shop owner?'

'I wouldn't know.'

'Exactly,' he said. 'You wouldn't.' He leant over her. She noticed he had a shaving rash under his jawline. A cheap razor. Probably a dry shave in the office before he came out. 'So why don't you leave the investigating to the experts.'

'I will… and when will they be arriving?'

He laughed in short strangled bursts. 'Very good, yes… very good.' He brought out a small card from his top pocket. 'Don't forget. If you remember something you should have told me… don't hesitate to get in touch.'

'Of course.' She took the card and watched him leave. When he reached the alleyway, she slipped the card into her wallet.

Astrid took a path that took a wide arc around the town – just to make sure she didn't bump into Harper again. She was pleased to have got the better of him in the end. Apart from that one slip-up, he'd revealed more than she had. Of course, she should have told him about the wet footsteps on the path. But she didn't trust him. To use another phrase of her mother's, he was as shifty as a one-eyed cat. Why had he been skulking around the antiques shop on his own… and in the dark? What was he looking for? Maybe it was all innocent enough. He was just a young police officer making a hash of his first real case.

Or maybe Kath was right? The English Trust had a darker side – 'like the mafia with cream teas', that was her phrase. A bit over the top maybe, but it was possible. If there was a billion pounds in the Trust's bank account, who knows? Harper could be covering up for some powerful people. Either way, as long as she stayed out of his way, she might as well carry on investigating. What harm could it do?

By the time she reached the riverbank forty minutes later, the sun had dipped behind the hills. The sky blushed peach and amber. A soft wash with a flat sable brush – that's how she would paint it. If she hadn't given up painting. Working with great masters made you realise how amateur your own work was – as Simon had always pointed out. Simon... she hadn't thought about her husband since this morning when Kath mentioned him. The investigation was taking her mind off him. It was also kind of fun. Sifting through the evidence. Narrowing down the suspects – who wouldn't enjoy that?

Through a gap in the reeds, she noticed her boat on the opposite side of the river. The name *Curlew's Rest* was painted down the side. This was the first time she'd seen it from a distance. It looked rather handsome. The prow shouldered the current, which slid past into gold and black V's behind the boat. The mast was perfectly vertical – a dark line scratching the sunset.

To get back to it took another ten minutes. Upstream to the wharf, over the bridge and back down the towpath. She could barely see where she was going now. Left hand out to make sure she wasn't going into the reeds. Right hand feeling for the hedge. How had she made it back from the pub that first night? She scrambled aboard the boat and shut the door behind her. Shoes off. The little curtains drawn over the portholes.

It was good to be back – safe and sound.

11

Monday, Day 6

At 8.40 a.m., her staff lanyard clearly on display, Astrid strode along the second floor of the house. This was the quickest way to get to the storeroom. Or it would be if she hadn't planned a detour to find Harold. The house wouldn't be open to the public for another ten minutes.

As she predicted, he was seated by the door. 'Ah, good morning to you, Astrid.' He rose slowly to his feet.

'Morning, Harold. I don't suppose I could ask you a couple of questions.'

'I'd be delighted. That's why I'm here.'

She wandered over to the window. When she turned round to find him he was in the middle of the room, his thumbs tucked into the pockets of his blazer. 'The eagle-eyed cinema goers will no doubt recognise this room from a film called *The Dark Knight*.' His voice was slow and considered, smoothing the bumps of a story he'd no doubt told word for word a thousand times.

'Sorry, Harold. I just…'

He returned to his usual voice. 'Terrible movie. I assumed it would be about a knight. It wasn't. It was about a man who dressed up as a bat.'

'Oh, right...'

He had an audience, and he wasn't going to lose it. 'The filmmakers used this room as the library for Wayne Manor. Which is adjacent to a bat cave. Although for some reason there weren't any bats down there. Just some rather unroadworthy cars and rubber suits.'

'Sorry, Harold.' She held up her hand. 'We only have a few minutes.'

'Of course.' He joined her at the window.

She pointed to the path that ran through the arch in the yew hedge, and on into the woods. 'This path through the hedge.'

Harold squinted. 'Yes?'

'Is that the only way to get to the icehouse?'

'It is.'

'There's no other way of getting into the woods then?'

'No. There's fencing all around it to keep people from sneaking into the grounds without paying.'

'Right. And why is the icehouse closed to the public at the moment?'

'Closed? No, no... it's open all day.'

'Really? There was a closed sign across the gap in the hedge.'

'Well, there shouldn't have been. It's only just been restored to working order. They cut the ice on the pond this winter and put it in there – as they would have in Georgian times. Of course, there were no fridges back then. Anyway...' he checked his watch, which had a black leather strap that hung loosely on his pale wrist '...I better get back to my post.'

'I've just got one more question.'

'Go on.'

'The top floor of the house. Is it open to the public?'

'The top floor?' Harold hesitated. 'No, it hasn't been for years.'

'Is it locked?'

Harold checked his watch again. 'Yes. Although I've no idea who has the keys. Why do you want to know?'

'Oh, well... no, I'm sure it was nothing.'

'Go on, Astrid. You can tell me.'

'Okay, the other day I was in the garden and I thought I saw a figure at the window.'

'A figure?' He shook his head. 'You know, the Trust store a lot of furniture up there. Maybe it was a trick of the light.'

'You're probably right.'

'Listen, I really must dash.' Harold smiled anxiously and set off for the door. His tread was soft and careful. He moved to the side of a floorboard that creaked when Astrid stood on it. 'I'm sorry I can't stay and chat,' he said. 'But there's supposed to be someone in the rooms at all times.'

'To welcome guests?'

'Mainly, but they also need someone for insurance reasons. In case anyone makes a grab for the antiques. Although I don't know if it would work. I'm still pretty sprightly, but I can't imagine Margaret wrestling a cat burglar to the floor. Can you?'

'I haven't met her.'

'She's just had her hips done.'

They reached the door. 'Well, thank you, Harold. You've been more than helpful.'

'I'm very glad. And by the way – if you are short of company, we volunteers have our lunch in the old boiler room in the basement. I'm sure the others would love to meet you too.'

'I may do that, thanks.'

He sat down, put his palms on his knees and watched the door for the first of the visitors.

On the way to the storeroom, Astrid mulled over what she'd learnt from talking to Harold. The case had got more intriguing. Maybe she had imagined the figure at the window. But there was one thing she was sure about. Whoever had gone into the icehouse after DeVine had drawn the closed sign across the hedge. Which meant they didn't want to be disturbed. Then they'd taken the same path back into the gardens – there was no other way out of the woods.

The problem was, it could have been any of hundreds of people in the grounds that day. Any visitor, member of staff or volunteer could have slipped into the woods. So where should she look now? For the time being, like the wet footprints on the path, the trail had evaporated.

For the rest of the morning Astrid went through the remaining collection. She worked steadily through the paintings, taking photos and notes and setting aside anything that might be worth featuring as the star of the show. Eventually she found what she was looking for. Wrapped in a white sheet was a small landscape, about twelve inches by ten. It showed a grey sea surging against towering cliffs. Along the headland were copses of trees. There was a white smudge for a building, a lighthouse presumably, near the edge of the rock face. She checked the signature, although she already knew who'd painted it. Sure enough, scratched in olive paint was the name John Constable.

She was going to take some photos, but her hands were shaking. This was too exciting. The landscape was smaller than most Constables, less showy than the watermill scenes and cathedrals he was famous for. No more than an afternoon's work. Perhaps it was a rough guide for a larger canvas he never painted. It may not be his finest work, but it was almost definitely a Constable. And if the Trust had paid less than five hundred thousand for it, they'd got a bargain.

Astrid checked the list again. The painting was noted on the other side. It had the date down as 1816. If she remembered correctly that was the year he'd married his childhood sweetheart Maria. They'd gone on honeymoon on the Dorset coast, staying with a local vicar, who was a friend of his. He must have brought his art materials with him. So was Maria in the painting? Astrid took out the magnifying glass and ran it across the canvas. There on a path that wound up the side of the hill was a tiny mark. Astrid looked closer. It was two quick brushstrokes. A dash of blue, a dab of hazel above it. There was no mistaking it. This was a figure – Maria walking ahead of him? Who else would it be?

Astrid stepped back and gave a little fist pump. It wasn't something she'd done before, but now seemed as good a time as any. Not only was she going to be working on a Constable, there was a story behind it. Paintings were always more beautiful with stories attached to them – and this was a romance. Cressida might get her 'blockbuster' exhibition after all. She left the painting on the table and gathered her bag. It was time for lunch.

Astrid eventually located the Orangery Café in part of a stable block at the back of the kitchen garden. It was busy. There was a crowd of people milling around the hot food area. A long line of families queued patiently to get to the chiller cabinets. At the front a child was grabbing a selection of snacks.

'That's six items, Josh,' hissed his mum. 'Put a yoghurt back.'

'Can I swap it for more crisps?'

'Okay… quickly.' Josh was dragged away as the next family shuffled forwards. 'Sorry.'

'Honestly, it's fine,' said the dad behind her.

But it wasn't – you could tell. Everyone was tense. The place had the same atmosphere as just before a riot in a prison canteen. Astrid skipped ahead and quickly bought the first sandwich in reach. Maybe it would be nice to have lunch with the volunteers.

The signs to the boiler room took her down a corridor in the basement, past some empty wine cellars, over a rope and round the corner. Astrid pushed open the big cream door and was struck by a warm fug of cosiness – a mixture of steam, coffee and shortbread. There was a long table in the middle of the room. Harold was sitting there with an elderly woman who was eating something brown and lumpy from a Tupperware bowl. She was wearing a shapeless floral dress that reminded Astrid of a flowering shrub she'd seen in the gardens.

'You made it.' Harold got up and took her elbow, steering her round to face the shrub lady. 'Margaret – this is my new friend Astrid. The art restorer I was telling you about.'

The woman peered at her. Like a conger eel drifting out from some crevice in a rock. 'I won't get up – it's my hips.'

'Margaret specialises in Georgian etiquette and fashion,' said Harold.

'Only Georgian. The Victorian stuff is a bit dull for my tastes.' She raised a spoon of brown food to her lips.

'How fascinating,' said Astrid. 'I love the Georgian era.'

Harold shuffled over to the sink area. There was a microwave, a rack of cups and a silver water boiler with a black tap at the bottom. 'Coffee, Astrid?'

'Oh, yes please. Just milk.' Astrid settled into a spare seat at the table. 'So, are you two the only volunteers today?'

'I'm afraid so,' said Margaret. 'It's just the three of us at the moment – me, Harold and Denise. There's a bit of a recruitment problem at the moment for volunteers. So when we have our coffee and tea breaks we have to pull the rope across some of the rooms.'

'There's some garden volunteers,' said Harold, pouring a dash of milk into a sage-coloured cup. 'But they knock off before lunch.'

'The garden volunteers are pretty much part-time,' Margaret said dismissively. She worked the spoon into the corner of the bowl. 'Not sure you'll get much sense out of them though. You have any questions about the house, you ask us.'

'I promise I will.'

Margaret pressed the lid down on the empty bowl and pushed it to one side. 'So why are the Trust restoring the paintings?'

'Oh, they're planning an exhibition before Christmas – the Treasures of Sherborne Hall.'

'I'm guessing this is one of Cressida's big ideas?' Harold raised an eyebrow.

'Yes, she's organising it,' said Astrid.

'Ughh… Cressida.' Margaret pretended to retch up a bit of food into her hand.

'Margaret's not a fan of Cressida,' said Harold.

'I got that,' said Astrid, suppressing a smile.

Harold came over with a cup of coffee and placed it in front of her.

'Thank you.' Astrid took a sip.

Harold sat down next to her. 'Help yourself to biscuits. They're free.' He pointed to the jar. 'One of the perks.'

'I might do later, thanks.'

'Do you know what they paid for the paintings?' said Margaret. 'I heard it was close to a million.'

'I honestly wouldn't know. My job is just to restore them.' Astrid reached into her bag and brought out her sandwich.

'One thing's for sure. Lady Sherborne needed the money,' said Margaret.

'Really?' said Astrid.

'Of course. The poor old bird didn't have a pot to piss

in after her husband died. She had to pay off a massive inheritance tax bill. She's still broke now.'

'Margaret... we're not sure if that's true, are we?' said Harold.

'It's a fact.' Margaret reached for the jar and tweezered out a stick of shortbread with two fingers. 'And boy, is she furious that the public are wandering around her house. I heard that she pushed a toddler over the ha-ha.'

'Listen, I'm sure Astrid isn't interested in all this tittle-tattle,' said Harold.

But Astrid was very interested. She'd just done a good job at not showing it. 'I don't mind, honestly.' She carried on eating the sandwich, as the others kept up a steady flow of gossip. Their conversation had a rhythm you only get with good friends. Each playing a part. Harold – the voice of reason. Margaret – judge, jury and hangman. Her most stinging comments were aimed at the 'bigwigs' in the Trust's central office in London, and nearer to home, Cressida, who she seemed to resent even more than Denise.

However much they complained, though, Astrid was sure that there was nowhere else they would rather be than here. In the basement of a stately home which, as they mentioned a couple of times, 'really belonged to the volunteers'. Without them to keep up standards, they were sure the whole place would fall apart.

They were in the middle of a heated discussion on the new changes to volunteer travel expenses – an extra five pence a mile if you cycled in ('pointless!' barked Margaret) – when there was a crackle from a heavy walkie-talkie on the sideboard. The voice was slow and deliberate. 'Denise to the volunteer hub. Respond please.'

Harold grabbed the walkie-talkie and spoke crisply into it. 'This is Harold. Over.' There was a twinkle in his eye, as if he'd been reminded of some successful army manoeuvre long ago.

There was a pause as everyone waited for Denise to reply. The walkie-talkie clicked a few times. 'Oh, dear.' Harold shook his head. 'She's forgotten you don't have to press the button. This handset is on the blink so you can hear everything all the time.'

Margaret tapped the side of the biscuit jar with a spoon. 'Tell her we're running low.'

Harold gripped the walkie-talkie. 'Denise. Can you please bring more biscuits from the stock room? Over.'

There was some heavy breathing, more clicking, then Denise's voiced crackled back. 'On my way. Over.'

'Honestly,' muttered Harold, placing it back on the side and covering it with a tea towel. 'It needs to get fixed.'

'We need to get Denise fixed,' growled Margaret.

'Oh, Margaret, that's a bit harsh.' Harold faced Astrid. 'Don't worry, it's only a bit of friendly rivalry. You see, Margaret and Denise are up for the same job. It's to do some private VIP tours in the evening.'

'A paying job at the English Trust,' said Margaret with a wistful sigh. 'They're as rare as hen's teeth. And Denise already gets Christmas shifts in the gift shop.' Margaret raised herself using a stick she had under the table. 'How's that flipping fair?'

'It's not, is it, Margaret?' sighed Harold, who was checking his tie in the mirror over the sink.

It was nearly two o'clock and lunch was over. And it had been very entertaining. Lady Sherborne's money problems,

Margaret and Harold's dislike of Cressida and Denise. Kath would have loved to hear it. It would confirm her theory that the Trust was a hotbed of intrigue and scandal. It was really only harmless office gossip though, no more than that. Wasn't it?

Astrid had wondered what she would do if they asked her about herself. How much would she tell them about her life in London and how she got here? But they never asked, which was a relief. Nor had they mentioned the death in the icehouse. News didn't travel as fast as she thought. Or Harper had decided not to do a thorough investigation. At DeVine's antique shop he'd revealed the icehouse was a 'crime scene'. So why wasn't the place wrapped up in yellow and black tape right now? That's how it worked on those TV shows. She'd have to keep a close eye on Harper from now on.

Astrid decided she needed to jot down some of the details of the case before she forgot. So instead of going straight to the storeroom, she made a detour for the gift shop – which was in the same stable block as the Orangery Café. Astrid located the stationery section, which was in the corner between a Welsh dresser loaded with jams and chutneys, and a rail of pastel cardigans.

There was a good range of notepads. Most had tasteful lino-cut covers showing hares leaping across cornfields or puffins on a cliff. But they were either too small, or the pages inside were plain or graph paper.

At the back she eventually found an 'official' One Direction notepad. It was a bit dusty, and having a boy band on the cover wasn't ideal – presumably that's who the four teenagers staring into middle distance were. But it was a good size with white lined paper. And it was eighty per cent off.

The cashier, a middle-aged woman in a William Morris print blouse, took the notepad from Astrid with an expression of revulsion. The way a hygiene inspector might lift a dead rat out from behind a chest freezer.

'Sorry, I've no idea how that got there – we've had an inventory problem recently.'

Astrid paid for it along with a nice silver ink pen and found a bench under the chestnut tree. She folded back the first page then wrote 'what we know so far,' and underlined it twice.

Below that she put down the details of DeVine's death and the discovery of the plain white chalk marks. This last bit was circled with an arrow to the word 'clue'. The next page was headed 'suspects', although there was nothing to fill in. Except 'Sergeant Harper', which merited two question marks at this stage. She stared at the almost blank page. It wasn't a great start. But it was a start.

At the bottom corner of the page was a headshot of 'Harry' from One Direction who, according to the daily 'fun fact', had a phobia of four-legged animals after being attacked by a goat when he was ten years old.

'What do you think, Harry?' she whispered.

'Hi there.'

Astrid jumped. Emily was standing in front of her, holding a pile of mail to her chest. 'Wow.' Emily pointed at the notepad. 'I used to love One Direction.'

'Uh… me too,' said Astrid.

'They were my favourite band at uni. Then Zayn left and ruined it.' She sighed.

'I know, what a disaster.'

'Anyway.' Emily perked up again. 'I don't suppose you've seen Margaret?'

'Not since lunch – sorry.'

'Don't worry. I have a letter for her. I'll put it in her locker in the volunteer hub.' She waved the letter. 'See you later, Astrid.'

'Yes, see you later, Emily.'

Astrid watched her cross the courtyard and follow the path back to the house. Then she snapped her notepad shut.

For the rest of the afternoon, Astrid went through the remaining paintings. She now had a good idea of the dozen that would make up the exhibition. There were a couple of vivid storm scenes that she'd added to the list. But nothing that would outshine the Constable. She packed up her materials and decided to call it a day.

Cressida must have heard her walking down the corridor. She'd just passed the door when it swung open and a cheerful voice called after her. 'Oh, good. It's you.' Cressida beckoned her over. 'Would you mind popping in for a moment?'

Astrid stepped into the office. Cressida hurried round her and firmly closed the door.

'I don't suppose you talked to the press about the accident in the icehouse?' She stressed the word *accident*. As if to embed it in Astrid's mind.

'I've only spoken to the police. They took a statement yesterday.'

'And did they, you know... suggest the Trust was in trouble?'

'No. Not at all.'

'Thank goodness.' She sighed. 'We can't let the Trust's brand be dented in any way.'

'I'm sure it won't be.'

'Fabulous.' Cressida was back to her usual self. She dodged round Astrid and swung the door open. 'Well, I won't keep you.'

Astrid stood where she was. 'Actually. I do have some other news for you. There's a really nice Constable among the paintings.'

'Constable? Right...' She played idly with her necklace, which was made of heavy amethysts. 'I'm sorry, I haven't got a clue about art.'

'You didn't have anything to do with the purchase of the collection?'

'No, that was arranged by central office.'

'Okay, well, it's a really lovely work, and I think it should be the centrepiece of the exhibition. There might be a romantic story attached to it.'

'Smashing – I'll leave it up to you then.' Cressida opened the door a bit wider. 'Have a lovely evening, Astrid.'

'You too.' Astrid stepped out into the corridor and closed the door behind her.

12

If there was one thing that Astrid liked, even more than pressed cotton bed sheets, it was an empty email inbox. Just thinking of the emails stacking up over the days set her teeth on edge. Sometimes she'd walk past colleagues' desks and see they had hundreds of unopened messages. It was a struggle not to say anything.

She arrived at the library about twenty minutes before it closed and booted up the laptop at her usual table. To her relief there were only about a dozen emails in the 'focused' file of her work account. HR clearly hadn't got round to shutting it down.

The first was Muraki checking if she was okay. She replied, thanking him for caring and saying she'd explain everything soon enough. How she would have loved to have told him she was knee-deep in a murder investigation!

There were a handful of other work emails from people outside the department who'd clearly not been told she'd left. She deleted them all – not her problem now – and scanned the twenty-two junk emails headed up by one titled *'Doctors are amazed by this home-made cure for shingles'*.

She was about to dump the whole folder when she

spotted an article at the bottom of the page – *'The secret signs that show you're heading for a divorce'*.

Her finger hung over the delete key. Had she really misread her marriage all this time? Hard to believe, but maybe worth checking.

She tapped 'enter' and a headshot of 'Relationship expert, Brenda Golden', a woman with a tight perm and reading glasses, popped up. Next to her was a picture of two wedding cake figurines with their backs to each other. Below that was a series of questions Brenda promised would show any cracks in a marriage.

The opener asked, *'What was his last birthday present to you?'* Astrid drummed her fingers on the table. Simon had given her an Amazon gift card. Nothing wrong with that. It meant she could buy something she really wanted. Brenda disagreed – unromantic gifts she said 'could be a clue that your love life has gone off the boil'.

Next question. *'Is your husband the first person you confide in?'* No. That was Gina. Astrid felt a stab of sadness, and quickly moved on to the next question.

But as the questions stacked up so, according to Brenda, did the signs of a marriage in trouble.

'Do you argue?' Not at all, thought Astrid. That had to be a good sign? Apparently not. Arguing showed 'the spark is still alive'.

She sat back in her chair and muttered. There was no science in this, was there? Probably not – Brenda Golden might have reading glasses but there was no sign of a PhD in psychology.

It didn't matter though – her marriage was over. Her husband, the man she loved, had left her. For her best friend, who she'd lost as well. She trapped her hands between her legs and the chair to stop them shaking. No crying, Astrid. Not here.

Someone had once told her that getting over a break-up is like standing with your back to the ocean. You think you're okay, then once in a while you're hit by a wave that takes you off your feet. Like now. This grief, and that's what it was, had floored her again. And she had nobody to confide in. That might be the worst part. Right now Gina was with Simon. This was like getting over two break-ups, and it didn't feel like she'd ever recover from either of them.

She emptied the junk folder. Then she ordered the restoration supplies she needed, putting the delivery address down as Cressida Giles, at Sherborne Hall. She began packing her laptop away, then another thought crept up on her. It had been four days and Simon hadn't been in touch to give her an explanation. The next time she saw him… oh, boy – big public embarrassment time. Jug of water over his head in a restaurant. Standing up at one of his lectures and telling everyone what a prize shit he was. That kind of thing. Right now, though, some answers would do. She was owed that.

She took out her phone, checked the librarian wasn't watching, and set up a text. Her finger quivered over the screen. Do it, Astrid.

You're a coward Simon… now tell me why you did it?

The path back to the boat was thick with scent. Little white flowers covered the hedgerows. Black flies with long dangling back legs floated clumsily between them. The reeds hushed in the breeze, sending a scatter of small brown birds. Like a handful of seeds thrown in the air. Everything was moving. Buzzing, humming, filling every space. In the distance the spire of the church shimmering in the heat. Early summer in England. How many beautiful days like this had she missed by working so hard?

At the boat she worked the key into the lock and pushed the door open. On the top step was a square white postcard. It must have been pushed under the gap of the door. She picked it up carefully by the corner and read it. In black marker pen were the words:

I KNOW WHAT HAPPENED TO DEVINE. MEET ME AT THE ARNE CAR PARK – 6 P.M.

She sat in the car and tapped in directions for the Arne on her phone. It appeared to be a nature reserve that jutted out into Poole Harbour. There was a single road that led into a wood and stopped at a car park. It was 5.40 p.m. The route would take fifteen minutes to get there – no time for second thoughts. Or to tell anyone where she was going – which, if she did, they'd probably advise her not to. Meeting a stranger in the woods who had information about a murder... when was that ever a good idea? Still, she needed answers about DeVine's death, and there was nowhere else to find them.

Right now, nobody believed in her. That's why she was going to crack this case. That's what they said on those TV shows, right? Crack the case... wide open. She'd failed at her marriage. But she wasn't going to fail at this. She was going to show people she was worth something. Especially Simon. She checked the phone. There was still no reply to her text.

The Arne car park wasn't much more than a square of dry ground, the size of a tennis court, which was surrounded by high beech trees. There was one other car there, a blue Volvo estate. It was newly polished, a Panama hat on the rear window shelf – hardly the car of a criminal. A few minutes later a middle-aged man wearing maroon cords appeared from the path and unlocked it. He knocked the dust off his hiking boots with his walking stick and drove off.

The only other sign of life was a log cabin that had a sign saying 'VISITOR CENTRE' over the door. There was a English Trust logo in the window. Astrid got out of the Mini and paced across the car park. A couple appeared from the path and carried on past her without breaking their conversation. She was on her own now. Maybe it was too risky?

She was about to get back in the car when a man came out of the log cabin and beckoned her to come over. He was shorter than average – five foot six maybe. Slim build. In his sixties with a grey goatee beard. He was wearing olive hiking trousers with a square patched at the knee and a green fleece. She sized him up. If it came to it, she might be able to overpower him.

As she walked over, he looked around the car park behind her. 'Is it just you?' His voice was high and nasal.

'Yes, I'm on my own. But I've told other people I was coming here.'

'Good for you,' he muttered, looking slightly bewildered. 'Let's go then.' On his back was an old canvas rucksack. The way it swung suggested there was something heavy inside.

She searched her pockets for something sharp. Anything. But there was only the key fob for her car.

'Do you think we should just stay close to the car park?'

'Car park? No, no. We need to go into the woods.' He stared at her. 'Is that a problem?'

Decision time. She needed answers or her investigation was over. Someone else, Harper maybe, would solve it. 'Okay.' Her lips were dry. 'After you.'

She hung back for a while, watching his rucksack swinging on his shoulders. Eventually he stopped at a fork in the path and she had to catch him up. To the right the trail weaved through the trees and back out into the sunlight. The sea glistened in the distance. To the left it headed deeper into the beech forest.

'Chop, chop,' he said, taking the left fork.

'Sure,' she said, keeping a few yards behind him.

He turned to face her. 'So do you know these woods at all?'

'Yes, I'm very familiar with them.'

'Good. People get lost in here only a hundred yards from the visitor centre.' He stepped over a log and there was a clink of metal from his rucksack. She looked around. There was nobody else in sight.

They reached a hollow and the man stepped off the path. He studied the trees in the dappled light. 'Yes, this is it,' he said, setting off again. When he was twenty yards ahead he stopped near a fallen tree that was covered in dark moss. He bent down and ran his hand behind the log. Then he waved her over.

She paused – but there was no going back. She had to see what he was looking at. When she was a few yards from him he held up his hand. 'Okay, careful. Stay there.' He took out a tiny red penknife from his pocket.

'If I'm not back before dark, my friends will be very worried,' she said.

'Oh, we'll only be an hour or so.' He flipped the small blade of the penknife open and got down on his knees. 'This is a lovely specimen.' He pointed to a cream-coloured mushroom that was poking up between the dead leaves. He cut the mushroom carefully at the base and held it up in the dappled light. '*Hydnum repandum.* The hedgehog mushroom.'

'Sorry,' said Astrid. 'Why are you showing me this?'

He stared at her again. 'Excuse me?'

'You lure me into the woods, and now you're showing me a mushroom?'

'I don't understand.'

'Come on – just tell me what you're up to.' She stepped back, ready to run.

He held up the penknife. 'I'll tell you why, madam... because this is the guided foraging walk. And mushrooms are one of the best things to eat.'

'Guided foraging walk?' Astrid burst out laughing. 'Oh no. That's hilarious.' She gasped for breath.

'Are you alright?'

She managed to compose herself. 'I thought you'd sent me a note.'

'Note?'

'It's fine. Sorry…' Astrid held out her hand. 'I'm Astrid.'

The man cautiously shook her hand. 'I'm Eric Wainwright. There's usually a handful of people who turn up so you're lucky to have me all to yourself.'

'You know what? I think I am lucky. Please, Eric, tell me more about the hedgehog mushroom.'

'I will.' He folded up the tiny penknife and slipped it into his pocket. 'Like all mushrooms they are really the fruiting body of an organism. The rest is a mass of mycelia that spread out in a circle under the leaf mould. You're standing in the middle of one now.'

She looked down and noticed that there were other cream mushrooms ranged around her.

'That's why you have to be careful where you're treading. Now then.' He held the mushroom up and waved it about. Even with an audience of one, he was enjoying himself. He passed the mushroom over to her. 'Smell that and tell me what you think.'

She brought it to her nose and inhaled. 'It's kind of earthy. Nutty maybe.' She sniffed again. 'A slight cucumber smell.'

He clapped his hands. 'Well done. You have a wonderful mushroom nose, Astrid.'

'Thank you. I can honestly say that nobody has said that to me before.'

He swung off the backpack and placed it on the ground. After loosening the string at the top he took out a linen bag and dropped the mushroom into it. 'So, we'll pick another couple of these. Then we'll see if we can find a saffron milk cap or two. Does that sound like fun, Astrid?'

'You know, it does sound like fun.'

They carried on along paths that cut through chest-high bracken. Out into bright clearings. Past fallen ancient trees, their broken limbs reaching back up to the sky. Birdsong ricocheted through the branches. Along the way Eric pointed out clumps of mushrooms among the leaves, or sprouting in fleshy ruffles from damp logs. Some had tempting names – 'chicken of the woods', 'penny bun', 'beefsteak mushroom'. 'Edible and excellent,' according to Eric. Others, he said, should be avoided at all costs, especially the ones with white gills – if the names weren't enough to warn you off. 'Destroying angel', 'sickener' and 'amethyst deceiver' were three he regarded as 'particularly nasty'.

After an hour they emerged onto a thin beach – the great bay of Poole Harbour was ahead of them. A few yachts were moored off a nearby island. For the entire walk she never saw another person. Other than Eric. He settled in the sand cross-legged and arranged the mushrooms around him. He couldn't have looked more like a pixie if he'd been sitting on top of a red and white spotted toadstool.

'Now, Astrid. I was going to cook some of these up. It's all part of the foraging tour.' He brought out a small cast-iron frying pan from his rucksack.

'It was a frying pan.' She laughed.

'Um, yes… a frying pan. Anyway. I was going to slice up the hedgehog mushroom, add some butter. Wild garlic. Maybe a pinch of samphire from the waterline. Mmm… humm.' He wrinkled his nose, already tasting the meal ahead. 'You're welcome to join me, but I guess your friends would get worried.'

'Oh yes.' It did sound mouth-watering. She was hungry now – but what could she tell him? That she'd thought he'd set a trap to bump her off because she knew too much? 'You know, I'd love to, Eric. But I better get back, they do worry about me.'

'I understand.' He started bringing out other ingredients. A half bottle of brandy. A square of butter in a little jam jar. 'Now remember what I told you. Never take more than you need. Then there's enough for everyone.'

'Thank you so much, Eric. I've had a fantastic time. Oh…' She patted her pockets for her wallet. 'Do I owe you anything?'

'Gosh no.' He wafted a hand at her. 'No, no. It's all part of the English Trust experience.'

'How lovely. Well, thanks again.' She looked up and down the beach, and back up the path into the woods.

'Oh, the quickest way back to the car park is along the beach. Then turn right.'

'Yes, yes,' she said, hands on hips. 'It's coming back to me now.'

She set off down the beach. There was still nobody around. A small rowing boat with *Sea Breeze* written on the side had been pulled up onto the shore. But that was the only sign of life. The scent of pine sap drifted from the woods. A bird somewhere in the trees cooed and whirred. Her stomach rumbled in reply. Time to forage some food of her own. On a plate this time.

The Angler's Arms was exactly as it had been the first night. Although this was a place, she imagined, that wouldn't change from one decade to the next. The restaurants she went to in London were always updating the menu – riding the latest foodie trend or revamping the decor. Looking around the empty snug it seemed like polishing the glass case of the stuffed pike was an annual event. Dolly came over with a glass of wine from the box as Astrid read the menu at the bar. 'You decided yet?' she snapped.

Astrid resisted the urge to blow gently on her to see if any dust rose up from her hair. 'The fish and chips.' She checked the menu again. 'What sort of fish is it?'

'Battered.'

'No, I mean. The type of fish?'

'No idea. I didn't catch it myself, dear.'

'Well, that's sold it to me.' She shut the menu. 'Fish and chips it is.'

Astrid chose the table next to the fire. Ten minutes later the food arrived. Dolly set down the plate and brought out a handful of red and blue plastic sachets from the front of her apron. 'Ketchup if you need it,' she said, leaving them in a small pile on the table.

The meal was surprisingly good. The fish, haddock possibly, was fresh from the sea. The chips, wedges of potato with the skin still on, had a satisfying crunch to them. The bright red ketchup added a bold splash of colour. She pushed the plate out onto the table and sat back in the pew.

The evening had worked out well. Although the more she thought about it, she had pushed her luck. Eric the forager had showed up, but who was supposed to meet her? And what would have happened if they did? Next time she'd definitely tell someone where she was going. Also, it would be nice to have someone to confide in – to share the drama with.

She took out her phone and dashed off a text, before she could change her mind.

Hi Kath. I'm in the Angler's Arms – can I buy you a drink?

If she really stressed how important it was to keep a secret, it would be alright to tell Kath. Wouldn't it? A text pinged up on her phone.

There in 5. Pint of Badger's – thanx.

Astrid waited until Kath was halfway into her pint, then checked that Dolly was out of earshot. 'Listen, Kath.' She leant forwards. 'There's something I want to tell you.'

Kath pulled her chair nearer. 'I think I know,' she whispered.

'Do you?'

'Gerald DeVine – right?' Kath gave up the whispering and went for a slightly gravelly version of her usual voice. 'Heard he came a cropper at Sherborne Hall. Everyone knows.'

'How does everyone know?'

'Someone knew the ambulance driver who loaded him up. Then they told Heather who runs Tea Cake Max, the café on the high street. Heather has marriage problems so she'll talk to anyone.' Kath shook her head. 'Honestly, I can't stand the gossip round here.'

'Is that right?' Astrid held back a smile and took a long swig of her glass of wine. 'Anyway, I still feel bad for not telling you when I saw you at the beach.'

'Don't worry – I get it.' She tapped the side of her nose. 'The English Trust have you in their grip.'

'Grip?'

She squeezed her fist together as if wringing the last bit of juice out of a lemon. 'Like a vice.'

'No, really... anyway. Kath, if I tell you what happened will you promise to keep it to yourself?'

'Of course,' she breathed. 'Not a soul.'

Astrid carefully explained what had happened. How she'd found the body in the icehouse, the wet footsteps up the path and the note that led her to the Arne. As she talked Kath sat wide-eyed. Every so often she interrupted to say 'no way,' or to get Astrid to go over the juiciest details. When Astrid finished the story Kath drained her pint and put her hands on the table. 'Well, I told you something like this was going to happen.'

'To be fair, I don't think you predicted this one, Kath.'

'Not exactly, no. But I did say no good would come of it.' She took a stray chip off Astrid's plate, dipped it in the puddle of ketchup and popped it in her mouth. 'Good news though – you've done the right thing telling me. I can ask around the village.'

'You know, you really don't have to.'

'What? Just try and stop me. It'll be like Thelma and Louise.'

'Um, not sure if that ended up so well for them.'

'Cagney and Lacey then.'

'Kath.' Astrid sighed. 'Alright then – you can ask around. But you have to be incredibly discreet.'

'Incredibly discreet.' Kath mimed zipping her lips shut.

'I've already had that policeman Harper warning me off.'

'Oh aye?' Kath took a paper napkin, wiped her fingers and balled it up on the plate. 'Wouldn't worry about him. He's new. And he couldn't catch a cold if he sat on a glacier with his pants off.'

'You might be right. We'll just have to see.'

Dolly shuffled over to the table and picked up the plate. 'Everything alright then?'

Astrid looked at Kath, who was sitting bolt upright with a deadpan expression. 'Everything is fine. Thank you,' she said slowly. Then winked at Astrid.

Maybe it hadn't been the best idea to tell Kath. There was only a slim chance that she would keep this secret – which she needed if she was going to keep ahead of Harper. But she was also the most amusing, open person she'd ever met.

Dolly picked up the empty glasses. 'Same again?'

Astrid smiled. 'Yes, why not?'

13

Tuesday, Day 7

It was 9.10 a.m. and the first visitors to Sherborne Hall had found their way into the gardens. From the high window of the storeroom Astrid watched them filter along the paths. Toddlers ran ahead of parents. Couples sat down on benches. Others leant over the hedges to read the labels. A gardener stepped forwards to explain more about the plants. Nods and thank-yous were exchanged. It was as polite a scene as you could imagine. Hard to conceive that something so grim had taken place a couple of days ago. Would the murderer return? Were they here now checking to see if the murder scene was being investigated?

Over by the yew hedge the chain had been lifted back. A handful of people wandered through towards the icehouse. If there had been an investigation, it had all been cleared away pretty quick. As far as the Trust was concerned, it was business as usual.

Astrid opened a couple of windows. It was a bright day and even without the new halogen lamp she'd ordered

– Emily had promised to 'keep an eye out' for the delivery – she had enough light to work with. At least for cleaning the less important paintings. She couldn't resist taking another look at the Constable again though. She dragged the table over to the window and unwrapped it from its sheet.

It was as thrilling to hold it again as it had been a couple of days ago. She laid the cloth out on the table and turned the painting face down. One of the first things that she'd learnt as a conservator was that the backs of paintings could be as revealing as the front. Especially the frames.

There was a single label pasted on the upper edge. It had turned yellowish brown with time but the words were still readable:

Thomas Agnew & Sons. Old Bond Street Galleries, London.

That made sense. Agnew's were a long-established art dealers specialising in Old Masters. They must have sold the painting at some stage.

She took out her magnifying glass and ran it over the frame. It was made of a light pine, again stained by time. The only other marks were the initials *L.B.C.* handwritten in a hard pencil, and the description – *Weymouth Cliffs 1816*. That was the same date on the list, the same year he went on honeymoon. The romantic story, Constable's love of painting taking him away from his new bride, would hold up.

Most of Constable's oil paintings were done on a canvas, which he later pinned out on a wooden frame. This appeared to be a hard board – a thin panel scratched and dotted with pin marks. That made sense. Constable would probably not have brought canvases with him from London. Was the board something he found lying around at the vicarage? There might be more clues if she could get the painting out of the frame.

There was a black tack in each corner holding the board in place. She went to her work case to get some fine-nosed pliers. As she leant over the case, she felt a draught of cold air on the back of her neck. She turned towards the door and gasped sharply. A woman with a walking stick was standing in the middle of the room staring out of the windows. She was wearing a tweed jacket, cinched at the waist. Cream riding trousers, short brown boots and a green and gold Hermès silk scarf knotted under her chin. She edged forwards towards the window without acknowledging Astrid was there.

Astrid studied her more closely. Her hair was brilliant white and candy floss thin. Slender arched eyebrows had been drawn in dark pencil. There was a tide mark of light foundation just under her ears, from which hung pear-shaped pearls.

'Hello?' said Astrid.

The woman pursed her lips and carried on staring out of the window.

'Are you alright?'

The woman's eyes were still fixed on the garden. 'You know which room this used to be?'

'I don't, sorry.'

She turned to face her. 'It was my nursery. As a child I used to sit by this window and watch the seasons change. If I wanted any flowers of a particular colour then someone would tell the head gardener. They'd plant what I wanted. I could paint the landscape.' The childhood memory had softened her for a moment. Then the meanness quickly returned. 'Now look at it. Families. Ice cream vendors. Just hideous.'

'You must be Lady Sherborne?'

'That's right.' Then she grunted something that sounded like 'char'. She had a habit of killing off her vowels if they got too close to each other.

'A chair?'

'That's what I said.'

Astrid brought over the wooden chair and put it down by the window. Lady Sherborne eased herself into it. 'Are you a painter?'

'I do paint... well, used to. But I'm here to clean and restore the collection of paintings. There's going to be an exhibition later this year.'

'Is there?' She crossed her arms.

'Actually, while you're here.' Astrid went over to the paintings she'd chosen so far. 'I wonder if I could ask you where some of these were hung? It will help me work out how best to clean them.' She picked up an oil painting of a vase of lilies that were yellowed by a dark varnish.

'That—' Lady Sherborne peered at the picture '—was hung over the fireplace.'

'That's useful to know. I thought there was a build-up of soot.' Astrid carried on picking out paintings. Lady Sherborne remembered only about half of them. There had been so many in the house, she explained, and the collection was always changing. Her late husband kept selling them to pay the maintenance bills, she said with a hint of annoyance.

After a few minutes Lady Sherborne began to shift in her chair. Astrid hurriedly reached for the Constable. 'If I could just ask you about this one.'

'If you must.'

'What can you tell me about it?'

'It was in one of the bedrooms. I don't know any more than that.'

'I see. Well, I think it should be the centrepiece of the exhibition.'

'No, no...' Lady Sherborne picked up her stick and pointed it to another painting by the wall. 'That should be the star of the show.'

It was a portrait – full length, a young woman about twenty years old in a light blue ball dress. The figure stared imperiously out of the frame. Astrid went over to fetch it then placed it against the table. It hadn't even come close to making her shortlist. The brushstrokes were uniform – soft, too flattering. The art equivalent of gauze over a lens. 'I'm not sure it really has much merit, to be honest.'

'Oh really?' said Lady Sherborne dryly.

'No, the colours are a bit sickly. The pose, it's a bit melodramatic. And the subject... well, she's beautiful... but so stern.'

Lady Sherborne was on her feet. 'And do you know who the subject is?'

'No, I don't.'

'It's me. That was painted when I had my coming-out ball.'

Astrid studied the painting again – buying some time, the back of her neck burning from Lady Sherborne's gaze. She turned to face her. 'I am so sorry.' She laughed nervously. 'But hey, I did say you were beautiful back then.'

Lady Sherborne stood in front of the painting and struck a similar pose. As if she was admiring herself in the mirror. 'Back then?'

Astrid pinned on a serious expression. 'Sorry, no... now as well.'

Lady Sherborne picked up her stick. Her knuckles whitened on the silver handle. 'If this exhibition has anything to say about the history of Sherborne Hall, this portrait should take centre place. The lady of the house must be there. Not some mediocre landscape. So start freshening it up.'

'I'm not sure if I have the final say.'

'Well make sure you do.' She narrowed her eyes at Astrid. 'Oh, and I never liked that bracelet I was wearing so you can change that too. Add a bit more sparkle to it. But let's be sure about one thing – my portrait will take pride of place.' She pointed her stick at Astrid then turned for the door.

Astrid made her way down the corridor to the volunteer hub. Lunch with some good company was a better option than freshening up a young Lady Sherborne. It would have to be done at some point – Lady Sherborne was clearly used to getting her own way. Now there was a ploughman's cheese triple pack from the Orangery Café to enjoy, and a jar full of the kind of biscuits Simon would disapprove of. Nothing took the enjoyment off a good biscuit more than Simon tutting at the other side of the table. Well, he wasn't here now so she was going to have as many biscuits as she liked.

She checked her phone.

No reply from Simon.

'I noticed you speaking to Lady Sherborne?' Harold shuffled his chair closer.

'Did you?' said Astrid.

'Um… yes. I was just taking a quick constitutional – don't tell anyone – and I saw her coming out of the storeroom.'

'Well, yes, I did meet her. She's quite formidable, isn't she?'

Margaret folded down the corner of her book on Georgian tapestry and put it to one side. 'Deadly, would be more appropriate.'

'You know I'm renovating the collection of paintings that she sold to the Trust,' said Astrid. 'Well, one of them is a portrait of her as a young debutante. And she wants this to be the star attraction of the exhibition.'

'Course she does,' snorted Margaret.

'And, I think you'll like this. She even wants me to paint in a fancier bracelet.'

'Really? And are you going to do it?' said Harold.

'I guess so.' Astrid looked at their eager faces. 'All part of the job. Some of the best-known paintings in the world have been changed over the years.'

'That's right. The *Mona Lisa* was changed many times,' said Harold.

'Yes, it was. So there's no harm adding a new bracelet. The painting isn't worth much – sentimental value really.'

'You should add a little picture in the background of Lord Sherborne waving for help.'

'Now really...' Harold gasped. 'That's a bit steep, Margaret.' It seemed that Margaret had crossed a line. 'Lord Sherborne was eighty-seven. If you fall off a horse at high speed at eighty-seven the odds aren't great.'

'Mmm... but why did the horse bolt in the first place?' said Margaret with a devilish grin.

Harold shook his head disapprovingly. 'Come on, Margaret. Lady Sherborne had all the money to start with. She had nothing to gain.' He turned to Astrid. 'I'm so sorry. You must think we are such awful gossips.'

'Not at all.' What she thought was, they were brilliant gossips – which could be very useful. Another few pairs of eyes and ears around the house. She just couldn't tell them about the investigation though.

The conversation bubbled on until it reached the thorny subject of the approaching 'Civil War re-enactment'.

'Obviously, with my military background,' said Harold, sitting up stiffly, 'I was the natural choice to run the event.'

It appeared that Cressida was keen to tick off the 'living history' brief on her list. So this weekend the front lawn of the Hall was going to be turned into an authentic Roundhead battle camp. There would be field tents, cooking, weaponry and hand-to-hand combat courtesy of the local battle re-enactment society.

'They're all rugby players so it can get a bit unruly,' said Harold. 'But don't worry, I'll keep them in order. I'm a former second lieutenant,' he added for at least the fifth time.

Unfortunately, Cressida had also booked a bouncy castle

to, as she'd said, 'bring in the families'. This historical inaccuracy hadn't been missed by the volunteers.

'A bleedin' bouncy castle,' huffed Margaret. 'I mean, what's the point of organising everything down to the last detail and there's a dayglo bouncy castle in the background?'

'I see what you mean,' said Astrid.

'Tip of the iceberg,' Harold chimed in. 'The English Trust needs to pull its socks up.'

'Cressid*urrgh*,' breathed Margaret.

The bouncy castle discussion continued until the voice of Denise crackled through on the walkie-talkie. Margaret and Harold began hurriedly tidying up. It was obvious that they were trying to get out of the room before she arrived. For what reason though? Astrid could feel a new page in the One Direction notepad coming up: 'Friends and Enemies'.

If they were trying to avoid her, it didn't quite work. A minute later, Denise bustled through the door. She was wearing the same maid's outfit from the other day and her usual sunny expression.

'Hi, everyone,' she said, making a beeline for Astrid. 'It's Astrid, isn't it? I'm Denise – I think I saw you when I dropped into Cressida's office.'

'Yes, you did. You had a wax kipper in your hand.'

'Don't ask.'

Astrid laughed. 'Okay, I won't.'

'The thing is,' Denise ploughed on. 'I used to be able to do the historic cookery demonstrations with real ingredients. But then Cressida came along and said we had to have wax food for health and safety reasons.' She shook her head. 'How can I make a Georgian coffin without real flour?'

'Coffin?' asked Astrid.

'It's a type of pie,' said Denise.

'I wish Cressida was in a real coffin,' mumbled Margaret.

'Me too,' said Denise. 'Health and safety. There's going to be even more accidents with her round here. Mark my words.'

'Okay, well listen.' Astrid thrust out her hand. 'It's very nice to meet you, Denise.'

Denise took her hand. 'Yes, it's lovely to finally catch up with you. I'm usually doing the rounds of the house – liaising with the garden volunteers. I'm the volunteer co-ordinator, if you didn't know.'

'Yes, we're all aware of that.' Harold rolled his eyes. In the boiler room he was outranked, and clearly not happy about it. 'Back to our posts then,' he said, squeezing past her to get to the door.

Margaret gathered her books and hauled herself out of her chair. 'So, is there any news from Cressida about the bouncy castle?'

'I think it's still going ahead,' said Denise.

'Well, you can tell her from me it's a bloody disgrace,' said Margaret.

'I'll pass on your thoughts,' said Denise, backing into a coat stand.

Harold turned from the door. 'I know it's tough, Denise. But this is leadership. Some people are born for it. Others aren't,' he said, adjusting his military tie.

14

The satnav suggested a different way back to the river. An accident had snarled up the traffic on her usual way home. The new route took her on a smaller, winding road closer to the harbour bay. She was in no hurry – window down, the breeze ruffling her hair. The kind of driving you always see in car adverts, but rarely experience in real life.

Around a tight corner she saw a flash of something that made her squeeze the brakes. It was the gateway to a drive. Two simple brick pillars with white stone balls on top, a black iron gate half-open between them. The scene shook loose another childhood memory. She brought the car to a stop. Her uncle's house had pillars just like that.

She backed the Mini onto the verge a few yards short of the entrance and got out. There was no other name on the pillars. Or on the metal gate. She pushed it open and carried on down the gravel drive. In front of her was a handsome three-storey house. It was painted duck egg blue. Her uncle's house had been white. But the door was the same – painted in a glossy racing green.

There were no cars on the drive. No lights on in the house. She took a deep breath and knocked on the door. Waited a minute or so, shifting from foot to foot. But nobody came. A quick look around then – what harm could it do?

She opened a gate that led down a stone path alongside the house and out onto a wide lawn. Astrid's hands trembled. This was it. There was no doubt about it. Every step out onto the lawn took her further back in time to her childhood. She could almost feel the straps of the sandals she wore as a kid. There was the apple tree – twice the size now. Images, smells, noises from the past drifted back, overlapping with the present.

Lying on the grass.

The hum of bees in the blossom.

She closed her eyes and heard him again. His voice was slow and gentle. 'Alright, Astrid. Let's get started.' He was next to her. A blue smock dashed with paint. There was an easel and a blank canvas in front of them both. 'I want you to squint at this view.'

'Okay.'

He held out a palette and she rolled her brush through a smear of aquamarine. 'You have to ignore the details now. Find the big shapes of the picture. See how they all connect.'

She ran the brush across the horizon in loose swirls.

'Later we'll add a detail that will reveal the truth. But not now.'

She swept clouds over a sky she'd already painted in her mind.

'Wonderful – you've a gift, Astrid.' His hand was on her shoulder, as warm as the sun on her forehead – the joy of a childhood summer distilled in a moment. She closed her eyes tighter. Holding the happiness close to her – a happiness, and she was sure of it now, she hadn't felt since.

'Can I help you?' Another voice jolted her back to reality.

She swung round. Standing by the back door of the house was a middle-aged man in chinos and a pink shirt. He was holding a canvas shopping bag that he put down at his feet. 'Are you lost?'

Astrid went over to him. 'Hi – sorry. I was being a bit nosy.'

He looked confused.

'I was driving past and I recognised this place from when I was a kid. My uncle, Henry, used to live here. I stayed with him for a few summers. He died recently.'

'Oh, I'm sorry to hear that.'

'Thank you.'

He smiled. 'Do you want to look around the house? You're more than welcome, although Jessica and I have done some major renovations so you may not recognise it.'

'No, no. I just wanted a peep at the garden.'

'I could make you some tea?'

'That's kind, but I couldn't.' She reached the gravel path and stood in front of him. 'I've really only one question.'

'Of course.'

'My uncle... do you know why he sold the place?'

'Ooh, let me think.' He sucked in a long breath. 'This was over fifteen years ago, so I can't be sure. But I think our solicitor said he wanted a simpler life. Buy a boat maybe. I never met him.'

'Okay, I see. Well, I better be going.'

'I'm sorry I couldn't be much help. But please, come back anytime if you think of anything else.'

'I will, thanks.'

Astrid took a last look at the garden, thanked the man again, and went back to the car.

Driving back to the boat, Astrid knew she wouldn't return to her uncle's old house. She'd seen enough. Her memories of the garden were best left unshaded by the present. There were more questions to answer now though. Why had he left the house? It was so perfect for a painter, with the garden and the views over the river. Maybe his paintings weren't selling and he'd had to drastically downsize? Her father might know – but he probably wouldn't tell her if he did.

She remembered really pushing him for an answer once. Why had they fallen out so badly? They were brothers after all. He told her 'not to be nosy'. Which had hurt. Then he pointed out that she didn't get on with her sister – so what's the difference? And that hurt even more because it was true. They just didn't seem to have anything in common. Astrid shrugged off the thought. She did need to repair her relationships with her family. Not now though. Now she needed to concentrate on the case.

She took the final turn down the lane, her mind changing gear back to the investigation. What about Lady Sherborne? Was she really as 'deadly' as Margaret suggested? She'd seemed more lonely than anything – bitter that her gilded life had started to tarnish, her beauty faded. Could that be enough to tip her over the edge? Or tip DeVine over the edge more like. Maybe he'd sold some other antiques of hers and cheated her out of the profits? Or maybe she was so furious at the Trust taking over her beloved house she was out to embarrass them. Ooh, it was all so... dare she say it, deliciously exciting.

Astrid made her way along the gangplank. Cobb was standing in the engine well in the rear decking, whistling to himself. He was wearing a T-shirt that was a very faint pink. Her mother once told her it was easy to tell how long a man had lived on his own. You just checked the number of vaguely blue or pink items they had that had been ruined by not going in the 'whites only' wash. Not that her mother ever did anything domestic herself. She had staff to do that kind of thing for her. At least before the divorce, when her father's business was doing well.

Cobb reached for a tool on the planks and bent back down.

'Hi, Cobb.'

'Hey, Astrid.' He pulled himself up onto the edge of the decking, his feet still hanging over the hole. She liked the way his muscles tensed on his forearms. Shame he was so arrogant. Best keep it friendly though – she needed the boat fixed. 'Can I get you a drink, Cobb? Tea? Coffee?'

'I'm good.' He reached for a cloth and wiped his hands on it. 'So, do you want the good news or the bad news?'

'Let's have the good news, then maybe the bad news won't seem so bad.'

He laughed. 'Alright then. Good news – the engine's in good condition. I need to change a few things. But there's no rust.'

'Great. Now the bad news.'

'A bunch of other stuff needs doing. New water pump. New batteries. I wouldn't mind changing the fuel lines.' He brushed his hand through his hair.

'So how much is it all going to cost?' That's it, Astrid, she thought. Keep it formal – don't stare.

'You might want to sit down for this bit.'

Astrid looked around the deck. There was a canvas fold-up chair in the corner. The kind directors on movie sets are supposed to have. She unpacked it, brushed some dried leaves off the front and squeezed into it.

Cobb stared at her in amusement. 'Yeah… it's just a saying. Like the shock will make you fall over.'

God, he was annoying. 'Well, I'm sitting down now, so let's hear it.'

'Right. It's a rough estimate. But with all the parts and my labour, you're looking at maybe six grand to get her shipshape.'

Astrid gulped. That was nearly all her savings. Still, it had to be done if she was to get a good price. She plastered on her best smile. 'Oh, that's not too bad. I was expecting a lot more.'

'In which case, it's eight grand.' He burst out laughing. 'Just kidding. Yeah – it'll probably be about six grand. I can get an exact quote for you later.'

'Alright. And how long will it take?'

'If I can get the parts – about a month.'

'Okay, I guess I could stay on that long.' She got up from the chair and held out her hand. 'It's a deal, Cobb.' He took it thinking she was helping him out of the hole. He pulled against her so she needed all her strength to keep her feet from slipping towards him. 'Thanks,' he said, clambering onto the deck. 'Hey – if you're around tomorrow we could take her out into the harbour.'

'Could we?' Astrid said, realising her voice was a bit high. A bit too keen. 'Only if you have the time, Cobb.' She dropped it down a notch.

'Of course. I need to see how she's running.'

'Okay, let's do it.' She shrugged. 'What time?'

'High tide's around ten tomorrow morning. Can you take time off?'

'Sure.' There wasn't much she could do on the paintings until the new materials arrived, so she might as well take a break. 'Let's do it.'

'Good.' He flipped the hatch over the engine well. 'I'll come over then.'

Cobb started packing his tools away. She stood over him. 'Out of interest. You know you keep referring to the boat as "she", "her". Do you know why they say boats are female?'

'Oh, I know this one.' He pushed his hair from his temples. 'It's because they're unpredictable?'

'No, Cobb. It's not. It's because back then ill-educated sailors believed in mother nature. That an ever-present goddess would save them.'

'Mmm... I never knew that.'

He carried on putting the tools away. She noticed that his thin silver chain had snagged on the collar of his T-shirt. That chain... it was still awful. So why did she want to reach out and touch it? Gently tuck it back into his shirt. The thought had ambushed her. No. No... she almost said out loud. That was a terrible idea.

He closed the toolbox lid. 'I'll see you at ten tomorrow morning then.'

'Yes... I'll see you then.'

It was another warm evening. Too nice to spend in the cabin. What she needed was a drink at a table outside the Angler's Arms. Not that there was anywhere else to go. Wallet, notepad, phone – check. Lock the door – keys in the bag. Two minutes and she was ready. That record was going to stick.

As she crossed the wharf she saw that Kath had got there first. She was sitting on one of a handful of wooden tables and benches that had been set out under the hanging baskets. Astrid hurried over. 'Hi, Kath.'

Kath looked up from her phone. 'Hey, Astrid. You got my text?'

'No, I haven't had a signal recently. I just guessed you'd be here.' She slid into the bench opposite. Her phone beeped in her pocket.

'That's probably it,' said Kath.

Astrid brought out the phone and read the text aloud. 'Meet me at the Angler's – I have news about the case. Kath x.' She looked up. 'And there's an emoji of a bull with steam coming out of its nostrils. Excellent.'

In the middle of the table was a tin can with knives and forks poking out of it. Kath pushed it to one side and leant forwards. 'So, you want to hear what I found out.'

Astrid set the phone down. 'Go on then.'

'Well, I've been asking around. Discreetly of course. Like you said.'

'Good.'

'It seems DeVine was in a lot of debt. The antique shop

was struggling and he'd borrowed money off some people who wanted it back. Sort of people you don't mess with.'

'What are the names of these people, Kath?'

'Not sure.' Kath took a swig from her pint.

'Not sure?'

'Well, that bit came from Frank, who's a bit dodgy to be honest. Sold one of my brothers a generator that turned out to be half-inched from the new development at Worth Matravers.'

'Kath? We need facts.'

'Yeah, yeah. I'm telling you – the debt part is definitely true.'

Astrid sighed. 'Alright then.' She brought out the One Direction notepad.

Kath's eyes lit up. 'Ooo... a 1D notepad. I used to love them.'

'Until Zayn left of course – then it all went downhill.'

'Ain't that the truth,' said Kath, shaking her head.

'Okay then...' Astrid turned to the first page, which was covered in scribbles and arrows. 'Let's go over what we know so far.' She plucked the pen from the spine. 'DeVine fell to his death in the icehouse. The railings were secure and high enough, so let's assume he was pushed over them.'

Kath nodded sagely. 'Although, you know what my mother used to say? Assume makes an ass out of you and me.'

'Hey, my mother used to say that too.'

'I think all mothers said that one.'

'Anyway – let's ignore our mothers for the time being and assume that he was pushed.' Astrid began underlining some of the words. 'The person who pushed him must have arranged to meet him there. Why else would they be in the icehouse?'

'Exactly.'

'Which makes it premeditated.'

'You mean…' Kath did her gravelly voice '…murrrder?'

'Yes, Kath – murder.' It was such an awful thing. But the word itself felt so satisfying to say. It tripped so smoothly off the tongue. 'Then after the murder they went down to check that DeVine was dead, or remove something from the body. Hence the wet feet. Then they left the icehouse, made sure the no entry sign was clipped across the hedge so no members of the public wandered in, and carried on into the gardens. Do you agree?'

'Yeah. But the thing I don't understand is…'

The door of the pub swung open and Dolly came out. She went over to the table. 'You eating?'

Kath shook her head. Astrid too. 'We're fine for the moment, thanks.'

Dolly collected up the tin with cutlery in. 'House red and a Badger's, then?'

'You know – I might try something a bit lighter. Seeing as we're outside,' said Astrid.

'The Admiral's Thumb is four per cent,' said Dolly.

'Four per cent? Sounds delicious. I'll have a pint of that then.'

Dolly brought out a cloth and wiped down the table. Her elbows were as worn as the rails of Astrid's boat. They both waited for her to finish, itching to get back to discussing the case. Dolly turned to Astrid.

'And don't worry – the drinks are on the house. After the ordeal you've had, love. Finding that body.' She flicked the cloth into the wharf in a spray of crumbs. 'Dreadful business,' she muttered and went back into the pub.

Astrid folded her arms and stared at Kath. 'Really? You said you hadn't told anyone?'

Kath held up her hands. 'It slipped out.'

'Kath!'

'Don't worry. She's the only one – and she won't tell a soul.'

Astrid sighed. 'Right – where were we?'

'I was saying… the thing I don't understand is what it's all got to do with Eric the forager's death?'

Astrid sat up sharply 'What! Eric is dead?'

'Shussh,' hissed Kath. 'Keep it down.'

Astrid glared at her. 'Why wouldn't that be the first thing you'd tell me?'

'I forgot. Anyways, you want to know what happened or not?'

'Of course.'

'Okay. Someone from the Purbeck Twitchers found him on the beach this morning at dawn.'

'Purbeck Twitchers?'

'Yeah – birdwatchers. They reckon he'd eaten a poisonous mushroom by mistake. He had a little pan out and had been cooking them up.'

Astrid's pen fell from her fingers. 'Poisoned?'

'You alright, Astrid?'

'Yes, I mean…' Astrid stumbled. 'He, he… asked if I'd like to join him for a meal.'

'No way? That was a close one.'

'I know. He was going to cook up the mushrooms we collected. He'd brought some cream and butter.'

'Ooh… cream *and* butter.' Kath smacked her lips. 'Is it wrong that I'm feeling really hungry right now?'

'Yes… it's a bit wrong.'

'Sorry.' She shook her head, as if trying to shake away the images of bubbling cream and mushrooms. 'Right, then. So, what would Cagney and Lacey do?'

'I'm not sure, Kath. But this is a major development. I think that's the kind of thing they say – a major development.' She picked up the pen again. 'The thing is – why would Eric mistake a poisonous mushroom for an edible one? He'd be the last person who'd get that wrong.'

'I dunno – even the experts get it wrong now and then.'

'Really?'

'There's loads of people who go out and forage for mushrooms round here. Once in a while they eat a nasty one.'

Astrid flinched. Something had rubbed against her shins under the table. She looked down and saw the white dog peering up, his jaw trembling with excitement. 'Oh, hello you,' she said, patting the bench next to her. 'Up you come.' The dog sprang up onto the bench, wheeled round a couple of times and sat with his head on his paws. Astrid rubbed the wiry top of his head, which made his ears perk up.

'Hey there,' a voice boomed behind them. Grub was approaching, his hands firmly in the pockets of his long oil coat. 'Getting them in early I see.'

'Five minutes ahead of you, big boy,' said Kath.

Grub eased himself onto the end of the bench. Astrid felt the bench legs start to lift. She shifted towards the other end to get the balance back. He patted the dog on its back. 'There you go, Sheepdip. You get comfy.'

'Sheepdip? Why do you call him that?'

He took an extendable dog lead from his pocket and put it on the table. 'Well, when he was a pup he fell in a sheep dip on a farm. He was bright blue for a week. Except the ears.'

Astrid looked at Sheepdip. He nodded, as if confirming the story. Grub brought out his wallet, which was bulging with receipts.

'You ordered drinks?'

'Yeah, they're on their way.'

'Brilliant. Now, Astrid.' He turned to her and took off his sunglasses. She noticed that the left arm was held together by a bent paperclip. His voice was sombre. 'Are you alright? Must have been a terrible experience.'

Astrid flashed a stare across the table. 'Kath?'

'What?' she said innocently. 'Well obviously I told Grub. But he's not going to say anything.'

'That's right. Not a word.' Grub brought a thick finger up to his lips.

'You see,' said Kath.

'And poor old Eric too,' said Grub. 'That must have been an even bigger shock?'

'Eric, what? Listen…' She turned to Grub then Kath. 'We've really got to keep this to ourselves from now on. Right?'

'Absolutely,' said Grub. 'What happens in the Angler's stays in the Angler's.' Grub stood up and Astrid hurried to the middle of the bench to steady it. 'Now let me chase up those drinks and get a bowl of water for Sheepdip. Then I'll tell you my theory.'

Astrid waited for Grub to leave, then wagged her finger at Kath.

'What?' she said, innocently.

'You know what, Kath Basin?' Astrid sighed. 'You can't keep a secret to save your life.'

'Sorry.' Kath paused. 'So, are we getting toasties or what?'

Astrid didn't stay too long – an hour and a half at the most. Two pints and a couple of toasties, which were very tasty. Astrid went over the discussion about DeVine and Eric's deaths as she showered. The conversation had ended up swirling in smaller and smaller circles. Grub and Kath debunked each other's theories as soon as they'd explained them.

Grub thought Kath's story that DeVine had dangerous enemies was 'utter guff'. Grub's suggestion that Eric might have deliberately killed himself – 'death by mushroom' – was rounded on by Kath. 'Rubbish!' Nobody, and Astrid agreed, nobody would want to go like that – a slow and agonising death according to both of them.

She dressed for bed and went over to the racks of books by the wall. As she'd hoped, there was a field guide to British fungi. She teased it out from behind the netting and got into the sleeping bag. Inside the guide were pictures of hundreds of mushrooms and toadstools. They were beautifully painted in watercolours. Sprouting up from foliage or bursting from tree branches. Meticulously logged at various angles to give the best chance of recognising them in the wild.

The chapters ran from 'Edible and Excellent' to 'Inedible',

'Poisonous' and 'Deadly'. Most of the mushrooms in the last section looked angry and revolting. But not all of them. A handful of 'deadly' ones were almost identical to others in the 'Edible and Excellent' chapters. The tasty Caesar mushroom was just like the vicious destroying angel. The fool's funnel – again 'edible' – could easily be confused with the grim ivory funnel. But Eric was no fool. Nearly all the most dangerous mushrooms had white gills. He'd warned her about that straight away.

So how could he, of all people, have made a mistake with such awful consequences? The worst result, according to the book, sounded horrendous – a medical nightmare including liver failure, seizures and paralysis. Sometimes, cruelly, the symptoms would disappear after a couple of days, only for the poison to suddenly take its fatal grip. Some of the very worst ones contained a toxin called muscarine. Eating them caused the victim to produce excess water. They'd drool, weep and sweat away their final hours.

Astrid closed the book and opened the porthole to get some fresh air. She dropped the book on the floor by the bed. Yawning deeply, she closed her eyes, trying to plant some nicer thoughts in her mind. Pleasant summer scenes. Her favourite paintings. But she knew – whether she remembered them or not in the morning – she was going to have some strange dreams about mushrooms.

15

Wednesday, Day 8

Cobb had said that high tide was ten o'clock that morning. That would give her plenty of time to give the interior of the boat a good clean. Not that she was doing it to impress Cobb. He didn't need to come down here. And if he did, it didn't matter what he made of the place anyway.

She went to the cupboard under the sink to get started. Cobb simply wasn't her type anyway. He was too unrefined. That swagger of his – as if he was in his own cowboy movie. The way he stared at her as if she was stupid. It was so rude. Nice eyes though. Hazel, with flecks of light yellow. His broad shoulders... her stomach gave a flutter – probably indigestion. Must be. She wasn't going to give him the satisfaction of having a crush on him on top of everything. 'We're not... are we, Astrid?' she said to herself, opening the cupboard.

Inside was an orange bucket packed with cleaning sprays for all materials – wood, glass, bathroom surfaces. Plus a handful of scrubbing brushes and a roll of bin bags. She took the bucket out and unpacked it, wondering where to start. She'd never met the cleaners at her apartment. They just showed up when she wasn't there. Everything was tidied up, as if by magic. 'Industrious elves' – that's what Simon called them.

When they first moved into the apartment, she'd cleaned the place herself – it was something she enjoyed. Getting her hands dirty. Then Simon told her cleaning was 'a bit beneath them.' And that was that.

She slipped on a pair of yellow rubber gloves and went over to the window. Then she took the curtains off the portholes and bundled them up in a black bin bag along with the bedding and her worn clothes. That could all go to the dry cleaner's later. Wherever that was. She spritzed the portholes with window cleaner then polished them with a dry cloth until they gleamed.

There was a different spray for the bathroom and shower. The sink and sideboard were attacked with another chemical that had a pungent smell that made her feel unsteady. The table was dealt with by a dollop of beeswax worked into the surface with a soft yellow cloth. After an hour and a half, she stood back and proudly inspected her work. The place was spotless. 'Well done, Astrid,' she whispered.

Finally, she lifted up the Persian carpet to take up to the deck. She'd hang it over the arm of the mast and hit it with a stick to get the dust out. But as she rolled it up, she noticed something. In the middle of the floorboards was a folded piece of notepaper. She unfolded it. Handwritten in black ink were the words:

Dear Astrid – You are where the ladders start. Uncle Henry.

She sat down at the table and examined the note, turning it over in her hands. The paper looked new. The ink was clear and sharp – a fountain pen probably. The message had been left for her recently. She peeled off the rubber gloves and dropped them into the bucket. Her uncle obviously wasn't referring to any real ladders – so what did it mean then? And why was it so cryptic? Couldn't he just tell her what she was supposed to do?

Boom. There was a thump on the metal roof. Then a gruff shout: 'You ready to go?'

According to Cobb, it was the perfect weather to test the boat – bright, and not a breath of wind. 'You've brought the good weather with you, Astrid,' he said as he untied the ropes from the jetty. 'Not a drop of rain since you arrived. Maybe you coming here hasn't been… such a…' he mumbled.

'Sorry, Cobb, what was that?'

He joined her at the controls. 'You know what they say though?'

'Go on.'

'A smooth sea never made a good sailor.'

'Oh, Cobb. You were just about to say something nice there, weren't you? And you just couldn't do it.' She laughed.

He held out his hand. For a moment she thought he wanted to take hers. Then he said, 'Keys?'

She felt her cheeks flush. 'There you go.' She dropped the keys on the cork float into the palm of his hand, avoiding his eye.

In front of them was a wooden dashboard. There were

about a dozen instruments ranging across it. A radio handset, a small black and white screen and a handful of dials with white numbers that veered up into red.

'I should tell you,' said Astrid, 'I've never sailed a boat before. So this feels like taking my driving test again... in a spaceship.'

'Hah! Don't worry, you'll get the hang of it.' He turned the keys over and there was a low gurgling behind the stern. Cobb eased a lever forward and the boat seemed to sit up on the water. As if it had woken up, and was keen to get going. He really did know what he was doing. It was impressive. She gripped the rail, hoping that he wouldn't turn round and catch her staring at him. But he was too concentrated on keeping the boat close to the bank. 'So, where do you want to go?'

She had a sudden flash of inspiration. 'Can we get out to the Arne?' This was a perfect chance to check on the scene of Eric the forager's death. Find some clues maybe.

'The Arne? Any reason?'

'Not really. I just saw it on the map.'

'Whatever you want.' He shrugged.

There was a small wooden wheel below the dials, like a cart wheel with hand grips around the rim. He spun it gently and the boat curved off out into the estuary. Another revolution back again and the boat straightened up. 'You want to take over?'

'What?' she said, trying to dampen the rising panic. 'Steer the boat?'

'You have to learn sometime.'

'Okay then.' She stepped over and took the wheel.

'Couple of tips then.' He slid the pane of glass in front of them to one side. 'See those two beacons?'

In the distance were a couple of marker buoys. They were made of black metal with a cone on top – one red, one green. 'Yes – I see them.'

'We're going out into open water so the green is on the starboard. The right side.'

'Got it.'

'Good. Now set a line in the middle of the two – that's the deepest part of the channel.'

She gingerly turned the wheel and the boat barely changed course.

'A lot more than that, Astrid. It's not like the steering wheel of a car. Be bold – then wait for the boat to react.'

She spun the wheel a full turn, waited, and the boat swung back to face the channel. 'Do I use the compass?' She pointed at an instrument that was like a snow globe with a small compass floating inside.

'No, no… we can see where we're going today. When we get past the marker buoys, line her up on a point on the horizon. Let's say… that dip in the ridge.'

The boat ploughed through the water, sending rounded waves fanning behind it. Cobb studied the dials, tapping some of them with a knuckle.

'Is everything alright?'

'Yup – not too bad.'

They passed the buoys and the wake of the boat rocked them on their anchor chains. A rusty bell on each rang out behind them – as if they were wishing them luck on their voyage. Astrid slipped the wheel through her hands and waited until the prow was aiming at the ridge. Cobb went back down the couple of steps and out onto the deck.

'Hey,' she said, not taking her eyes off the horizon. 'Where are you going?'

He smiled. 'You've got it, Astrid.'

She watched him as he strode out down the side of the boat. His step didn't falter as he picked his way between the ropes. She still had to grip the side rails when the boat was moored. For him – it was as if he was still on dry land. He began coiling up the ropes, looping them between his hand and elbow, then stowed them neatly to one side.

When it was done, he joined her in the cabin again. 'You don't want ropes lying around, Astrid. Not if you're sailing on your own.' He paused. 'Although you shouldn't be out sailing on your own.'

'Really?' Astrid raised an eyebrow. 'I'm sure I can get the hang of it.'

'No, no,' he said firmly, 'I need to make sure the engine's safe. Then you've got to learn the instruments.'

'It's my boat, Cobb.'

'Fine. But remember – the water you sail on is the same water that'll swallow you up.'

She groaned. 'Are there going to be many of these maritime sayings, Cobb?'

'Lots more… unless you promise not to take her out on your own.'

She opened the other glass panel. The breeze ruffled her hair. 'Okay,' she said. 'I promise I won't.'

'Good.' He took the wheel, turning it half a revolution towards him. 'Thing is – there's some big currents out here that you don't know about. When the tide goes out all the water funnels through the gap between Sandbanks and Shell Bay. Between those islands... see?' He gestured into the distance.

When she'd been cycling high up on the heath she could make out the individual islands. At water level they blended in a line of trees and low cliffs. She peered out, trying to sort out the pieces of the jigsaw. 'Yes, near the big island.'

'That's it. The big ferries out to France and Spain run through there. The chain ferry crosses it. Very dangerous on a falling tide.'

'Got it.' She scanned the bay. It was a beautiful scene, but she was here for a reason – to work out where Eric's attacker had come from. There had been no other cars in the car park, so maybe they arrived by boat? They might even live on one of the islands. 'And the other islands – are they inhabited?'

'Some are English Trust. Some are privately owned.' Cobb pointed to the nearest one on the left. 'That's Green Island. Nobody lives on that one.'

The island was only a few hundred yards long, with pine trees growing down to the shoreline. There was a narrow channel between that and the next island. It was twice the length, with a yellow, orangey cliff that sloped to a stony beach. A long wooden pier jutted out into the water.

'And that one?' said Astrid.

'That's Long Island. There's about ten houses on there.'

'Green Island? Long Island? Very inventive.'

He laughed. 'Yes, but you know straight away though.' He took off his battered baseball cap and hung it over the compass. His hair was ridged where the hat line had been. He inhaled deeply. 'Right, keep her straight ahead.' She adjusted the wheel slightly as he went to the back of the boat.

They ploughed on for a while, Astrid looking over the side at the water now and then. Sometimes it was crystal clear. Deep. Dark patches of weed swaying on the seabed. Then it quickly became shallow and silty, the wash of the boat lapped up on grey sandbanks. Small wading birds hovered up to get out of the waves and settled back down – dabbing their bright orange beaks at the mud.

Cobb spent the time tinkering with the engine. Every so often there would be a *crack* and a curl of bluish smoke would puff up from the stern just above the waterline. After a while the engine sounded less angry about his interference. He put the hatch down and came over. 'Right – take her in.'

When they were about thirty yards from the shore he held up his hand. 'Shut the engine down.'

She pulled down the lever and the boat slowed, sinking slightly into the water. When it came to a stop, he put his thumb on a button by the wheel. 'This is your anchor release.' He pressed it and there was a grinding metallic sound at the prow as the anchor chain rattled out.

'Right then. Can I get you a drink?' she said.

He wiped the sweat off his forehead with the back of his hand. 'Yes, water. Thanks.'

Back down in the living quarters she poured a couple of glasses of water from a bottle in the fridge. A thought struck her. She'd just sailed across the bay in her own home. How odd not to have realised that earlier? But how exciting. She could just pull up the anchor and set off – no need to pack. No need to wait until Simon could get time off work, then have him dictate where they would be going. For the first time in years, she could do exactly what she wanted.

The boat rocked gently. She had spent so much time watching life move around her through the big picture window of the apartment. Now she was immersed in it. The bay, the river... the open sea. They were all connected. Waiting to be explored.

Up on deck, Cobb had opened out the folding chairs so they faced the shore. She handed him the glass and sat down next to him. Ahead of them was the beach of the Arne. The spot where Eric had made his fire was a little further up the sand.

'So, Cobb – can we get any closer in?'

'No – it's too shallow, even at high tide. You need a tender.'

'Tender?'

'Small rowing boat – a dinghy. I have an old one at the yard you can have.'

'Thanks.' She drained the water. 'So basically, you anchor here, row the tender in and pull it up on the shore?'

'That's it.'

Astrid ran through her last moments with Eric. She'd left him by the fire and walked straight up the beach. She didn't remember seeing any other footsteps on the sand. But then, why would she have been looking out for any? If she was right, and Eric had been poisoned by someone – they probably arrived by boat. A much larger boat moored out in the bay. Yes, she remembered now, a dinghy had been dragged up the beach. She closed her eyes. What was the name on the side... No – it wasn't there. Not yet.

'You okay, Astrid?'

She opened her eyes. 'Yes, thanks. I'm fine.'

'So… the engine. You want to hear it?'

'Go on.'

He put his glass down by his feet. 'It's not in too bad shape. I was right – with all the parts it's going to cost about six grand, maybe seven.'

Seven grand? That was well over her budget. But why couldn't she tell him no? Because she wanted to see him again? She pushed the thought away. 'That's good news then.'

He leant down and rubbed at the low rail along the boat. A big flake of dried varnish came off on his fingers. 'You want me to sand down the woodwork and paint it?'

'No, I'll do all the exterior work.'

'Seriously?'

'Yes, I'm an art conservator. I restore paintings. It's a bigger scale but the same materials. Paint, varnish…'

'Good for you. I'll drop a box of sanders and tools round for you.'

'Thanks.'

She looked out across the shallows. A shoal of grey fish patrolled the channels between the reed islands, their fins carving slowly through the surface. Cobb was staring serenely at the water.

'Have you always loved the sea, Cobb?'

'Yes – and boats. And fishing. I was on the water more than on dry land as a kid. I learnt to read from a tide table.' He snorted. 'Anyway, that's what they said.'

'Fishing. Is this a good spot here?'

He turned to her. 'You really interested? Or just being polite?'

'I'm never polite, remember?' She laughed. 'No, really…
I want to know.'

Truth was, she liked hearing him talk. When he wasn't
arguing with her, or barking instructions about the boat,
he had a beautiful voice. Deep, mellow, the words tumbled
over each other in a soft stream.

'It's too shallow here. The fish are too small, and mostly
mullet. Hard to catch – fickle, and they taste of mud. You
want to try for the bass in the deeper channels.'

'Maybe I will.' Since they'd sat there, the tide had slowly
begun to turn. Another few inches of reeds were showing
on the mudflats. 'So how long has your family had a boat
business?'

'Three generations. My grandfather bought the land and
set up the yard. My father worked there all his life.'

'And when did you take over from your father?'

'About ten years ago. I was travelling and this place
seemed to be calling me back. My two brothers weren't
interested. So, the dumbest son got the job.' He nudged her
with his elbow.

'I'm sorry about that,' she said, sheepishly. 'Not the best
start, was it?'

'No—' he laughed '—but the best journeys usually have
the rockiest starts. That's what I've found anyway.'

Did he really mean that? 'Maybe they do,' she said quietly.

They sat together in silence. There was some kind of static
in the air. Was the weather changing? Or was it between
them? And could he feel it too?

She looked ahead, avoiding his gaze. The fish had
retreated to the safety of deeper water. It wouldn't be long
before the keel of the boat would hit the sand. Then, they'd

be stuck. They would have to stay there until the next high tide. Hours together. He, of all people, would know that. She closed her eyes and waited, aware of her heartbeat.

Then he got up and glanced over the side of the boat. 'We'd better go,' he said.

16

Uncle Henry had written to her – sort of. It was just a scribble on a card, but it was something. When she'd seen Dutton that first day, she thought it was strange that her uncle hadn't left a letter for her. If you give someone everything you own, don't you explain why? There definitely wasn't any other paperwork though. Dutton was sure of that. So these notes – this was how he was going to talk to her.

She stood in the car park and turned the card over in her hand for the tenth time. *Astrid – You are where the ladders start.* That's all there was.

So how did he know that she was going to stick around here? Long enough at least to clean the place up herself. She could have sold the boat on quickly and the new owners may never have noticed his notes.

Then there was a more ominous question. How had he predicted his own death and quickly drawn up the will? Dutton had said it had been written about a year before, so Uncle Henry must have been keen to make arrangements. She took one last look at the card and slid it in the side pocket of her hiking trousers.

*

She searched for information on the Purbeck Twitchers on her phone. Their website came up straight away with a home page offering a *'big feathery welcome'* to anyone who was interested in Dorset birdlife. Newcomers especially. She shut down the page and tapped in the phone number. A moment later a deep voice replied.

'Glen Maynard speaking.'

'Oh, hello. My name is Astrid Kisner. I wondered if I could speak to someone about…' What did she want to talk about? The murder? Better ease into that. 'I'm interested in bird life.'

There was a rustle on the other end of the line. 'Super – do you want to sign up for a bird-spotting course?'

'I'm not sure – possibly. Maybe I could have a chat with you first, if you're not too busy.'

'My wife Philly and I will be down at the hide on Brownsea Island this evening, if that suits you?'

'That's great. What time?'

'Shall we say 5 p.m.?'

'Okay – see you then.'

According to Glen, it would take about forty minutes to get to Brownsea Island if she was lucky with the ferries. There were two to navigate. The big chain ferry to Sandbanks then a smaller one out to the island. This would mean she'd have travelled on three different boats on one day. More than she'd probably done in a lifetime.

The first crossing involved parking up at a car park on the

eastern side of the channel then taking it from there on foot. She queued up in a short line of passengers. They were families – kids in shorts clutching buckets and plastic spades, parents weighed down with bags of towels. Cyclists with all the gear – Team Ineos outfits, mirrored specs, pink necks. There were hikers with walking sticks. Runners with backpacks. Nobody seemed to want to relax in the countryside.

The cars drove into the central section and the passengers climbed the steps to the top level. A few minutes later, the metal ramp clunked up and the ferry surged out into the current. She watched over the side as the waves buffeted the hull. Cobb was right. The current here when the tide was turning was fierce.

The ferry took five minutes and didn't stop for anything. Small boats held up to let it pass then tucked in behind. Or made a last dash to get in front of its prow.

On the other side, the passengers hurried down the gangplank and set off in all directions – most out to a beach round the breakwater. The Team Ineos cyclists steamed off up a road through the pines to get ahead of the cars. Everyone else marched off to another smaller banana-yellow boat called *The Maid of Poole*. She followed them and queued up. A ticket collector, a man in an orange hi-visibility vest that revealed nut-brown arms covered in vague tattoos, worked his way down the line. She held up her English Trust lanyard.

'Yer good,' he grunted.

'Oh, can I check? The birdwatching hides. How do I get there?'

'Uh, yeah. Follow the signs to the lagoon on the east side of the island. You can't miss it.'

'Thanks.'

The Maid of Poole headed back into the harbour against the tide. From her seat by the rail she had a good view of the dozen huge homes that ran along a short bulge of waterfront – clearly the prime location round here. They were mansions made from smoked glass and steel. Manicured lawns sloped down to private moorings – most with a smart yacht tied up. It was the sort of thing that made estate agents drool in their sleep.

Ten minutes later the boat drew up to a wooden jetty that ran out from a steep beach of big round pebbles. To the left was a red-brick castle. On the other side was a row of cottages near the water's edge. Ahead, guarding the way, was the English Trust Visitors' Centre. Again, the lanyard sorted out a quick entry to the other side where she quickly found herself in a shady woodland.

As the ticket collector had said, the lagoon was easy to find. It was well marked with a new path of planking that snaked through the trees. She paid the *'voluntary contribution'* of £2 and took a fork to a bird hide tucked back in the trees. Inside it was empty. There were a series of small open windows that looked out to the water. On the wall was a poster of all the varieties of bird you might see. Next to it was a chalkboard of recent *'bird sightings'* – none of which she'd heard of before.

Sandpiper.

Little Ringed Plover.

Whooper swan!

An exclamation mark? Obviously a rare one.

Out in the lagoon hundreds of white birds were tiptoeing around in the mud. A flock of larger grey ones skimmed over the water. What was the point of bird-spotting? The next day they could just fly off to who knows where. Or you could just pretend you saw one. Who would know?

The door creaked open and a couple edged into the hide. They had roughly the same physique – tall and slim. They were wearing matching camouflage fleeces and bucket sun hats. The man was holding a folded-up tripod with a camera still attached. The lens was about a foot long, covered in the same camouflaged material as their jackets. With the right vegetation behind them, they might both disappear.

'Astrid?'

'Glen?'

'Yes, yes…'

They both stalked over, their arms behind their backs. Like two herons picking their way through a muddy channel. 'And this is my wife, Philly.' He swept out his hand towards her. She was in her mid-fifties, a good decade younger than him.

'Hello, Astrid,' she said, then peered over her shoulder to look at the sightings board. 'Oooh… Glen. Look. A whooper swan. Do you believe that, dear?'

'I very much doubt it.' He raised an eyebrow. 'Earliest sighting you'd expect would be late autumn. I suspect someone has been having a bit of fun.' He took a cloth from a peg by the board and wiped off the name. 'The whooper swans are winter visitors, Astrid. The birds you see now are here all year – the lagoon gives them somewhere to roost at high tide.'

'That's good to know,' said Astrid.

Philly went to the window and raised her binoculars, sweeping them slowly across the horizon. 'Terns, sandpipers... mmm, no spoonbills,' she scoffed.

Glen craned his head towards Astrid. 'Right – you said you had an interest in bird-spotting?'

'Well, um...' She tried to remember something about birds. Anything – just one fact she could plump up into a conversation. The last birds she'd seen were a gang of pigeons hanging round the bins in Trafalgar Square. That's all she had. 'To be honest, I wanted to ask you about something else. It's a bit delicate.'

'Delicate?'

'Yes, I don't suppose you were at the Arne yesterday morning. I heard that someone from your club discovered the body of Mr Wainwright.'

Philly put her binoculars down. Her lenses had left a ring around her eyes, which added to her sense of wonder. 'Yes, we did. But I'm not sure we can really talk about it... I mean, unless you're close family?'

'Well, actually. The thing is, I was with him on the evening before he died.'

'Oh, I see,' said Philly with a knowing smile. 'You have to be discreet? Is that it?'

'Discreet?' She knew exactly what she meant. 'Yes, I do, Philly. So, you must keep this to yourselves.'

'Don't worry – we all know about Eric's reputation with the ladies. Don't we, Glen?'

'It was common knowledge.'

'Was it?' said Astrid.

'Indeed – Eric was a very handsome man.'

'Do you think so, Philly?' said Glen.

'Absolutely. He was very commanding. And he knew more about foraging than anyone in the county.' She turned to Astrid. 'Don't worry. We won't tell anyone,' said Philly. 'Will we, Glen?' Glen nodded earnestly.

'Thank you for understanding.' Astrid smiled weakly. It looked like she would have to keep it up – it was the only way to get some information on Eric. 'So what time did you find him?' She put her hand to her forehead. A tragic pose best suited for a goddess in a Renaissance masterpiece. 'I mean, dear Eric.'

Philly hurried round her and shut the door of the hide.

'Well…' said Glen. 'We had heard that there had been a sighting of some Dartford warblers. They're a lovely little species. A very tuneful call. Philly can do a rather good impression if you'd like to hear it.'

'Perhaps later.'

'Of course.' He carried on. 'So, we must have been on the beach at about 6 a.m. – first light. We were coming down the path and then we saw what looked like a pile of clothes lying in the sand.'

'But no, it wasn't clothes,' Philly chimed in, 'it was Eric. Flat out. Eyes to the heavens.'

'You could see there was no point trying to resuscitate him,' said Glen. 'He'd clearly been there for some time.'

'We found his backpack about thirty yards up the beach,' said Philly. 'And the remains of the fire he must have made from the night before.'

'It looked like he'd walked down the beach from the fire?'

'Staggered more like,' said Glen. 'Wouldn't you say, Philly?'

'Oh yes, Glen. There were footsteps that sort of snaked along the sand.'

'I see. And can I ask you one more question? When you found him lying there, was there anything unusual about him?'

They looked at each other. As if deciding to reveal this last piece of information. Glen nodded and Philly drew in a breath. 'Well, it looked like he'd been crying.'

'Crying?'

'Yes,' said Philly. 'His cheeks were wet with tears.'

'And the shirt, Philly?' Glen nudged her.

'Oh, yes – his shirt… it was drenched in sweat.'

Astrid made her way back to the English Trust visitors' centre and took out her phone. She found Sergeant Harper's card in her wallet and rang the number. He should really know this. It might even stir him into action.

'Astrid Kisner.' He answered firmly. Obviously, he'd taken the time to put her name down in his contact list.

'Sergeant Harper. I've some information about Eric Wainwright. The man who died at the Arne on Monday night.' She heard the *brrrh* of a sigh.

'Is that right?'

'Yes, something that proves that he was poisoned.'

'And how did you get this information?'

'I was with him on the night he died.'

There was a muffled conversation, as if he was talking to a colleague. Maybe asking for a pen. When he spoke again his tone was more urgent. 'Where are you?'

He was waiting for her on the slipway when the ferry came in. He wasn't wearing a uniform. Just a pair of dark pressed trousers and a white shirt rolled up over his pale arms. Which was a relief – being picked out of the line of passengers by a policeman would have been mortifying.

When she got to the bottom of the gangplank he steered her over to a bench that looked out over the channel. He took out his notebook and rifled through to a fresh page. 'Now, you said that you were with Mr Wainwright on Monday night, before he died. Is that right?'

'Yes. Someone left a note on my boat to meet them down on the Arne.' She reached into her trouser pocket and found the note. He plucked it out of her fingers. 'Are you not going to put it in a clear plastic bag. Have it examined?'

He ignored her. 'You went off for this secret rendezvous at the Arne and met up with Mr Wainwright.'

'Correct. Although he clearly wasn't the person I was meant to meet. He was doing his usual mushroom foraging tour in the woods and assumed that's why I was there. We wandered around in the woods for an hour or so and ended up on the beach. That's when he offered to cook up some of the mushrooms he found.'

'And did you stay to eat these mushrooms?'

'No, no. I felt I'd taken up too much of his time already. I went back into Hanbury and had a drink with a friend.'

'Who was the friend?'

'Kath Basin.'

'Basin?' He made an expression as if he'd bitten into a sour apple.

'Do you know her?'

'No – I've not met her. But I've had a few run-ins with those brothers of hers.'

A man squeezed past them with a fishing rod in one hand. In the other was a bucket with something that smelt like sardines that had been left out in the sun. He clambered down the boulders of the breakwater and began to set up his rod.

'Where were we?' said Harper. 'Right… so you left Mr Wainwright at what time?'

'Probably about seven-twenty. Because I was in the Angler's Arms before eight.'

He jotted it down in his notepad. It was about the only thing that was on the page.

'Now let me tell you how I know that Eric was poisoned.'

'Go on then.'

'Well, on the walk in the woods he told me he had certain rules about collecting mushrooms because there were some dangerous ones out there. He said that he never touched the ones with white gills. Some of them contain muscarine – that's a deadly toxin. He was most insistent.' He'd started writing again but she couldn't quite read what it said. 'Anyway, the main symptom of muscarine poisoning is excessive water production. Crying, sweating… did you see his body on the beach?'

'I did.'

'And it was drenched in sweat. Right?'

He shut the notepad. 'And how would you know that, Mrs Kisner?'

'I just spoke to the birdwatchers who found him.'

Another bite on the sour apple. Even sharper this time. 'Right. So what exactly is your theory then?' He leant back on the bench. His sandy hair, she noticed, was the same colour as the terracotta tiles of the Haven Hotel behind him.

'Alright then. I suspect that there's a connection between the DeVine death and Eric's. Both took place on English Trust estates. Both were made to look like accidents. What you need to do is work out who had access to the Trust and why they'd want to kill them both.'

'MMO.'

'What? That awful kickboxing sport?'

'No, that's MMA,' he said, impassively. 'MMO is a police term. Means, motive and opportunity. The three driving forces behind any crime.'

MMO. That was good – she was definitely using that one. 'Sergeant Harper, when are you going to investigate these two murders?'

'Murders? Is that what they are?'

'Yes – DeVine was pushed to his death. And Eric would have been the last person to accidentally poison himself by eating mushrooms. Then there's the note.' She took it from him and stashed it back in her bag. 'Someone was trying to tell me what that connection was – but for some reason they didn't show up.'

'Is that right?' Harper let out a sharp laugh that sounded more like a whistle. 'You know what my theory is, Mrs Kisner?'

She shook her head.

'You're a bored trophy wife who's come down from London to set up a second home on a boat. You've got nothing else to do except make up some crime mystery to pass the time between shopping for sailing gear.'

Astrid scowled. 'Trophy wife?'

'I did my research. You're married to the head of some big London gallery.'

'I worked hard to get that job.'

He was up on his feet, his hands planted in his pockets. She couldn't make out his expression because of the angle of the sun. But she could hear the disdain in his voice. 'If you say so, Mrs Kisner.'

'Fine – but whatever you think of me, you need to investigate this.'

'No, I don't. What we're looking at here are two freak accidents. Someone leans out over the railing in an icehouse. A tour guide accidentally eats a deadly mushroom. That's it – there's no connection between the two of them. Of course...' He put his finger on his chin, as if the thought had just come to him. 'Except you were there both times – weren't you?'

'Yes – but, only at the second scene of the crime because someone had lured me there with a note.'

'That's ridiculous. Why don't we leave it at two accidents and hope you don't show up at any more... for your sake.' He turned and set off towards the car park.

She balled up her fists. 'Ugh...' That had not gone as expected.

The big chain ferry was drawing in to the harbour. The two huge chains that ran out underneath it juddered and thumped on the concrete. It slowed as it approached the slipway and the iron plate scraped to a halt. A man in a grimy polo shirt waved at the drivers in the central bay and they turned their engines on. The wash splashed up the breakwater rocks. The fisherman picked up his bucket and went to find a better spot.

She should get up and catch the ferry back to her car at the other side. The next one back would be another half an hour. But she had some thinking to do. Trophy wife? How dare he. Kath was right – he was incompetent. 'Mister No Pants', sitting on his glacier.

It took a good ten minutes for Astrid to calm down about Harper, and for another train of thought to steal up on her. Whoever had lured her to the Arne must have known she'd been investigating the death of DeVine. She had thought she'd been discreet, but obviously someone had noticed. But who were they?

17

Thursday, Day 9

Astrid woke up at 8.45. Back in London, she'd feel guilty about getting up so late. Now it felt lovely and decadent. She stretched out in bed, the remnants of a dream evaporating before she could piece them together. She dressed, made a coffee in her favourite tin mug and went up on deck. The estuary was blanketed in fog. This was the first overcast day since she'd arrived. It was still beautiful though. Murky. Cool. The damp air draped around her. A good day to work on Lady Sherborne's portrait.

In the morning, she did a thorough clean of Lady Sherborne's features, hair and dress. She left the background alone so it would appear that the freshly restored subject had defied the effects of time. Lady Sherborne was bound to like that. In the afternoon, she added a dozen square-cut diamonds to the bracelet. She used watercolours so they could be easily removed if they didn't get approval. When it was finished, she propped the painting by the wall and admired her work. It had been a simple job, but she'd done it well. She looked out over the garden. If only Harper had been so diligent with the case. There had never been a proper investigation of the icehouse. Thank goodness she was going to get to the bottom of it all.

The next day she slept in even later. It was well past nine when a call from Emily wrenched her awake. The art materials had arrived and could she *'pop in to Cressida's office'* to pick them up. This was good news. She now had everything she needed to start restoring the Constable.

On her way to Cressida's office, Astrid realised she hadn't explored the other half of Sherborne Hall. It was still early and the house had yet to fill up with visitors. A good time to dash around then.

She took the corridor to the left of the foyer and turned in to the first doorway she came to. Two elderly couples in light hiking gear were standing in the middle of the room and laughing out loud. In front of them, Margaret was waving her hands around and talking excitedly. Astrid found a leather bench by the wall, sat down and watched.

'The thing is, Margaret,' said a man with a white goatee, reading her name badge. 'This is the dining room, but there's no big table.'

'Ah, you've fallen for it haven't you? All that *Downton Abbey* tosh. The long table with what's-his-name at the top.'

'Hugh Bonneville,' said one of the women.

'That's the one. No, this is much earlier. This is the Georgian era – 1714 to 1837. The Georgian aristocracy were really naughty buggers.' Margaret cackled. 'They drank, had affairs, and they were addicted to gambling.

So, at dinner they'd get the staff to lay out a collection of card tables, depending on the number of guests. They'd eat quickly then clear the plates to start gambling. Card games like Faro, or dice games like Hazard. In fact, they were so obsessed with winning they wouldn't go off to the bathroom. You see those screens?' She pointed to a pair of black inlaid room dividers in the corner. 'They'd go behind them, and do their business in pots. The waiters would then carry the contents off to the loos.'

The four visitors laughed again. Margaret spotted Astrid by the wall. 'Listen, I'm going to take a break. I hope you enjoy your day at the house.'

The four of them thanked her, then wandered off towards the door. Margaret watched them go, smiling. Something Astrid had never seen before.

'Oh, hello.' She sat down next to her on the bench.

'That was brilliant, Margaret.'

'Ah… no, I've just been doing it for a long time,' she muttered. 'What can I do for you, Astrid?'

'You know I was just about to see Cressida and I thought I'd explore this part of the house.'

'Oh, I don't suppose you could ask her if she's heard anything about that VIP tours job?'

'Of course.'

'Not that I stand a chance.'

'Why not?'

Margaret hung her head. 'They'll give it to someone young and energetic, like Denise.' She smacked her lips. 'I'm too old – old and overlooked.'

'No, that's not true.' Astrid waited until Margaret looked

up at her. 'I've just seen you in action. You had those visitors eating out of the palm of your hand.'

'Yes, the visitors appreciate me... but the Trust? I love this organisation – it's the greatest institution in the world. But they've forgotten volunteers like me. Sometimes I wish something would happen to take them down a peg or two.'

'What kind of thing?'

'Oh, I'm just thinking aloud. Forget I said it.'

'Sure.'

'Anyway...' She watched another half a dozen visitors file into the room. 'I better get back to work.'

Margaret started to get up. Astrid hooked her arm through hers and helped her to her feet.

Cressida was hunched over a big cast-iron radiator under the window. 'I can never get the right temperature,' she said, drawing her camel coat tighter. 'The windows are painted shut so it's either roasting or too chilly.' She adjusted a valve by the side and patted the radiator. 'Ooh, lovely – it's working.'

Astrid looked around. There were some cardboard boxes neatly stacked up in the corner. 'Are these the art materials I ordered? Emily said they'd arrived.'

'Oh, yes... I think they are. I'll get Emily to give you a hand.' She tapped in a text and settled in behind her desk. 'So how are you getting on with the collection, Astrid?'

'Great, thanks. I bumped into Lady Sherborne – she's keen to have a portrait of herself in the exhibition. I said we could probably arrange that.'

'I don't see why not. I'll pop it on the spreadsheet.' Cressida shuffled a few things around on her desk. She seemed more distracted than usual this morning, lining up paper, stuffing biros back into the pen pot on her desk.

'And good news on the Constable,' said Astrid. 'It's in excellent condition so it only needs a minor surface clean.'

'Uh? Oh, yeah... that's super news,' she said, peeling off a bright pink Post-it Note from a pad.

'And the story of Constable and his honeymoon is great. I could write up something for the exhibition – along the lines of the love that inspired one of England's greatest romantic painters.'

Cressida looked up from the Post-it Note. 'That's a fab idea. If you could get me a few paragraphs ASAP, I'll send them to the designers to incorporate into the display material.'

'Sure. Oh, and Margaret was asking about the VIP tours job. Is there any news?'

'Margaret?'

'One of the volunteers.'

'Right, no... the VIP tours have been outsourced to a company called Legacy Experience. They'll be in touch if she gets an interview.'

The door opened and Emily squeezed in with a cup of coffee in one hand, and a small plate of biscuits in the other. She hurried over to the desk and put them down. 'I got you some of those amaretti biscuits you like.'

'Oh, you're a sweetheart, Emily.' She turned to Astrid. 'She really is the most brilliant assistant.'

Emily beamed. 'Can I get you a coffee, Astrid?'

'No, thank you. I'd better go.'

Cressida sipped her coffee and closed her eyes with pleasure. 'Oh, that's just what I need. Thank you, Emily.' She put the cup down. 'Now would you be a dear and give Astrid a hand with the boxes?'

'Of course,' said Emily. 'I'm here to help.'

They headed down the corridor, each with a box in both arms. Emily was still glowing from the praise in the office. 'She's terrific, isn't she?'

'Yes, she's great.'

Emily was wearing the same blue suit, with a matching velvet scrunchie. Her hair was chestnut – as rich and glossy as the picture on the side of a hair dye box. Astrid realised she hadn't asked Emily anything about herself. And over the months, she was sure Cressida hadn't either. 'So, you went to uni in London, Emily?'

'Yes, three years in hotel and hospitality management.'

'You enjoy it?'

'Not much – to be honest.'

'Oh, really?'

They slowed down next to a corner and carefully steered the boxes round a table with a large vase on it.

'I was born and raised in Dorset. I grew up on a farm so I really missed being in the country. So, after graduating I came back and started looking for work.'

'You must have been pleased to get a job at the Trust.'

'Yes, it's a dream come true.' She smiled, a pinkish flush high on her cheekbones. 'I'm only on an internship at the moment. But I'd love to make it a permanent job.'

In the workroom, Emily stood by the door until Astrid told her to put her box down on the table.

'Well, thanks again for helping me.'

Emily was staring at the Constable, which was wrapped in a sheet. 'I hope you don't mind me asking... is that the Constable? I heard Cressida talking about it.'

'Yes, it is.' Astrid unwrapped the painting and centred it on the table. 'It's one of his smaller landscapes – probably painted at the location. Actually...' Astrid stepped aside as Emily took a closer look. 'You're from the area – do you know where this is?'

Emily peered at the painting. 'Yes, I do – it's about five miles west of here, along the coast. It's a bay just before Weymouth.'

'Do you know exactly where he would have set up to paint the view?'

Emily studied the painting again, then she shook her head. 'The strange thing is – he would have had to paint it from out at sea.'

'Is that right?'

She pointed at a rocky outcrop. 'Yes, I know this beach. He would have been at least a hundred yards off shore.'

'Are you sure?'

'Yes, positive.' She checked her watch and snapped back into faultless assistant mode. 'I'd better get back. Cressida has a list of things for me to do.'

'No problem. Thanks for the information, Emily.'

When she had gone, Astrid opened the boxes and set up the new halogen lamp on a tripod. She put on a new headpiece magnifying glass and went over to the Constable. He was one of her favourite artists – driven to capture English weather in all its grumpy, grizzly moods. A lifetime spent agonising over how shadows played on fields of long grass or oak leaves. He wanted you to be there with him. To feel the wind. To see the light sparkle between the branches. Many artists of the time just used a blank wash for the sky. Or painted clouds as static puffy pillows. Not Constable – his clouds moved. Air falling through air. Weightless, pushed on by approaching storms.

She leant over and scanned the brushstrokes. Constable's paintings were alive. The animals and people in them too. Horses shuddered to shake the dew off their backs. Millwheels creaked round in crystal streams. She gently touched the ridge of the headland and ran her finger up through the brushstrokes. Then she took her finger away as if it had been too cold to touch. This painting wasn't alive. The brushstrokes were measured and deliberate. There were none of his carefree flourishes. Maybe he wasn't inspired that day? Or his new bride, calling from the path, had distracted him.

As she looked again, the feeling that something wasn't right began to build in waves. It was still a good painting. Just not good enough for a master at the height of his powers. And now she'd noticed something else. Something even more worrying. All varnishes dry in a pattern over time. They create a jigsaw of random cracks known as 'craquelure'. Over decades the varnish sinks into the paint beneath it. It creates a fingerprint that's hard to copy. After two hundred and fifty years the cracks should be more intricate than this. More random. These were too regular

– a sign that the painting might have been forced to age quickly by some unnatural drying process.

She took out a swab, found a low-concentration solvent and worked at an area in slow circular movements. The cotton wool came back light grey. Underneath she could see the varnish more clearly. It hadn't fallen into the cracks in the paint. Which meant it had been layered on recently. There was only one explanation for it – the Constable was a fake.

Astrid went to the window. Raindrops tracked down the diamond panes. This was exciting in a way – as exciting as when she found the painting and thought it was authentic. This was the first time she'd discovered a copy – she was almost certain that's what it was. Lady Sherborne would be pleased. She'd be centre stage at the exhibition now. But the Trust? If they'd paid as much for it as the rumours said, then this was going to be embarrassing.

She laid out a sheet of paper and turned the painting over. Using a pair of long-nosed pliers she carefully prised out the black tacks and the frame came away from the board. Turning it over, she checked down the edge that had been concealed by the frame. The colours of the paint matched the rest of the picture. They shouldn't do – hidden from sunlight for centuries, the colours should be brighter and fresher than the rest of the painting. She was sure now. Better take a sample just in case.

Aiming the point of a scalpel in a small corner of the board, she teased a flake of varnish from the surface. Pinching it with tweezers she put it in a small clear plastic sample jar. If she could get it analysed back in London – Muraki might be kind enough to help – then she'd have the absolute proof she needed.

She went to the window. The rain had stopped. A bank of clouds, thick as bonfire smoke, had been pushed away by a band of cobalt blue. Constable clouds. He'd know how to hold this moment for ever. The real Constable would.

18

Astrid had been expecting Cressida to have a meltdown about this latest piece of news. Hot on the heels of a suspicious death on English Trust grounds, it would be the last thing she'd want to add to the spreadsheet. But when she told her the Constable was a fake she barely raised an eyebrow. 'Are you sure about this, Astrid?'

'Almost positive. I'm sending back a sample to the National Gallery so we have the chemical proof.'

'Yes, good idea.'

Emily was behind them both, prising a screwdriver into the gap in the painted-up window frame. The screwdriver kept falling from her grip and rattling down the back of the radiator. Cressida turned to her. 'Emily, darling. Maybe that can wait.'

'Of course.'

'Perhaps you could go through the mail instead?'

Emily put the screwdriver on the ledge and gathered up the pile of mail from Cressida's desk. Then she took a seat in the corner.

'So, where were we?' said Cressida, cheerfully.

'I was going to ask,' said Astrid. 'Do you know who authenticated this painting before the Trust bought it?'

'Yes, we asked some independent assessors to value the collection.' She put her hand to her mouth. 'Oh, no. The assessors have made a huge mistake here – don't you think?'

'It looks that way.'

'Whoo,' she whistled. 'An expensive mistake too. I do hope nobody gets in trouble over this. Although, at the end of the day the buck has to stop at Head Office, doesn't it? Not me though, right. Astrid?' It was the first time she'd looked worried since hearing the news.

'I think you're in the clear.'

'Phew...' she sighed. 'I mean, they're a great bunch at Head Office. Harriet, Jasper... but if you make mistakes, you pay the price.'

'I guess. So the assessors – do you know who they were?'

'No idea. As I say, the art collection had nothing to do with me.' She got up from the chair and edged round the desk. A second or two later, Emily hurried over to open the door.

'Right. I'll head off,' said Astrid.

'Ace,' said Cressida. 'And thanks for telling me about the painting. Keep it to yourself for the time being though – until we're absolutely sure.'

'I will. And shall I keep restoring the rest of the collection?'

'Yes, please. We still need to put on an exhibition at some stage.'

Astrid went back to the room and picked up her things, including the sample of varnish from the Constable and her work briefcase. It would have been too difficult to concentrate on the other paintings. She couldn't stop thinking about the Constable. Who had made it, and when?

The answer to the second question was easier – fairly recently, given how similar the brightness of the paint was on the margins. The ageing process, the drying of the varnish, had been done speedily. Probably by a hairdryer. A few hours over a smoky fire could have added the soot. The next question then – yet another big flat stone to be turned over and inspected underneath – had the fake painting been sold to the Sherborne family? Or was the English Trust the first sucker?

In the corner of the room, the portrait of Lady Sherborne stared at her. Astrid went over and picked it up. In her late teens she really was impossibly beautiful. Refined. Enigmatic. From the pose you could tell she knew it too – and the power it would give her in high society. As her mother said – 'it's survival of the prettiest, Astrid'. So how do you cope when all that power has gone? Best find out.

It wasn't hard to work out where Lady Sherborne's living quarters were. Most of the signs around the Trust's part of the hall were clearly marked. There were cheery pointers everywhere to the estate's highlights – the Herb Garden, Pan's Temple, the Scallop Fountain, with plenty of options to lighten visitors' wallets along the way. Chalkboards every hundred yards were marked up with temptations – *'Delicious organic Dorset ice cream'*, *'Cream teas in the Orangery Café all day'*.

Towards the West Wing, though, were the kind of warnings more suited to indicating uncleared minefields.

'*Danger – Keep Out! Private Property.*' There was a sign with a silhouette of a guard dog against a yellow background.

Astrid carried on and pushed open a heavy wooden door in a red-brick wall, the portrait of Lady Sherborne under her arm. Beyond the door was a cobbled courtyard. It was shaded by a high stable block with mossy tiles. A rusted weathervane of a hunting hound rocked in the breeze. Inside one part of the stables was an old Land Rover Defender.

She crossed the cobbles towards a dark green door. Either side were two short flights of stone steps. There were no railings to stop you falling. This must be where you dismount from your horse. Then someone would take it back to the stables for you. Not now maybe. The place was well past its glory days. The paint on the door was peeling off in flakes the size of holly leaves. An ivy, thick as a forearm at its base, took over much of the side of the house. It had crawled upwards over the years, obscuring windows, getting its fingernails into the gutters.

The house had stood here for five centuries. Now nature was coming back to claim it. However much the Trust had paid for the rest of the estate and the art, there had been little left to fix Lady Sherborne's remaining part of the house. Margaret was right – Lady Sherborne was broke.

Astrid climbed the stairs and found a brass doorbell that was almost hidden amongst the ivy leaves. When she pressed it there was a tinny rattle and a flurry of sparrows flew out from the ivy. A minute later and the door slowly swung open. Lady Sherborne peered out from around the frame.

'I've told you lot before. Just leave the package on the steps.'

Astrid stepped forwards. 'It's me – Astrid, the art restorer.'

Lady Sherborne opened the door a few more inches. 'Right… yes. Thought it was the Amazonians. They always want me to sign their electronic thingy.'

Astrid held up the painting. 'I've finished working on your portrait. I thought you might like to take a look at it?'

'That was quick,' said Lady Sherborne.

'It was just a simple clean and touch-up job.'

Lady Sherborne folded her arms. 'Was it now.'

'Yes. It was such a beautiful painting to start with, I didn't need to do much with it.'

'Mmm…' the slightest curl of a smile. 'Well, you better come in then.'

Astrid was ushered down a gloomy corridor then round a sharp right into a drawing room with high ceilings. If the Angler's Arms was a shrine to the art of fishing, then this was a museum of hunting. Anything that was worth chasing around the countryside and shooting dead was here. On the panelled walls were a range of animal heads – deer, antelope, some sort of African buffalo. There were twisted horns and antlers of all shapes and sizes.

Over the fireplace was a large oil painting of a fox hunt. Nothing too interesting – the usual red-coated, red-faced men on horseback charging over a field. It was the only art on the walls – although other paintings had clearly been taken down. Darker rectangles were dotted across the panels.

The rest of the room was filled with antique furniture – grandfather clocks, Chinese cabinets, a mahogany sideboard covered in trinkets and pictures in heavy silver frames. A bunch of withered flowers drooped in a Lalique vase. It was as cluttered as DeVine's antique store. Except these were classic antiques. Worth a fair amount – or would be if they were in good condition. Everything was scuffed and dusty.

Lady Sherborne edged round a chipped oak table near the fireplace. There was a fat dog on the carpet in front of the fire. She stepped over it. 'For goodness' sake, Beezer, you lazy cur.' She turned to Astrid. 'Marvellous dog in his day though.'

Astrid leant the portrait against a table and went over to the dog. 'Hullo, boy.' The dog raised its muzzle slightly, opened a cloudy eye then closed it again.

'What sort of dog is he?'

'Beagle hound. We've had some good rides out – haven't we, Beezer?' A smile, if that's what dogs do, creased up at the corner of its muzzle.

'Do you hunt?'

'No.' She looked round the room at the antlers and heads. 'I'm not sure I could kill anything.'

Lady Sherborne snorted. 'This generation has gone soft if you ask me. Children are stuck behind those video screens. I was bloodied on my first hunt at five. I'd bagged my first 22-pointer at nine. Everything you see in this room I shot. I hunt to this day and I'm...' Her voice trailed off as she caught herself revealing her age. 'In my autumn years.'

Astrid studied the painting of the hunting scene. There was a flash of ginger in the hedge. A pack of hounds bearing down on it. 'I'm not sure it seems that fair to me. The odds of it. A fox versus all those people.'

'Uhh...' Lady Sherborne crossed her arms and sat back

on the corner of a table. 'You sound like that ghastly Cressida woman.'

'Cressida?'

'Yes, the marketing lady. She's gone and taken down all the hunting trophies around the house. Says they're no longer "relevant" in this day and age. That's why they're all in here.'

'I see.'

'She's nothing more than a "counter jumper" if you ask me.' Lady Sherborne still had another barrel to unload at Cressida. 'Sitting around as if she owns the place. She has no idea about the history of the Hall. The work my family have put in to keep up the standards of a big house. And the English Trust – they're grave robbers.' She went over to a log basket, pulled out a log and tossed it on the embers. 'Now I'm stuck here.' Lady Sherborne began clearing a space on the table, sweeping aside paperwork and putting inkpots and blotters to one side. 'Now then. Let's see my portrait.'

'Of course.' Astrid took the sheet off the painting and laid it out on the table.

Lady Sherborne bent over the canvas. She was silent for a while, then her hand reached out slowly and stroked at a curl of hair on the painting.

'Divine,' she whispered. Then she brought her hand back to her own hair and twirled a wisp above her ear. 'My "coming-out ball" – I remember every moment. Every dance. The flowers in the hall. Everyone said I was beautiful.'

'Well, I'm so glad it's bringing back happy memories.'

'Yes, such happy memories.' Her bad mood had been

dulled by sadness. This was a fragment of the past that sang softly to her. 'Where does the time go, Astrid?'

Astrid shrugged. 'I'm not sure,' she said, although the question wasn't due an answer. 'And you're happy with the jewellery? The bracelet has some more stones now. And I've added drop pearl earrings.'

Lady Sherborne rubbed the corner of her eyes. 'Oh yes, yes… well done. That's much more impressive. Don't you think?'

'Yes, I'm glad you're pleased. I've restored self-portraits before but usually the subject of the painting is, well… no longer around.'

Lady Sherborne raised an eyebrow. 'Is that so?' Her gruff demeanour returned. 'Now, have you persuaded Cressida to include my portrait in the exhibition?'

'Yes, I've sorted it out.'

'Excellent.' She picked up the painting and sat it in an armchair. 'I'll hang on to it until then. Spend some time with her. Now, if that's all. I have to take Beezer out or he'll be planted next to the fire all day.'

'Actually, I did have another question about the Constable.'

Lady Sherborne took out a heavy stick from a copper bucket by the fireplace. 'I've told you all I know.'

Astrid went over to her. 'Yes, but if you could just tell me when your family bought it? Do you have any paperwork?'

'No, there's no paperwork.'

'So, it might not be authentic?'

'Authentic?' She growled. 'Of course it is. My family bought from the best galleries and dealers around the world.'

'Sorry.'

She pulled out a dog lead from a drawer in a bureau. 'Ah, there it is.'

'Can you tell me anything else about it?'

'We've got to go.'

Astrid blocked her way. 'All I need are a few details. Then I can get on with the exhibition, and we'll have all the guests in the main house, admiring your portrait… your ladyship.' Astrid wondered if the ladyship bit was laying it on a bit thick. But Lady Sherborne rose to it.

'Well, it's been in the family a while. Grandfather picked it up. He was the big art collector. I think it's in a photo somewhere.' She went over to the mantelpiece and scanned the gilt frames above the fire. There were so many that they overlapped. She gently levered one out. 'There we are.' She placed it on the table. 'That is a picture of my grandfather. He'd be in his fifties here.'

Astrid studied the black and white photo in the frame. A man with his chest puffed out, and a face like thunder, was staring back at them. Behind him were a few pictures on the wall. One of them was the Constable. Even in black and white you could just make out the cliffs above the sea.

'That's all I have, I'm afraid.'

'That's more than enough,' she said. 'Thank you.'

'Bravo. Now, can you show yourself out?'

'Of course.' Astrid turned from the door. Behind her she heard the rattle of Beezer's chain being clipped on, a 'come on dog,' then a *wuffling* humph of protest as Beezer hauled himself up from the warm carpet.

*

Astrid checked her phone to make sure what day it was – Friday. That was a first. In London she'd never lose track of which day it was. Her week was well marked out – by meetings, lunches and sessions at the gym. The gym – she hadn't missed that recently. Thinking about it, why had she wasted so much time in there, sweating herself to distraction – and paying for the privilege? When she could just get on a bike or go for a walk along the river, like she did now? Simon had kept an eye on her gym routine too. 'Remember how good you looked in those wedding photos?' he'd said. 'You don't want to let things slip, do you?'

No more gym then. It was walking and biking from now on. Anyway, Kath had told her the nearest thing to a gym session round here was the Tuesday Zumba class at the church. Which was best avoided, according to her, because the vicar worked up too much of a sweat.

Astrid decided to drop into the volunteer hub before heading back to the boat. On the way she thought about the Constable in the photo. Lady Sherborne was almost certainly right – her family wouldn't have bought a forgery. So the original must have been carefully copied at some point. But when exactly?

She got to the hub at ten to two and was surprised to find the place deserted. The biscuit jar was untouched, the hot water urn switched off.

There was a faint fizz of a conversation from the walkie-talkie on the sideboard. She picked it up and pressed the button on the side. 'Hullo. It's Astrid in the volunteer hub. Is anyone there?'

She heard Denise rounding off a conversation in the

background. *Click*. 'This is Denise speaking. We're all on the front lawn. Come and see us. Over.'

The gardens were, she thought, probably as lovely as they could ever be. The flowerbeds were filled with foliage, fat buds and shoots. Every colour in a furious upwards race. Dusky pink and orange roses climbed the trellises. A bush with white flowers with yellow centres rambled over the brickwork. On the gravel path ahead of her an elderly couple stopped to read plant labels then sneaked a cutting into their bag.

On the main lawn was what looked like an old-fashioned Scout camp. Six cream canvas tents had been set up – three on either side of the lawn. They were a simple tepee style – a wide circular base with wooden poles sticking out of the top. Denise appeared from the open flap of the nearest one and hurried over. As usual she was wearing her maid's outfit, a clipboard in her hand. 'What do you think?'

'It's great. It's the battle camp tomorrow isn't it?'

'Exactly.' She swept her hand in front of her. 'What you see now is the same scene that would have greeted Cromwell's supporters on their long march to London. Follow me.' She strode down the line of tents. 'I will be manning this first tent and giving a demonstration of bread-making. Cressida finally relented and is letting me use actual ingredients because a tent is classed as an outdoor space.'

'That's wonderful news.'

'It is. I'll be able to show how bread was actually made...' her voice became airy '...in those faraway times.'

At the next tent Denise pulled back the door panel and

tied it back up with a toggle. Margaret was inside sitting next to a square wooden frame on which was stretched a section of cloth. Around her feet were balls of wool and glass jars filled with purple and blue dyes. 'Come on, you bugger...' she grunted as she tried to work a spindle into the cloth.

'Ah, Mar-gar-ret,' said Denise, 'what fair tapestries art thou weaving?'

Margaret glowered at her over the frame. 'Give it a rest, Denise.'

Denise let the flap of the tent slide back. 'Let's press on, Astrid. Margaret is a bit busy in there.'

The next tent was larger than the others. It was set near the edge of the lawn, which dropped straight down, eight feet or so, to the open field. Inside was a long table covered with a range of weapons – crossbows, swords and pikes. Harold was at the head of the table. He turned to greet them. 'Ah, Astrid... Denise. Welcome to the armaments tent. What do you think?'

Astrid looked around the room. There was a rail of clothes at the back. Everything a soldier might put on for battle. The back wall was draped in regimental flags. 'Very impressive.'

Denise carefully picked up a stick with a short chain attached to it. There was a spiky ball on the end. 'This looks lethal, Harold.'

'Don't worry – they're reproductions. And anyway, I'll be standing here to keep an eye on things, just in case any sticky-fingered kids get in.'

Denise ran her finger down the side of the sword. 'Yes, that's blunt enough. I'll still have to write it up in the risk assessment for Cressida.'

'You do that, Denise.' Harold turned to Astrid. 'I hope you can make it tomorrow.'

'I was planning to.'

'Excellent. I've got a couple of chaps coming in from the local battle reconstruction society in Poole. They'll be putting on a hand-to-hand combat display every hour from ten o'clock.'

'Don't worry, I'll be there.'

'Good, and oh… let me show you something else.' Harold went over to the rail and brought over a heavy, short-sleeved shirt. He cleared a space on the table and laid it out. 'Now this is something I am an expert on – chain mail.'

Astrid ran her hand over the shirt. It was made from thousands of small metal rings. 'This is real craftsmanship. Well done.'

'Thank you, Astrid.' Harold beamed. 'I forged every single link from fourteen-gauge wire. Every rivet too.'

'Wow – how long did that take?'

'Oh, about nine months.' He held it up. 'This tunic would have a padded doublet underneath. The combination could stop any seventeenth-century arrow.'

'You two!' Denise called from the doorway. 'You've got to see this.'

They lined up on the lawn in front of the tent. Ahead of them a white van was backing onto the grass. On the side in large bubbly letters were the words *Bournemouth Inflatables*. A bald man with no top on hopped out of the cab. Denise exhaled. 'Unbelievable.'

'Unbelievable,' echoed Harold.

'Sorry, what are we looking at?' said Astrid.

'It's the bouncy castle, Astrid.'

'Oh, right.'

The bald man smiled and waved over to them. Denise and Harold crossed their arms. Margaret was hurrying towards them – faster than Astrid had ever seen her move. She joined the end of the line and glared at the van. 'Disgraceful,' she hissed.

'I know,' muttered Denise. 'What is it that Cressida is always saying she wants?'

'Heritage,' said Harold.

'Exactly,' said Denise. 'And she hires a bouncy castle! After all the effort we've put in to keep things historically correct.'

'You know how I made that blue dye for the wool?' said Margaret.

Everyone shook their heads.

'Indigo mixed with my own urine. You think I have been peeing in a bucket for the last three weeks so the Trust can make a few quid from a bouncy castle?'

'Ooh, Margaret.' Denise brought her sleeve up to her mouth. 'I might have to add that to the health and safety forms.'

Margaret gripped her stick. 'I'm going to say something.'

'No, Margaret – don't get involved.' Harold put a hand on her shoulder.

'Fine. But this isn't the end of it… mark my words.' Margaret turned and stomped off back to her tent.

'You know,' said Astrid uneasily, 'I think I'll head off.'

'Yes, yes…' said Harold, eyes still trained forward. 'See you tomorrow.'

19

The woman in the post office promised Astrid that her package, the varnish sample addressed to the National Gallery, would definitely arrive the next day. 'We're the post office. There's nothing we can't do,' she said with the certainty of a top motivational speaker.

She was a bit worried that she was putting Muraki in a difficult position, but he'd insisted he wanted to help. So, in a few days' time, she'd definitely know if the Constable was a fake. If it was, then she'd stumbled on a more sinister plot. Right now though, there were too many questions she couldn't answer on her own. Harper may have dismissed her as a bored 'trophy wife' – that still stung – but she was going to give him one last chance.

She had some more information to trade now – the forged Constable. Quid pro quo. She'd tell him about the forgery, and the chalk – and he'd tell her what he knew. He'd have to.

It was five o'clock – if she was quick, then she could catch him at work and find out what he knew, if anything.

Poole Police Station looked very similar to Hanbury Library – the same squat breeze-block building from the

1950s. In the reception there were just as many posters on the walls. They included an advert for Neighbourhood Watch schemes, a grid of head shots of wanted criminals and a warning not to leave dogs in cars in the summer.

Astrid stared at a poster that had a man in a balaclava wedging a crowbar into a car window. Underneath it said: *'Don't leave your valuables in your car'*. Did criminals really wear woollen balaclavas? Maybe this was just someone who'd been on a skiing trip and was rescuing a sweltering dog? Probably not, but you couldn't rule anything out. That's the way her mind was working these days. She was thinking like a detective.

'You alright?' a deep voice echoed from the front of the room. A police officer was standing behind a desk that ran across the back third of the room. He was bald with a thick block-like head. A pink neck bulged over the collar of his shirt like the top of a muffin.

She went over. 'I'm looking for Sergeant Harper.'

The name made him chuckle. 'Harpo? You sure?'

'Yes, Sergeant Harper.'

He chuckled again and sauntered over to a door that led to an open-plan office. She could see a few empty desks and computers. 'Hey, Harpo,' he shouted into the office. 'It's your lucky day. A lady wants to speak to you.'

Harper appeared a minute later at the door and nodded at Astrid. The other officer stood back and watched him come round the front of the desk. 'There he goes, Inspector Clueless.'

He led Astrid to the back of the reception. 'We'll have a bit more privacy here,' he said, pointing to a couple of seats next to a drinks vending machine. 'Ignore my colleague. It's just office banter.'

'Okay,' said Astrid. 'You're probably wondering why I'm here.'

'Not really. It's the English Trust case, isn't it?'

'Yes, and I have some very important new information.' She paused, expecting him to say something. But he just shook his head. 'And I thought we could, you know... exchange notes. You scratch my back and...'

'I told you before,' he interrupted. 'I have your statement – that's all I need from you.'

'Sergeant Harper,' she said firmly. 'Let me remind you, there's a killer out there and they could strike again.'

'Strike again?' he said in a shrill voice that she wasn't sure was because he was annoyed, or it was a bad impression of her. 'This isn't a TV show, Mrs Kisner. I'm investigating this thoroughly and you will know the outcome at the same time as the rest of the public.'

She edged her chair towards him, which rucked up a carpet tile. 'Right, well I'm going to tell you anyway. Because this is a major breakthrough.'

'Is that so?'

'Yes – I have discovered a forgery of a very valuable painting at Sherborne Hall.'

There was a flicker of interest. 'A forgery? Are you sure?'

Astrid hesitated. 'Not completely, not yet. But I expect to have proof any day now.'

He sighed. 'Well, you let me know when you're sure.' He was about to get up but the other officer was sauntering over to the drinks machine. He lingered over the buttons, clearly trying to tune in to their conversation.

Harper stared at his colleague.

'I'm having a chicken soup,' said the bald man,

deliberately popping the 'p' at the end of 'soup'. He looked at Astrid. 'Would you like a soup?'

'God no… who drinks soup that's come out of a vending machine?'

'Oooh… feisty,' he said under his breath. He started loading coins into the slot.

As they both waited for him to leave, Astrid realised just how much younger Harper was than his colleague. He was probably only in his early twenties, not long out of police training.

'Don't mind me. You carry on,' said the bald man, winking at Astrid.

Astrid turned back to Harper. 'Then there's the white marks on DeVine's sleeve. I'm sure you saw them?'

'Of course. Although you didn't mention you'd examined the body before.'

'It slipped my mind.'

The machine rattled and a small plastic cup popped out. It was followed soon afterwards by a hiss of steam that smelt faintly of chicken.

'I ran a test of my own and it turns out it was chalk.'

'Chalk, yes. I can concur,' said Harper earnestly, one eye on his colleague. 'That's exactly what my forensics team said.'

The other policeman roared with laughter. 'My forensics team!' He took the cup of soup in his hand. 'That's made my day.' He wandered back to the reception desk.

'As I say – a bit of office banter there,' said Harper. But she could see he'd been wounded by the mockery. His ears were bright red. He closed his notebook and got up. 'Thank you for coming. And if there's anything else, let me know.'

'I will,' she said.

So there it was. Harper hadn't been trying to bury the evidence for someone powerful. He wasn't incompetent. He was just a junior cop out of his depth. A big case had fallen into his lap and he had no power to do anything about it. And if Harper couldn't sort it out, it was up to her. Only she could catch the killer now. She strode out of the police station. If this was one of those TV shows, this would be the bit when the fat police chief would call her back into his office. Then he'd say, even though she was an art restorer, she'd make a 'damn good detective'. Damn right she would.

Kath sank back on the folding chair on the deck of the boat, drained a thin blue and silver can of *Booster* energy drink, crushed it in her fist and nodded knowingly. 'Told you, Astrid. The English Trust – it's rotten to the core.'

Astrid sipped her coffee. 'Kath – before we go through your thoughts on what's going on here... can I just check on something?'

'Anything.'

'Do you believe that we landed on the moon?'

Kath leant forwards and rummaged in a white plastic bag at her feet. 'I can't believe you're even asking me that.'

'Well?'

'Course not – you've seen the pictures of the American flag. It's pointing straight out when we all know there's no wind on the moon.'

'And Elvis is still alive?'

'Probably.' Kath brought out a muffin in a clear plastic wrapper and handed it over.

'Thanks.' Astrid took the muffin. 'Listen, Kath, what I'm saying is – let's try to not get carried away with the conspiracies at this stage and just focus on the facts so far. Agreed?'

'Agreed.'

Astrid unwrapped the muffin and took a cautious bite from the corner. She closed her eyes in delight. 'Mmm... oh, that's fantastic.'

'Toffee and banana,' said Kath. 'I nick them from the café. Definitely top five in Kath Basin's "lush list".'

'Good choice.' Astrid wolfed down the rest of the muffin in a couple of bites. 'Okay, so what do we know? Two people are killed on English Trust property within days of each other – one was pushed to their death, the other poisoned. Then just after that, a fake of a very valuable painting turns up at Sherborne House.' Astrid carefully folded up the wrapper and set it down next to her. 'Nothing bad ever happens at the English Trust, right, Kath?'

'That's why people go there.'

'So these three remarkable events have to be connected.'

'Definitely. And remember, DeVine was an antique dealer. So he probably had something to do with the fake painting.'

'Yes – that would seem to be an obvious link. But his shop – he was clearly struggling. If he'd made a lot of money from forgery he'd hid it well.'

Kath reached for another energy drink in her bag.

'You sure you should have another one, Kath? The stuff they put in those – it's not good for you.'

'One more. It helps my brain.' She tapped her temple, then cracked the ring pull on the can.

'Okay. Let's go through the suspects – which means?' She glanced down at her bag.

'Checking in with 1D?'

'You got it.' Astrid reached into her bag and pulled out the One Direction notebook, quickly flicking through to a page around the middle. Along the top it said 'Means', 'Motive' and 'Opportunity' and there was a grid of 'suspects' below it. 'Right,' she tapped a finger on the page. 'My boss – Cressida?'

'Guilty,' shouted Kath. 'She's up to her neck in it.'

'Kath! You've never met her.'

'Okay,' she said sheepishly.

'The volunteers make her out to be a monster, but I think she's really nice. A bit obsessed with marketing but that's her job, I guess. And she knows absolutely nothing about art.'

'That right?'

'Yes, she wouldn't know the difference between a Constable and a Sergeant.' Astrid laughed.

'I'm assuming that's an art joke?'

'It is, and a really good one.' Astrid dusted the muffin crumbs off her trousers. 'Now, what about the volunteers?'

'Who are they again?'

'Okay, there's Denise. Mid-thirties – bubbly, the other two hate her. She dislikes Cressida because she's brought in lots of new health and safety rules, which means she's not allowed to do any cooking demonstrations. Then there's Harold – former military man, might have money problems. And Margaret – the oldest, might have anger issues. They both dislike Cressida as well. The thing is – they still seem too nice to commit grand fraud and murder.'

'They could just be pretending? So they can hear how you're getting on with the case.'

Astrid took the pen out, and scribbled a note down next to the volunteers about keeping your enemies closer. She would have liked to be scratching names off the suspect list – narrowing it down. But, for now, there wasn't enough evidence.

'What about Harper?' said Kath.

'No, he's just a junior cop.'

'A "rookie" cop. Let's get the jargon right, Astrid.'

'Nice one. Yup, he's a rookie cop. I just went to visit him at the police station and he's a bit of a laughing stock. I actually feel really sorry for him.' Astrid tapped the bottom corner of the notepad. 'Hey – quick One Direction fun fact… Louis has tinnitus in his right ear from all his screaming fans.'

'Yeah – I knew that.'

'Good for you. Now what about Lady Sherborne?'

'Guilty.'

'She's scary enough. All that shooting gear lying around the place. But would she know how to poison Eric the forager with a mushroom?'

'And you're sure he was poisoned?'

'Positive.' She reached into her bag and brought out the note and handed it to Kath. 'And remember this? Someone said they had information but they didn't turn up that night. Or they did and changed their mind at the last minute.'

Kath flipped the note over in her hand. 'Did you see anyone in the car park, or the woods?'

'No. Except… there was a big yacht out in the bay off

the Arne. And there was a tender brought up onto the beach that must have belonged to that. It was called… it was called…' She punched a fist into her palm. 'Got it! The name on the side said *Sea Breeze.*'

'*Sea Breeze?*' Kath shook her head. 'Dunno. But I can tell you, all the fancy yachts are moored up at the marina at Sandbanks.'

'On the other side of the chain ferry?'

'Yeah – the Royal Motor Yacht Club. It's very fancy. Might be worth checking it out some time.'

'Not a bad idea. I might have a nose around this evening.'

'I'd come with you but I've got a shift at the Angler's. Dolly is visiting her sister on the Isle of Wight.'

'Dolly has a sister?'

'Yeah – and she's even ruder than her.'

'Wow, is that even possible?' Astrid got up. 'Hey, I'm going to get another refill of coffee. You want anything?'

'Nah, I'm good.'

Astrid went down to the cabin and quickly made the coffee – instant granules tipped from the jar, no milk – which felt nice and lazy. When she got back on deck, Kath was gazing out over the estuary. 'It's blooming gorgeous out here, isn't it?'

Kath was always so positive. If she thought about it, Gina never had much good to say about anything, or anyone. She hadn't noticed it before but Gina had a mean streak – if running off with her best friend's husband wasn't proof of that. Simon not replying to her text for, what was it? Four days now… That was bad. But Gina not reaching out to her since this all happened. That was really cruel.

'You alright, Astrid?'

'Yeah, I'm great.' She forced a smile and chinked her coffee cup against Kath's can. 'Cheers.'

'Cheers my dears!'

They sat without saying anything – admiring the view. Eventually Astrid broke the silence. 'You know my husband has left me?'

'Yeah, I know,' Kath said, her eyes still on the river. 'I knew it when I first saw you.'

'Is that why you've been so kind to me?'

Kath turned to her. A smile creased her face. 'Well... maybe at the start. But then I got to know you. I think you're brilliant – even if you can't see it.'

'You too, Kath.'

'Aww... thanks, mate.' She punched her playfully, high on her arm. 'You know... whoever your husband is. He's a mug to throw you away.'

'It's a bit more complicated than that. But I appreciate it.' She clapped her hands. 'Hey – do you fancy coming to this battle re-enactment at Sherborne Hall tomorrow? I can bring a guest.'

'Oh, yeah... Men knocking seven bells out of each other – what's not to like?'

There was the growl of an outboard engine. A grey inflatable dinghy appeared round the bend in the river. Kath straightened and brushed the crumbs from the front of her jumper. 'Hang on, Astrid. Look lively.'

Astrid peered out over the water. Cobb was sitting on the back plank of the dinghy, his hand on the rudder.

'Afternoon, sailor!' Kath shouted.

He tipped the peak of his cap and ploughed on towards the boatyard.

'Seriously Astrid – you should definitely see him about fixing your boat.'

Astrid shifted in the chair. 'Actually, he's already agreed.'

'Oh, aye…?'

'We went out on the boat to see how it was running.'

'Uh, and I thought he was, what did you call him… an oaf?' Kath dropped her jaw in fake shock.

'What can I say? Maybe he's not too bad.'

20

Astrid carried on towards the end of the car park past a line of smart cars – a lot of brand-new Jaguars, open-top sports cars, black Range Rovers with matching tinted windows. The place screamed mid-life crisis, and she hadn't even got to the yachts.

She carried on past the boatyard to her left, which was as big as an aircraft hangar, then through an arch with a blue and white crest above it. The words *'The Royal Motor Yacht Company'* swirled round an anchor entwined by a pennant.

It was the first time she'd worn smart clothes (her cream Mugler shift dress) for over a week. It felt like going for an interview, for a job you didn't want. She ran her fingers through her hair, finding the braids Kath had done. She'd forgotten she had them in. Then she slipped on her sunglasses and marched through the archway.

A wide boardwalk wrapped round the marina. Flanks of gleaming white yachts were moored up alongside. She walked on, trying not to catch her heels in the gaps between the boards. Not that anyone was watching. The yachts, it seemed, were all empty. They sat silently in their own grey reflections.

Further out, the water changed sharply to a turquoise blue. Deeper water. Stronger currents. This was where the smaller, scruffier boats were anchored. They swung on their moorings, nodding at the bigger boats.

Halfway down the marina she'd spotted the yacht she'd seen off the Arne. The red sail cover was still lashed to the mast. It was much larger than her own boat – three times the size, at least. Everything was white and chrome and new. The deck was freshly varnished. On the prow in large, gold letters was the name *Sea Breeze* – the same name was written on a tender hanging off the back of the boat.

There was also a small *For Sale* sign hanging off the rail with a telephone number underneath. She reached into her bag for her notepad. When she looked up a young man was staring at her over the rail. He had long sun-bleached hair and was wearing blue overalls and short yellow rubber boots. 'Everything alright, madam?'

'Yes, fine. I'm just taking the number down. It's still for sale, right?'

He nodded. 'Actually… the owner is on the terrace. You could have a word with him if you like.'

'Terrace?'

He pointed to a building set back from the boardwalk. 'The clubhouse terrace. Ask for Stevie Greshingham.'

ROYAL MOTOR YACHT CLUB – the white letters against the blue background of the clubhouse were huge. Six feet tall and stretching about one hundred feet above the sliding glass windows of the upper floor. Big enough, presumably, to be visible far out in the harbour if you were heading in from the water. Or just to remind everyone within three miles that this was the place to be. If buildings could talk, this one would bellow out across the bay like a foghorn.

The upper terrace was about the size of a tennis court and filled with tables and benches. There were only a dozen people around – middle-aged couples mostly – a silver wine bucket between nearly all of them. In the corner nearest the water was a man in a bright pink polo shirt with tight white shorts. He was hunched over a newspaper.

She approached him and he didn't look up even when her shadow fell on him. He was reading the back page, running his finger along each line. A couple of sovereign rings flashed on his left hand.

'Stevie Greshingham?'

He turned to her and sighed wearily. He had a pinkish face with hooded eyes shaded by a ledge of silver hair. 'Alright then – give us your phone.'

'Sorry?'

'Let's get it over with.' He stood up and leant against the glass railing, his shirt stretching over a bulging stomach. 'You squeeze in here then,' he said, patting the railing next to him.

Astrid stayed put.

'Come on.' He put his arm out to the side. 'Don't be shy.'

'What?'

He looked confused. 'You want a selfie or not?'

'Why would I?'

He tilted his head on one side. 'You know who I am, right?'

Astrid shook her head.

'Stevie Greshingham. Southampton. Seagulls...' He kept

going, as if one of these words would somehow jog her memory. 'Match Report. Manager of England?'

'You managed England? I think I would have remembered that.'

'Football... I was the manager of the England football team.' He sat down at the bench again. There was a glass schooner with some amber liquid up to halfway. He drained it in one easy gulp. She noticed that his knuckles were rough and scarred. 'So you seriously don't know anything about football then?' he said, incredulously.

'Nope. Never watched a single game.'

'Why not?'

'I just can't see the appeal. Lot of overpaid men running around chasing a ball. What's the point?'

He glanced over her shoulder towards a waitress who was standing by the clubhouse door. 'So why are you here then?' He raised his glass and shook it until the waitress nodded and went inside. She noticed that there was a faded tattoo on the inside of his forearm. A simple crest – a football club probably. The words underneath were too blurred to read.

'Your boat... I might be interested in buying it.'

'In which case, grab a seat.' He gestured to the opposite bench. Astrid set her bag down and squeezed in. 'So what can I tell you?'

'Well, to start with. Why are you selling it?'

'I've never used the sails, to be honest. So there's all this kit just lying around – ropes and stuff.'

'There would be, yes.'

'So we're getting a motor yacht – Sunseeker, probably. Missus wants something with a bit more room below to entertain people. We'll still be keeping James.'

'James?'

'Kid who looks after the boat. He does everything – just hands me the keys and away we go. You got a boat yerself then?'

'Yes, I have a houseboat – a Hillyard, nine-tonner.'

'No idea.' He shrugged.

'I'm moored near the Arne. You know it?' She watched him closely.

'I think so.' He folded the newspaper up and pointed it out into the bay. Ahead of them was Brownsea Island. The birdwatching lagoon in front of it. 'It's through that channel… near that little green island in the distance, right?'

'That's it. Have you ever been up there?'

'Yeah,' he said blankly. 'I was up there a couple of nights ago.'

'Oh right. For any reason?' She took her sunglasses off, scrutinising his face again for a twitch that might betray him.

'Just going for a wander. Only place I can get a bit of peace. You know… being a celebrity round here, I can't just walk about the place.' He shook his head and cackled. 'Seriously, you never seen any football?'

'Hard to believe, but no.'

The waitress came over. She was wearing a blue skirt the colour of the club emblem and a crisp white shirt. She lifted a schooner of beer from a round tray and set it down in front of him. 'There you are, Stevie.'

'Thanks, darlin'.' She picked up the empty glass. 'Hang on.' He swirled his fingers in front of Astrid. 'You want one?'

'I'm fine, thanks.'

He supped the foam off the top of his drink and patted his stomach. 'Lovely... so, if you don't like football, what do you like?'

'Lots of things. Good food. Exercise. Fine art is my real passion though.'

'Oh yeah... art? My missus loves it. She's made a bomb buying and selling.'

'What kind of art?'

'Modern stuff. What's his name? The bloke who pickles the sharks.'

'Damien Hirst.'

'That's the fella. She bought a couple of his spinny paintings. Think I could do better myself to be honest. But she made a lot of cash from them. Same with that American guy who does the pool inflatables out of steel. Jeff...' He snapped his fingers trying to conjure up the second name.

'Koons?'

'Yeah, probably. They look really realistic but they weigh a ton. When the nephews come round they try to push it in the pool.'

'Which one was it? A dog? Dolphin?'

'Lobster. Wife sold it a year later and made a packet.'

Astrid sat on her hands. She could feel her pulse tapping at her temple. 'And that's the only reason she buys them – to make money?'

'Course. She doesn't like them much either. But they always make a profit. That lobster paid off the mortgage on the house.' He thumbed up to the line of houses along the edge of the water.

'And does she ever buy fine art?' said Astrid.

'Fine art?'

'The grand masters. Portraits, landscapes, English classics.'

'Nah – tougher market to make quick money, according to her. Now then.' He folded up his newspaper. 'Let me tell you about the boat.'

Astrid folded her sunglasses and put them on the table. 'Of course, the boat.'

'Right – it's about seven years old… I think. Six berths. Lovely decor. Engine runs like a dream. I'd be looking for something close to half a mill.' He studied her closely now.

She didn't flinch. 'Half a million? Okay. And does it come with the mooring?'

'That's paid up for ten months. Plus club membership. I have a jetty up at the house, but it's easier for James to keep an eye on it down here.'

'Got it. And are you out on the boat this weekend?'

'Nah, I'm away. Championship League semi-final against Barcelona.'

'Is that a fact?'

There was a couple coming over to them. They were staring at Stevie and nudging each other, a phone in each of their hands. Astrid got up. 'Thanks for your time,' she said.

He got up. 'Anytime. But listen.' He pulled her closer by the elbow and whispered to her. 'If you aren't really interested in the boat, I'll be very upset.' The words unfurled in a slow snarl. 'One thing I hate is reporters digging around in my private life. Got it?'

Astrid pulled away from him and he smiled innocently.

'I'm not a reporter.'

'Then you'll be alright then.' Then he waved the couple over. 'Fans… eh. What can you do?'

'Yes, what can you do?'

She watched him stand back against the rail and put his arms out. The couple tucked in either side. They mumbled something to her as she left, maybe about taking the photo of all three of them. But she wasn't stopping to find out.

21

Saturday, Day 11

Kath had the passenger seat pushed back as far as it would go – her bare feet resting above the glove box, purple-painted toes pressed against the windscreen. It was just past 10 a.m. on the dashboard clock. 'You think he's lying?'

Astrid gripped the wheel, setting the Mini on a smooth line round a bend. 'I'm not sure, Kath. It's all a bit fishy – he says he was just going for a quiet walk on the Arne – to get some peace from his fans. But then he seemed delighted when people wanted selfies with him.'

'That's celebrities for you.'

'And he was really threatening, at the end. Accused me of being a reporter.'

'Well, the press haven't been that nice to him.'

Kath flipped open the glove box in front of her and rooted around. 'I don't suppose you've got any snacks in here?'

'No, sorry. Don't worry – we can get something at

Sherborne Hall soon. What do you mean, the press haven't been nice to him?'

Kath snapped the glove box shut. 'Well, he had a bit of a dodgy past. He went to jail when he was in his twenties for fraud – hates it being brought up by the papers. He's smacked a few reporters in his time.'

'Ooh… well there you go.' Astrid drummed her fingers on the wheel. 'He's violent. A former criminal. And his wife buys and sells art. Maybe some deal involving the fake Constable went wrong and he took his revenge?'

'Nah.'

'Why not?'

'I mean…' Kath pressed a button in the door until the window was open halfway. She closed her eyes, as the cool air rushed into the car. 'It's Stevie Greshingham.'

'So?'

'The guy's a legend.'

'Maybe. But he's still going on the list.'

'Alright. But I hope it's not him.' Kath put her hands behind her neck. 'The Seagulls won't find a better manager.'

Emily hurried over from the main gate and quickly handed over a guest ticket for Kath. 'I've taken the liberty of reserving a couple of seats for the first demonstration.'

'That's kind, Emily, thanks,' Astrid said.

'They're front-row seats so you and your…' she looked Kath up and down; she was wearing faded denim dungarees with flowers scribbled in marker pen across them '…your guest, are on the front row.'

'Brill.' Kath hooked her thumbs under the straps of her dungarees. 'Front row – the VIP treatment.'

'Enjoy yourself.' Emily hurried off into the house.

A crowd of about a hundred people had already gathered on the front lawn. Small queues had formed in front of the demonstration tents. There was a much longer one, all children, in front of the bouncy castle. It was huge – bright yellow, with a turret in each corner that wobbled in the breeze. On one of the turrets was a crudely painted picture of a knight looking up at a long-haired woman, who was leaning out of a small window.

In the centre, a dozen children were ricocheting off the walls. Half of them were crying. A mum had taken off her shoes and was on all fours trying to rescue her child. Her weight sunk the bouncy castle in the middle, dragging a handful of toddlers on top of her. A small boy ran over her head.

'Listen,' said Kath. 'I'm going to have a nose about at the icehouse.'

'Why?'

'You know… scene of the crime and all that. Maybe you missed a clue.'

'Okay – it's in the woods.' She pointed to a gap in the hedge. 'Be quick. You don't want to miss the show.'

Astrid watched her go. As she went through the gap in the hedge, Lady Sherborne appeared at the end of the lawn. She marched forwards, shooing visitors out of the way with her stick. Astrid was about to go over and say hello, when Denise stepped in her way. 'It's really quite hideous, isn't it?' Her eyes were trained on the inflatable castle. 'A monstrosity.'

'Yes, it's a bit tacky. But it seems like the kids are enjoying it.'

'I guess… now come with me.' Denise headed over to the first tent. At the front was a table on which were a dozen round loaves. They were dark brown with whirls of flour on top. Some had been crossed with a knife on top, so they looked like they were about to burst open.

'You have been busy, Denise,' said Astrid, hoping she might not be asked to try one.

'I've been making them all this morning in an authentic seventeenth-century clay oven.' She pointed to a small arched construction inside the tent. Orange embers glowed from deep inside it.

A couple and two kids, their noses no higher than the top of the table, edged closer. Denise handed a loaf to one of the children, who struggled to stop it dropping on the floor. He tipped it back onto the table with a thump.

'It's a no-knead recipe from France,' said Denise. 'An army could march on these.'

'Or fire them out of a cannon,' said Astrid.

Denise gave her a stern look.

'Sorry, Denise… carry on.'

'Anyway,' Denise addressed the mother and father. 'In those olden days they didn't have a dry yeast. So what did they do? I'll tell you…' Denise barely left a pause before answering her own question. 'They used something called barm, which is a by-product of the brewing process. The rye would first be…'

'I'm so sorry, Denise,' said Astrid. 'But I just want to say hi to the others before the show starts.'

'Of course, I'll catch you later,' said Denise.

★

In the next tent, Astrid found Margaret hunched over the loom. She was surrounded by children pressing in to see what she was making. 'Geroff...' Margaret grunted at them. They pressed in closer, laughing at what they assumed was an actor playing the part of an angry old weaver. Astrid backed out into the sunshine.

In the final tent, Harold was fussing with a soldier's costume. 'Oh, Astrid... how fantastic. You came.'

'I wouldn't miss your big day, Harold.'

'Bless you.' He glanced at his watch. 'I'd grab your seat quick though. We're starting in a couple of minutes.'

She hurried from the tent to the first row of seats, which had white *'reserved'* cards on them. There was one for her *'guest'* – although there was no sign of Kath. Cressida swept in from the lawn and sat on the chair on the other side.

'Isn't this wonderful?' she said, craning round to admire the crowd. All the other seats were taken. Handfuls of people were standing by the end of the rows, or sitting crossed-legged in the aisles.

'It's a good turn-out.'

'Fantastic – we're going to get some great pics for the magazine.' She pointed over to a photographer on the lawn. He was aiming his camera at the audience and snapping away.

'The bouncy castle is a big hit too,' said Astrid. The line for the inflatable now stretched along the hedge.

'Yes – it's bringing in the young families. That's a core demographic for us right now.' Cressida turned back to face the field. 'You know, I'm super excited about what the volunteers have planned.'

'Me too.'

Kath hurried down the front row and squeezed into the seat next to Astrid. 'Has it started?' she said.

'Just about to,' Astrid whispered.

There was a drum roll from the last tent on the left and a short man in a long leather coat emerged from the doorway. He marched onto the lawn beating out a simple rhythm on a small drum held at waist level by shoulder straps. He stopped in the centre of the lawn and put his drumsticks in his pocket. A moment later and Harold, dressed in a dark blue suit, glided out from the armaments tent. He waited for silence and brought a microphone to his lips.

'Good morning.' His voice rang out. 'In the summer of 1642 the view that you see now would have been the same one that greeted the arriving troops of Oliver Cromwell. They had come to ransack the town of Poole, which was a staunch Royalist stronghold. These troops...' He turned to the tent. 'These Roundhead troops,' he said louder. There was a pause and a large red-faced man burst out of the canvas. He was dressed in a mustard-coloured tunic with a tin breastplate, long leather knee-high boots, and a metal helmet shaped like an almond. He strode over to the middle of the lawn, his sword clanking at his hips. Then he spun round to the audience and planted his hands on his hips.

Harold stepped aside and looked him up and down – like a Savile Row tailor about to take an inside leg measurement. 'It is something of a myth that Roundhead soldiers and Cavaliers had a particular uniform,' he said into the microphone. 'Many would have been wearing what they could get their hands on. Often armour that they'd picked up from previous battles.'

There were still a dozen kids on the bouncy castle shrieking with laughter. Harold stared at them disapprovingly and raised his voice. 'To avoid confusion, soldiers would have worn shrubbery or vegetation in their hats or helmets.'

The soldier took off his helmet and fluffed up a sprig of leaves that had been poked into the rim. The photographer dipped down on one knee and steadied his lens at the soldier.

Kath waved at the photographer, who waved back. She nudged Astrid. 'Good mate of mine. He's called Pete.'

'Right,' said Astrid.

Harold swept his hand over to the tent and another man stomped out. He had a chain mail vest over a greenish tunic. A similar tin helmet to the first soldier. 'And lo and behold,' Harold shouted, 'the enemy has arrived – a Cavalier soldier under the rule of Charles II.' The second soldier strutted forward, drew his sword and shook it at the crowd. He pulled a face and roared.

There was some booing from the audience. Harold waved his hand at them. 'Honestly, there's no need – it's not panto.'

'Oh, yes it is!' shouted Kath. There was a roar of laughter from the crowd.

Harold reddened and carried on. 'Anyway. The poorer soldier wouldn't have been able to afford a musket. Hence he would have to be well versed in the art of swordsmanship.'

The Roundhead unsheathed his sword with a flourish and squared up to the Cavalier. They slowly circled each other, the points of their swords touching.

Harold stepped back a few steps and continued to commentate. 'Watch how the two combatants are sizing each other up. Working out the weak points in their opponent's armour.'

The Cavalier lunged at the Roundhead and struck him on the helmet with his sword, knocking it over his eyes. There was a 'whooo' from the crowd. The Roundhead fixed his helmet as the Cavalier lapped up the applause – but just for a few seconds.

The Roundhead stepped forwards and slammed a flat sword blade against the Cavalier's back plate with a resounding clang that dropped him to his knees. The crowd cheered even louder. Kath thumped her fist into her palm. 'Go on, son!' she shouted.

The two combatants squared up to each other again. More cautious this time. They wheeled round on the lawn, their swords grinding against each other. Determined expressions that suggested they weren't playing anymore. Harold stepped back for his own safety.

The Roundhead stabbed at the Cavalier's chain mail vest, but the strike was deflected by the swipe of a sword. The Cavalier barely paused before rushing forwards and kicking his opponent in the shins. The Roundhead hopped from foot to foot, groaning in pain. Then he collected himself to land a similar but much harder kick.

Kath was up on her feet now, cheering each move. The rest of the crowd rose from their seats, cameras aimed in front of them at the duelling soldiers – a smash here, a well-aimed boot to the backside there – the battle became more and more furious. For a good few minutes, they thumped and thrashed as Harold watched from a distance, shaking his head.

Cressida leant over to Astrid. 'This is very convincing.'

'Isn't it though?' said Astrid.

Neither had the upper hand until the Roundhead delivered a hefty blow to the top of the Cavalier's helmet that left a deep dent in the metal. The Cavalier staggered back towards the front row, until he was only a few feet from the three of them. There was a sharp hiss in the air. The Cavalier's sword fell from his hand, which went quickly to his chest.

But instead of celebrating, the Roundhead watched in silence as his opponent zig-zagged forwards and fell to his knees on the edge of the lawn. First his helmet tipped off. Then, the heavy metal vest unbalanced him, like a kid's slinky toy, dragging him slowly over the ha-ha. The last thing the audience saw was the Cavalier's boots diving out of view. The crowd went wild – stomping their feet and baying for more, for a good minute or so. Kath was the last to stop clapping. 'Wow, that was amazing.' She turned to Astrid, who was staring at the edge of the ha-ha. 'Everything alright?'

Astrid got up slowly. 'I'm not sure.' She'd noticed that Harold was looking anxious. He hurried to centre stage. 'Well, that concludes the hand-to-hand combat demonstration. Obviously, the Cavaliers were supposed to win that one. But you know… anyway. Thanks for coming.'

The crowd began to disperse, still chatting excitedly. Astrid, Kath and Cressida hurried over to Harold and they all peeped over the edge. Staring up at them, pale and moaning weakly, was the Cavalier. He was on his back, one hand clutching the end of a short arrow that was protruding from his midriff. A small patch of oily red glistened from the metal.

Harold shook his head. 'That's fourteen-gauge chain mail. That should have stopped an arrow. Very odd.'

'Harold – I'm going to call an ambulance,' said Astrid.

'Yes, Astrid. Good idea.'

Astrid and Kath stood on the gravel path and watched the air ambulance take off. Cressida had made a swift exit back to her office – no doubt to work out how she could appear blameless. This was the second unfortunate accident at Sherborne Hall. And this one was going to be harder to brush off.

The helicopter levelled itself about fifty feet above the lawn and thundered off towards the coastline. The blast of air rocked the hedges and knocked over a few foldaway chairs. The audience, still in a state of high excitement from the combat, cheered wildly.

They both watched the helicopter recede into the distance until they couldn't hear the sound of the engines. Kath put her hands on her hips. 'Well, I've got to say. For pure entertainment, that had the lot.'

22

Astrid and Kath sat down at a small table outside the café in the shade of a fig tree. It was quiet. The crowds had yet to disperse from the lawn. Most had hung on to see if there was any more to the show. Astrid had bought a couple of cans of lemony drinks that had Italian writing on and a tinfoil lid over the top. She also got two small tubs of organic honeycomb ice cream. Kath dug in with a small plastic spoon that looked like a tiny spade.

'How much were these?'

'Three pounds each.'

'Told you.' Kath took a mouthful, trying her best to pretend she wasn't enjoying it. 'They've got you over a barrel. I charge one pound twenty for a tub and it's twice the size. Plus it has a ball of bubble gum at the bottom.'

'You should put your prices up then.'

'Mmm... might do that.' She carried on eating as Astrid started on her ice cream. 'So... what was that all about then?'

'Incredible, wasn't it?' said Astrid. 'Thankfully, they're saying the arrow didn't go too far in and he's going to be alright. I had a word with Harold, the volunteer who organised it. Poor guy.'

'The Cavalier or Harold?'

'Both really. This will be the end of all the volunteers' historic re-enactments for a while. Cressida will make sure of it.'

'That was the person sitting next to you?'

'Yes, and she's an absolute stickler for health and safety.'

'Kath chased the last of the ice cream round the tub. 'Okay. So why did a real arrow get used in a reconstruction?'

'Actually, Harold says it was a crossbow bolt. It was one of the weapons laid out on the table in the final tent. Whoever fired it must have sneaked into the tent when everyone was distracted by the show.'

'You reckon?'

'Here, let me show you.' Astrid finished off her ice cream and put it on the table. 'There's the tent.' She moved the two cans of lemon drink to the side of it. 'And these are the two soldiers – Roundhead and Cavalier.'

'This going to take long? I'm thirsty.'

'Only a minute. And this…' she took a napkin from her pocket and laid it behind them '…this is the audience. I'm sitting on the front row with Cressida and the Cavalier.' She shifted the can towards the napkin. 'The Cavalier stumbles back from a blow from the Roundhead and is hit by the arrow.'

'You sure? He didn't stumble back because the arrow had got him?'

'Positive. I heard this hiss as it was fired.'

'So, what are you saying?'

'Okay, this is my theory.' Astrid picked up a can and passed it over to Kath, who began unpicking the foil lid.

'The Cavalier wasn't the target. He accidentally got in the way of the arrow.'

'Who was the target then?'

'Ah, well I have two ideas. First – the bouncy castle.'

Fzzzt – Kath had the ring pull open. She slurped at the drink. 'Bouncy castle? You're not serious?'

'There's a lot of bad feeling about the bouncy castle from the volunteers. Someone could have been trying to puncture it.'

Kath shook her head. 'Imagine the headline – "Cavalier hospitalised by arrow fired at English Trust bouncy castle."'

'I know – it sounds ridiculous.' Astrid opened her drink. 'But don't forget we could have already had the headlines "Forager poisoned by mystery mushroom" and "Antique dealer falls to their death in icehouse".'

'Good point – so which volunteers are in the frame for this one?'

'Well, Harold is off the hook because he was on stage. So that leaves Denise and Margaret.'

'Okay then – so what's your second idea?'

Astrid took a slow sip from her drink and smacked her lips. 'You know, the arrow might have been aimed at Cressida.'

'Really?'

'She's not popular – all the volunteers hate her. And Lady Sherborne absolutely loathes her.'

'Bottom line though—' Kath sat back in her chair and scanned the grounds '—anyone who walked into the Trust today could have done it. Visitors, staff, Lady Sherborne...' A line of people trailed up the gravel path. Most were checking their phones – no doubt going through the footage of the battle re-enactment. 'Anyone could get into that tent.'

'Yes, I guess you're right.' Astrid sat up. 'Hey, that photographer mate of yours – Pete. Maybe he caught something on his camera?'

'Good thinking. I'll give him a shout and get him to go through his photos.'

'Thanks, Kath.' Astrid noticed a family approaching the table. 'So anyway… what did you think of the icehouse? Any thoughts?'

'Oh, yeah. It was a bit creepy to be honest.'

'Anything else?'

'I agree with you. That railing is too high to fall over – DeVine was definitely pushed. No doubt about it.'

The family were standing near their table. The mother sighed loudly. 'We'll just have to wait here in the hot sun until someone's kind enough to finish up,' she muttered in their direction.

'We should probably go, Kath.'

'Give it a minute – there's no rush,' she said, crushing the can in her hand.

Even though it was well into lunchtime, Kath was in no hurry to get back to work. Despite her protests at the English Trust's 'stranglehold' on local cafés, the Shell Beach Café had very relaxed opening hours.

They sat there for another few minutes as the family hovered next to another table. Then they got up and arranged to split up – Kath agreeing to wait by the Mini while Astrid picked up a couple of things from the storeroom.

On the way there Astrid mulled over the recent events, trying one more time to assemble the pieces. So far, there had been two deaths, an attempted murder and the discovery of a fake painting. All these crimes had to be connected.

The forged Constable seemed the most likely starting point. Selling that off as an original would have made someone a few hundred thousand pounds – enough to make them desperate to cover their tracks. But how was that connected with DeVine, Eric and then, most bizarrely, the crossbow incident this morning?

There was a beep from her phone. An 'urgent' email had come in from Cressida. So far Cressida had marked all her emails as 'urgent', whatever they were about. The message simply said *'My office. Tomorrow. 10 a.m.'.*

It probably wasn't going to be about keeping quiet about the crossbow 'accident' as she would no doubt call it. With a couple of hundred witnesses, all armed with phones, this was bound to make it into the local paper. She'd just have to wait and see.

Astrid turned the corner and walked down the path alongside the scallop fountain. It was a large marble structure set in the middle of a circular pond. There was a man sitting on the edge, hunched over his phone. A beige jumper was tied loosely over his shoulders. The sleeves fell over a crisp white linen shirt.

She stopped abruptly. A pair of wire-frame sunglasses were tucked into the V at his neck. They were Ray-Ban Aviators – expensive. And she should know – she'd bought them for him. 'Simon?'

He slipped the phone in a trouser pocket and crossed his legs. 'Astrid?' His eyes swept slowly upwards from her shoes. 'I hardly recognised you.' He studied her hair. 'I mean... are those braids?'

'Simon?' So far she had stared at him and said his name twice. Repeating his name as he sat elegantly framed by a giant shell hadn't been on the list of revenge scenarios she'd planned.

'How did you find me?'

'Oh, I have your phone registered on that Find My Phone app. If you ever lost your phone I could locate it for you. Remember?'

'You've known I've been down here in Dorset from the start.'

He nodded.

'Then why didn't you come down straight away? Or answer my text? You just ghosted me – your own wife.'

'Honestly?'

'People say "honestly" when they're about to tell you a lie.' She twirled a braid. She liked them even if he didn't. 'But go on, Simon, let's hear it.'

He unclipped his sunglasses from his shirt and carefully put them on, pushing them back with a finger onto the bridge of his nose. 'Because I had some thinking to do, Astrid. I've made the biggest mistake letting you go and I want you back.'

Astrid folded her arms. 'So why did you cheat on me with Gina?'

'That's a question I ask myself every day, every hour. Why? Why, Simon?' He punched his hand into his palm, as if to punish himself.

Astrid gave him a slow hand clap. 'Oh, that was terrific, Simon. An award-winning performance.'

Simon gave her an injured look. 'It happens to be true... I want you back, Astrid.'

'What the... want me back?' She almost coughed the words. 'That's never going to happen, Simon.'

'I just want to start again. No lies this time.'

'Okay – then if you're in such a candid mood. Maybe you can answer a few questions.'

'Sure.'

'You and Gina. When did it start?'

'Astrid... there's no point going over the details.'

'Oh, I think there is.' Astrid felt the anger rising. She directed it down to her clenched fists. 'Are you going to tell me or not?'

He shook his head.

'Right, then you can get up and go back to London. We're done.'

'Actually, I'm staying for a few days.'

'Why?'

He brushed his hand across the knees of his dark blue jeans. Not his purchase – he never wore jeans. That was probably Gina's influence. 'Because I've been asked to give a second opinion on the Constable.'

Astrid's heart skipped a beat. 'The Constable?'

'From the movement of your phone I could see you were working at this place. So I got in touch with your boss, Cressida, and she told me all about the Constable. That's when I offered my expertise.'

'Because you didn't think I can do my job?'

'Not at all. You're an excellent conservator – I taught you well.'

'Listen, Simon, you didn't teach me anything. Except one

lesson – never to trust anything that comes out of that thin mouth of yours. You have a dark hard stone for a heart and if I could drown you in that fountain and get away with it I would.'

'Finished?'

She looked around the perfect gardens. The English Trust – it was almost too polite a setting for an argument. That was probably tucked away in the small print of the membership. No taking plant cuttings. No squabbling. She dropped her voice. 'I am far from finished, Simon. For some screwed-up reason you've come down here to try and ruin my life. But I won't let you and I'll never have you back. Get it?'

'Astrid. You've got it all wrong. I can explain everything…' he held up his hand '…but only when you're less emotional.'

'Emotional… arrrg!'

'That's exactly what I'm talking about, Astrid. Listen, when you're feeling more composed we should meet up. I'm staying at the Haven Hotel – we can have lunch.'

'Only if they serve rat poison.'

Simon shook his head and tutted. 'Really, Astrid, that's a bit beneath you.'

He'd always been so calm in arguments. In the past she'd admired the way he could coolly pick people apart. Now, it was just infuriating. 'Let's try and be more civil tomorrow at the meeting with Cressida.'

'So that's what the meeting is about – the Constable.'

'Yes, I'm going to give my opinion on the painting.'

'Good – well until then, you can get lost.'

Simon smiled serenely. 'Oh, Astrid.' He got up and took a few steps down the path. She called after him. 'Wait.'

He turned to face her.

'Is it over?'

'What?'

'You and Gina?'

He fixed her with a look between sympathy and pity. 'Yes, of course it is.'

A gardener appeared down the path with a wheelbarrow. He read the mood and made a slow three-point with the barrow without making eye contact. Astrid waited until he was out of sight. 'She dumped you, didn't she?'

He shook his head again, as if he couldn't believe she'd suggested it. 'I finished it – I promise.' Then he wandered off down the path.

She watched him go, not knowing whether to believe it or not. He was wearing burgundy loafers, a flash of bare skin at the ankle. No socks? That was new as well. There he was – her soon-to-be ex-husband right there, a man trying to look ten years younger by not wearing socks.

She waited for her heart rate to drop, then headed towards the car park. When she got there her fury had subsided to around fix or six on the anger scale. She'd been dreading meeting him again, but it hadn't been too painful. It felt like some of the wounds were starting to heal.

When she got to the car, Kath was leaning against the bonnet, soaking up the sunshine.

'Right, Kath, let's go.'

She stared at her, concerned. 'You okay, Astrid?'

'Not really. I've just seen a ghost.'

'Wow…' Kath gasped. 'I saw a ghost once. It was staying in this old pub up in Worth Matravers and in the night I heard this bumping sound…'

'No, Kath, I meant... you know, it's just some stuff from my past.'

'Got it, well...' Kath put her arm round Astrid's shoulder. 'If you want to talk about it, I'm here.'

'Thanks, Kath.'

'Angler's Arms tonight – couple of cheeky beers?'

'Actually, I'm doing something this evening, and tomorrow. What about Tuesday?'

'Yeah – I've arranged to have a few with Grub. That okay?'

'Of course. The more the merrier.'

23

On the way back to the boat, Astrid took a detour to the newsagent to buy the evening edition of the local paper. She wanted to see if the incident with the crossbow at Sherborne Hall had made the news. It had – a front page 'newsflash'. Two paragraphs below a photo of the air ambulance taking off on the front lawn. The piece was rounded off by a quote from Cressida explaining that the chance of this sort of thing happening was 'incredibly small' – no kidding – 'and nobody should be put off visiting Sherborne Hall this summer'.

Astrid got herself a coffee and spent the next ten minutes checking to see if the Trust's other two deadly incidents, the deaths of DeVine and Eric the forager, had made it in. They hadn't. But right at the back of the paper in the social section was something that caught her eye. A picture of Stevie Greshingham mingling with guests at, as the caption explained, a 'drinks party to celebrate the English Trust's acquisition of the art collection of Lady Sherborne'. Well, well. You do know a bit about fine art then, Stevie?

Now another plan, a mini-plan, was crystallising. Not only was she going to show Simon what a brilliant conservator she was at the meeting tomorrow, she was also going to reveal exactly where the original was – at Stevie Greshingham's house in Sandbanks. The more she thought about it, the more her theory sounded plausible. He definitely ticked both M's and the O. He had connections with the Trust. He made a lot of money trading art. And he wasn't too far from Sherborne Hall. He could have bought the original, got someone to fake it, and swapped it back without anyone noticing. Except her, of course.

She went to the bookcase and ran her finger along the lines of books until she found what she was after – *Tide Charts*, the latest edition. Greshingham was away for the weekend, that's what he said – so it had to be now. She'd take the boat over to Sandbanks, tie up in his mooring and have a snoop around. There would be no need to break in – most of the house was surrounded by glass. Would he be stupid enough to hang a stolen masterpiece on the walls? Well, he called Damien Hirst 'that bloke who pickled the sharks', so that was entirely possible.

She opened the tide chart book at the table. Each page was set out the same way – a grid for each week of the year showing a series of waves and troughs. There was tiny text underneath – sunset times, local currents... She squinted and put the book down. Maybe she shouldn't risk it.

Then she noticed the corner of a pink card tucked in between the cover and first page. She teased it out. It was the same card as the note Uncle Henry had left under the carpet. The same pen. This time it said:

Set sail, Astrid – fortune favours the brave. Uncle Henry.

Astrid turned the card over. There was nothing on the back. Now it made more sense. Her uncle was encouraging her, each step of the way. She'd found the first note because she'd decided to clean the boat, right down to turning the carpets over. Now she'd checked tide times because she was going to take the boat out on her own. She'd thought it was strange he'd not left her a letter along with his will. This is what he was doing instead – hiding little notes to keep her going. She smiled – what a clever, tricksy man he was.

She picked up the tide chart again – of course she could work this out. She rifled through to the correct day. The high tide – the tip of the peak of the wave, was about twenty minutes from now. Time to go.

Up on deck she moved quickly down the side rail, unhooked the rope and cast it loosely on the stern. The boat began to drift slightly from the boardwalk so she hurried back to the controls and started the engine.

Swinging the stern round towards the harbour she found the line between the green and red marker buoys and pushed the throttle up. The boat rose in the water and steamed ahead. Past the boatyard – no sign of Cobb, thankfully – and out into the channel.

Out of the shelter of the mooring the wind was brisk. Chilly even. Astrid noticed an old wax jacket hanging from a peg below the dashboard. She put it on, rolled up the sleeves and tightened the belt at the waist. Up on the headland, the sun was still shining. The shadows of clouds raced over the heath, turning it from purple to grey. Ahead of her were Green and Round Island. Beyond them Brownsea Island was cloaked in a low steely cloud that had pushed in from the sea. Darkness seemed to be seeping into the bay, even though there was still two hours of daylight left.

Twenty minutes later she rounded Brownsea Island and saw the English Trust jetty to her left. To her right, the chain ferry was docking at the tip of the peninsula. All clear – a burst of speed and she was out into the main channel. The boat thumped into bigger waves, sending up a spray that cleared the stern. She slid across the window above the controls and zipped up her jacket.

At the other side of the channel she turned the boat into the current and slowed down. The houses along the shoreline were much larger than she'd realised. Three storeys, most with wrap-around glass balconies. Huge windows on every floor that reflected the bay – and the wealth of the owners. Four million pounds – for starters.

Stevie Greshingham's was one of the largest. It was a huge block of smoked glass and brushed concrete – textbook Bauhaus – hard to believe he had such good taste. She guessed if you had the money you could buy the architects who did.

She tied the boat up on the pontoon and walked confidently across the lawn, which was made of bright green AstroTurf. At one end were white plastic goal posts. In the middle was a painted circle with a seagull on it – the emblem, no doubt, of his beloved football team.

At the front patio she cupped her hands against the glass and peered in. A white leather sofa sat in front of a large flat-screen TV on the wall. That was the only thing on the walls. Down the side of the house was a glass door that gave another angle on the living room. Again, there was no sign of any paintings. She pulled the jacket sleeve over her hand and tried the handle. It was locked.

A few seconds later there was a beeping sound above her head. She looked up and saw a small yellow box high on the wall. There was an outline of a dog on the side and a tiny red light underneath that was flashing. Time to go.

At the pontoon the rope was now running taut from the post. The tide must have turned. She steered the boat forward to buy some slack then dashed back to the post to untie the rope. Then she hurried back to the controls as the boat scraped alongside the mooring – the red plastic buoys grinding against the beams.

Spinning the wheel through her hands. Fighting the current to get the prow out from the shore. The waves slapped against the side – she'd made it. But the boat was now sliding round too far. She yanked the wheel back and pushed up the throttle as far as it would go. There was a cracking noise from the engine. 'Noo,' she breathed. A dark plume of smoke was curling up from the back of the boat.

Throttle down, then up again. *Crrunnge* – a noise that sounded like a cutlery drawer being pulled out. Then nothing. Except her voice – 'Damn it!'

On the dashboard the dial hands were settling back to zero. The light was off below the starter key. She turned the key again and again, the panic rising. Already she'd floated back past a couple of houses on the shore. The boat was side-on now, drifting out of control. She could feel the current rocking the hull beneath her feet.

Out in the bay the chain ferry was coursing across the channel. She tracked it for a moment, working out how quickly it was closing the gap. Fast enough to put her on a direct collision course. A couple of boats had held up in the current waiting for the ferry to pass. A man at the wheel of one of them shouted something at her but she couldn't make it out. The chain ferry, its funnel steaming, carried on. It was halfway across the channel and showing no signs of stopping. She'd slam into the side of it in less than a minute.

On the upper deck of the ferry a few people had gathered at the rail and were pointing towards her. How did you stop a boat in a current? There was no way she could raise the sails in time – wouldn't know what to do if she did. It would be too deep here for the anchor.

She left the wheel and rushed to the stern. Maybe if the ferry captain saw her? She waved with both arms in front of her. 'Helppp!' Her words were lost in the wind. That was it then. 'Astrid,' she whispered. 'What have you done now?'

'Throw the rope!'

She looked over the side of the boat. Cobb was standing in the back of his dinghy, his hand on the steering arm of an outboard engine. 'Throw the rope – now!' He swerved closer, almost bumping into the red buoys.

She gathered the rope in loose coils and threw it to him. He quickly found the end and lashed it round the last seating plank. She knew the ferry was close – she could feel the thrum of its engine in her chest. Hear the waves crashing off its hull. But she couldn't look.

Cobb gripped the accelerator and the rope went taut. Slowly, the prow of her boat turned into the current until it was in line behind his boat. He twisted the accelerator and the water churned and boiled between them. The outboard engine was more powerful than it looked. Together they slowly moved away from the ferry. The houses on the shore retreated. Out across the channel – the wake of the ferry chasing them into the quiet waters of the bay.

When they were alongside the lagoon on Brownsea Island, Cobb cut the engine of the outboard and steered alongside. Astrid went to the rail. 'Thanks, Cobb.'

He clambered aboard and walked straight to the control cabin. She caught up with him. 'So how did you know I was here?'

'I dropped by your boat and it was gone. Thought I'd check the harbour for you.' He worked the key into the ignition and grunted a couple of times.

'Don't you think I tried that?'

He scowled at her. 'I told you the boat wasn't safe to take out.'

'Yeah.' She crossed her arms. 'Well, I needed to do something.'

He tapped at the fuel gauge with a knuckle. It stayed flat down on zero. 'You know – if I hadn't rescued you, you'd be under that ferry.'

'I didn't ask to be rescued, Cobb.'

'Huh… is that right?' He went to the back of the boat, knelt down and worked the engine panel open. She watched him run his hand over some valves. 'Toolbox. Small dog grip spanner,' he said, without looking up.

She went into the toolbox and held up the first spanner she found. 'That it?'

'Yeah.' He held out his hand and she slapped it into his palm. 'Good job I got to you first – if the harbour master had spotted you, you'd be in big trouble. That's a big fine right there.'

'Look, Cobb, as I said – I'm not helpless.'

'You could have fooled me.' He cranked the spanner somewhere down in the engine well, muttered something under his breath and stood up.

'Did you sort it out?'

'Think so.' He wiped his hands on his overalls. 'The fuel line had come off from the engine mount. So basically, you were running on the fuel in the pipe. Only a matter of time before the engine would cut out.' He took the panel and slid it back into place. 'You been tinkering with the engine, Astrid?'

'No.'

'It was alright when I last saw it.'

'Only person who's been tinkering around down there is you, Cobb.'

'Hey, now listen – you can say what you want about me, but I know what I'm doing with engines.'

'If you say so,' she said firmly. 'No need to get moody.'

'I'm not moody, Astrid.'

'Fine. Shall I start the engine?'

'No, I'll take you back in.' He walked past her and lowered himself into his boat, avoiding her gaze. Which was fine. Okay – he might have saved her. But then, if he'd screwed up the engine in the first place, it was his fault. She went to the back of the boat and sat on a folding chair. And he was moody, whatever he said.

When they got back to the river he unclipped the rope and tied it up on the post. It was almost dark now. He swung his boat out into the estuary, carving a deep turn in the water. Not looking back. Stubborn... AND moody.

24

The next morning Astrid woke from a bad dream. She'd fallen from the boat in a storm and was sinking below the surface. A tangle of seaweed held her legs, stopping her from swimming back to the surface. No surprise maybe, given the near-disaster yesterday.

She got out of bed, opened all the portholes and breathed in deeply. The air smelt different on either side of the boat. On the bank side it was dry and sweetly scented. Salty and damp by the river. Now the chill of her nightmare had gone, replaced by an excitement about the morning ahead. The kind of buzz she felt heading out to the airport for a holiday – bags packed the night before.

Her phone beeped. It was a text from Muraki. He'd run some tests on the sample she sent him and it was conclusive – it was a modern varnish. She thanked him and said she'd be in touch soon.

This was going to be a good day. Simon could give his opinions about the Constable. But now she had the evidence.

It was definitely a fake, and he'd have to agree with her. His trip down to Dorset to patronise her was over. Bon voyage, Simon.

She showered, dressed, crammed in a couple of slices of buttered toast and was at Sherborne Hall a few minutes before nine.

Simon had arrived well ahead of her. He was leaning against the edge of Cressida's desk, winding up an anecdote about a dispute with a minor royal that, having heard it at least a dozen times, she knew took at least ten minutes to tell.

'That's astonishing,' said Cressida, clapping her hands, 'just amazing.'

'All in a day's work,' he said, playing with the sleeves of the beige jumper that was knotted over his shoulders.

The entire outfit was the same as yesterday. If he found a combination of clothes that 'just worked', as he used to say, he'd go out and buy three of each of the items. Then he'd line the outfits in the wardrobe in 'quadrants' for each of the seasons. At the time, it seemed to make sense. Now, it was just... *yugggh*.

'Right then – shall we get on with this?' Astrid sat down in the chair.

'Let's do it,' said Cressida.

Simon reached into his briefcase and brought out a thick wad of A4 notes. Then he went over and stood next to the Constable painting, which was on an easel by the window. 'So, this painting – Weymouth Beach, dated 1816. It is a rather gorgeous piece,' he said, as if he were an auctioneer introducing it to an audience of potential buyers. 'Before the sale to the English Trust it was appraised by a private dealers called Hassocks and Cole in Bond Street. Now luckily, I'm good friends with James Hassocks, who gave me access to all their research and tests.'

'Good friends? I didn't know that,' said Astrid.

'Astrid, please.'

'Don't mind me.'

'And by the way, Astrid, I've already explained our situation to Cressida. In case things become volatile.'

Cressida looked between them and nodded sympathetically. 'Please, Simon, carry on.'

Simon split the wad of notes, laying one half on the corner of the table. 'So these are your copies of the tests I carried out, Cressida.'

'Thanks, Simon,' said Cressida.

'Okay. So there's something called a dendrochronology test. It's used to establish the age of the frame from the pattern of growth rings in the wood. The result of that test, along with the labelling and signatures, shows us that the frame is authentic.' He looked towards Astrid. 'Would you agree, Astrid?'

'Yes, the frame was made within ten years of the painting.'

'Excellent.' He studied the notes again. 'The FTIR test then – it's an infra-red technique to see what elements have been used in the paint sample. Pigment binders such as linseed oil and egg white.'

'How fascinating.' Cressida nodded.

'It's honestly not, Cressida,' said Astrid. 'It's quite boring really.'

'Thanks, Astrid.' Simon shuffled his papers. 'So basically, we're looking for a recipe of paint that the artist was known to have used. And the good news is that the chemical composition of the paint in this work is peculiar to Constable.'

Astrid smiled to herself.

'You want to jump in here, Astrid?' said Simon.

'No, no. You carry on.'

'There are another couple of tests... ultraviolet, digital fingerprinting. Hassocks have really been thorough and...' he put his half of the notes down on the table '...everything confirms that this is indeed the work of John Constable.'

'Really? And you're sure about that?' Cressida got up from her chair and turned to Astrid. 'I don't understand... You said this was a fake.'

'Because it is.' Her voice was taut with excitement. 'Simon, you're wrong. The brushstrokes are too deliberate – it's not the hand of a master.'

'Is that right?'

'And I've had a varnish sample tested and it's come back as a modern varnish.'

'Who did the test?'

'Doesn't matter – it proves beyond doubt—' Astrid pointed at the painting '—that is not a genuine Constable.'

'Okay, time out, guys,' said Cressida. 'Which is it? A fake or the real thing?'

'I'm so sorry Cressida,' said Astrid. 'Simon has clearly come down here to try and humiliate me. It's all a bit tragic really.'

Simon shook his head. 'Not now, Astrid, please.'

'Good try, Simon.' She got up and strolled confidently over to the painting on the easel. 'You can tell by just looking at it.' She studied the painting. The sea, the path with the figure, the headland with the lighthouse. She ran her finger delicately across the surface. Then she pulled her hand back, as if she'd had an electric shock. 'No... umm.' Her jaw dropped.

She studied the rest of the painting for a few seconds. The cliffs, the path, the clouds. The clouds especially. They were gorgeous. Weightless. Luminous. As if someone had reached up to the sky with a stick, rolled them up like candy floss and cast them over the canvas. It was a masterpiece – God had breathed over this painting. There was no doubt – it was a Constable.

'Are you alright, Astrid?' said Cressida.

'It can't be.' She couldn't take her eyes off the canvas. 'This is not the painting I worked on.'

'Sorry?' said Simon.

'It's been swapped... this is the original,' said Astrid.

'Oh, so did you take any photos of this mystery forgery?' said Simon.

'Well, actually...' It dawned on her. 'No I didn't. I was so excited to discover it I couldn't hold the camera still.'

Simon shook his head at her. 'Honestly, I'm disappointed in you, Astrid.' He began packing his notes into his briefcase. 'And who would have swapped it?'

'I don't know. I mean...'

'Okay.' Cressida flipped open her laptop. 'So, what should we do now, Simon?'

'Well, if I may humbly suggest. You have a major art discovery on your hands. You should get this in front of the press as soon as possible.'

'Super idea. We have a special moment here – I'll set up a press launch for Tuesday... Get all the big papers in, and TV.'

Simon moved round the back of her desk. They carried on chatting as if Astrid wasn't there. 'And it would be a good way of publicising the whole exhibition later in the year. I would be more than happy to give the presentation.'

'That would be brilliant – thanks.' Cressida started typing on the laptop.

'And you know, I could also finish restoring the collection. I could take time off and stay longer.'

'Finish my work?' Astrid leapt up from her chair. The brakes were off. 'You've got to be bloody joking.'

'For the record—' Simon turned to Cressida '—can I say that all ties with Astrid were cut by the National Gallery a long time ago. Did she not mention that?'

'Oh, give it a rest Simon – you creep,' said Astrid.

'No, you didn't, Astrid.' Cressida got her phone out. 'So maybe the Trust should draw a line under your work here.'

'Hang on,' she protested.

Cressida tapped a number into her phone. 'I am so sorry, Astrid – but I think that sounds like the best way to proceed.' The call connected. 'Ah, Emily,' she said brightly. 'Could you pop into the office and give Astrid a hand with her things. She's leaving us.'

In the storeroom Astrid and Emily collected her belongings in silence. Emily folded up the tripod while Astrid tidied the art materials into her work case. They were halfway down the corridor when Emily spoke first.

'So will you stay in Dorset now – on your boat?'

'No idea. I need to get some time on my own to get a plan together.'

'Well, I'm sure you'll work it out.'

'Thanks…' They passed a Chinese vase on the table. 'Look, I just need to say goodbye to Harold.'

'Of course, I'll take your things to your car.'

'Thanks, Emily.'

Harold was at his usual station in the gallery room. He was sitting with his hands on his knees, deep in thought. She had to say his name a couple of times before he looked up. 'Ah, Astrid. A bad business at the weekend, don't you think?'

'Yes. How is your friend?'

'He's well on the mend. They reckon he'll be out of hospital this afternoon – thank goodness. But I feel awful about the whole thing.'

'You shouldn't, Harold.' She put her hand on his shoulder. 'Your chain mail saved him.'

'I guess.' He smiled slightly. 'There's not going to be any more historical re-enactments for a while though. Cressida has banned them.'

'She's not a huge fan of mine at the moment, either. In fact, I won't go into it, but I'm afraid this is my last day here.'

He got up from his seat. 'No, no. That can't be right.'

'I'm afraid so.'

'Well, that's such a shame. It's been so nice to meet you.'

'And you too. Will you say goodbye to Margaret and Denise for me?'

He stood to attention, as if he'd been given an order. 'I will.' Then he pushed out his elbow, as if she should put her arm through it. 'Now may I escort you to the door, Astrid?'

'How very gentlemanly of you, Harold.' She linked arms and they headed towards the door.

They made their way down the corridor, Astrid slowing her pace to make sure he could keep up. They walked in silence, until they reached the corner. There was a door leading to their right, and as they passed it Astrid felt the slightest breeze against her neck. No more than a kiss of cool air. She stopped and unlinked her arm.

'This door. Where does it lead to?'

'I imagine it's up to the third floor.'

'Yes, I think you said.' She remembered the time she'd crossed the lawn and thought she'd seen someone watching her from a window on the third floor. Astrid reached for the doorknob and slowly pushed the door open. 'Oh, didn't you say these doors were always locked?'

'Yes, they're supposed to be.'

Astrid stepped through the door. 'Shall we have a quick look?'

'No, no... I'm not sure that's a good idea.'

'What are they going to do? Sack me?'

Astrid took the narrow flight of stairs, Harold not far behind. The steps rose steeply then curved round into a corridor that was filled with furniture. It was pushed up against the walls leaving only a small gap to squeeze through. A faint smell of cooking and tea led her on.

On the other side was a large room with a big square carpet in the middle. Some of the furniture had been arranged around it. A wardrobe, a wing-back chair, a fold-out bed with a stack of books next to it. By the wall was a small camping stove and a kettle on a short flex plugged into a socket by the wall.

She worked it out straight away. Someone had secretly set up camp here. And when she saw Harold's expression, a mix of shame and nervousness, she knew exactly who it was.

'Harold?'

He walked past her, head down, and sat on the end of the small bed. There was a sleeping bag and pillow neatly laid out.

'You won't tell anyone, will you?'

'Tell them what, Harold?'

He glanced round the room. 'This is where I live, Astrid. In the evening when everyone goes home, I just slip round the corner and stay up here.' He brought out a heavy key from his pocket. 'I must have forgotten to lock the door this morning.'

'I see… and how long has this been going on?'

'It started about a year ago. Just the odd night. But then I just sort of made things cosy and stayed.'

'Have you nowhere else to go, Harold?'

'I had a bungalow, but then my sister wasn't well and I sold it to pay for her care. And my pension from the army isn't much.'

Astrid put her bag down. 'Don't worry, I understand.'

'No… I have to explain.' His pride was dented. 'I know I shouldn't have, but then is it really fair? A big house like this with so many empty rooms and all this beautiful furniture gathering dust.'

'You're right. It's not.' Astrid went over to the window

and looked out. There was a perfect view of the gardens. 'So that day I saw someone at the window. It was you, wasn't it?'

'Yes, it was. I'm sorry I couldn't tell you the truth.'

'That's alright, I understand. And don't worry, Harold, I won't tell anyone.'

'Thank you, Astrid. Can I get you a cup of tea?'

Harold glanced at the kettle. Next to it was an ornate silver tray on which were a couple of bone china mugs. She chuckled – he really had made himself at home. 'No, that's kind. But I really should be going.'

'Before you do. I should tell you something else.'

'Go on.'

'I'm not the only one who stays on in the house. A few evenings I've heard footsteps on the floor below. Someone sitting in the furniture. Even lying on the beds. I'd never do that, of course.'

'That's interesting. And did you ever hear their voice?'

'No, never. I lock myself in and keep very quiet until they go. I know how to be very quiet, you see.'

Astrid remembered when she first met him and he stepped to one side to avoid a loose floorboard. He knew every plank and nail, every creak in this old house. 'Right, well thank you for telling me.'

He stood up from the bed. 'My pleasure. And remember Astrid – if you ever pop back in, I'll always be here. Well, I'll probably be downstairs on my chair.' His voice faded again. The reality of it sunk in. He would be there. In the corner of that room, where the shadow of the big curtain swung round and left him in the shade after two o'clock.

Waiting in case someone had a question for him. Waiting to be needed.

She took a couple of steps towards the open door. Then she stopped. 'You know, Harold.' She touched the doorknob. 'I've noticed something about all the doorknobs in the house. On one side they have this intricate marigold design. On the other side they're just plain. Why is that?'

'Oh, that is interesting.' He'd cheered up again. 'You see, back in the glory days of the house, you would have a servant at every door. Their only job would be to open it ahead of a Sherborne family member.' He moved to the other side of the door. 'They'd stand on this side and touch the simple part of the doorknob. You see, there was no need for the servants to be touching a fancy handle.'

'Now that... is fascinating.'

'Thank you.' He stood there, not wanting to say goodbye.

'You see, Harold – this house needs you. You and Margaret and Denise, all the volunteers. You are the heart of the English Trust. Don't forget that.'

'I won't.'

25

She left her work case behind the door of the boat, locked up again and returned to the towpath. The verge was filled with tall plants with thick green stems that rose to umbrellas of cream flowers. Dusty bees zipped between them. In the distance, the spire of the church shimmered in the heat. England – early summer. Had she ever been so unhappy on such a divine day?

She decided to take the path past the town to see where it took her. To carry this new sadness. To feel it on her shoulders and know she could bear its weight. Just when she thought she'd got her life back on track, Simon had returned to betray her again. He'd even taken her new job.

How much more of her life did he want to steal?

How much more was there to take?

She marched on down the path, past the bridge and into a meadow. The river wound through the long grass ahead of her. The water was slow and crystal clear. Just under the surface swathes of bright green weed snaked in the current. Millais could have painted Ophelia here. Drowning. Serene. Her dress slowly dragging her down.

She took off her jumper and carried on. No, Simon wasn't going to watch her drown. She dabbed at the corner of her eye with the sleeve of the jumper. Her last ever tear for him. One day she'd get her own back and it would be as cool and sweet as this river.

At the end of the meadow she crossed a stile. The path was thinner – less worn by footsteps. Wildflowers hung in her way. As she walked she began to run over the twists in the case. The painting she saw today was the original Constable. At some point it had been swapped for the fake she'd worked on – there was no arguing with that. So who knew she'd discovered the fake? She'd only told Cressida, but given how chatty she was, word would have got round pretty quick. Simon? No, it seemed like he'd just showed up and grabbed his chance to muscle his way back into her life – even if that meant wrecking it yet again.

So who had had the original painting until now? They must have been nearby to swap it at the last minute. There was no point going back to Stevie Greshingham's house to find out. She'd have to break in and the security was too tight.

She carried on through a copse of trees where the path was not much more than a streak of dried mud. The trail of clues was running out too. The same questions going round and round. Who could have pushed DeVine? Who would have known how to poison Eric? Or fire a crossbow?

The path climbed up and away from the valley. The river was more of a stream now, rushing over rocks somewhere in the trees below her. She kept going. Past an old church, an old farm set back behind a thick stone wall, through open gates, over more stiles. Higher and higher until she could see over the trees behind her in the valley. The answers still just out of reach.

There was a beep from her trouser pocket. It was a text from Harper. A couple of voicemail alerts too, which were probably his.

The text said: *'Astrid. Call me – it's urgent.'*

She sat down on the grass and rang him. He picked up immediately – he sounded serious, and she could tell that he wasn't putting it on this time. 'Where are you?' he said.

'Out walking. A few miles west of Hanbury.'

'Good. Meet me at the wharf as soon as you can.'

When she got back to the square, he was sitting on the steps below the stone cross. She sat next to him on the step, and loosened her feet out of her shoes. 'So, what's this all about, Harper?'

He glanced around the square, which was deserted. 'Were you not expecting a visit from me? After what happened yesterday?'

'The crossbow incident?'

'Yes, it turns out you were right there on the front row.'

'There were a lot of other people there too... if you're suggesting that I had something to do with it.'

'No.' He turned to her, a look of concern. 'Astrid. I think you were the intended target.'

'What?'

'Whoever fired from the tent was trying to kill you, but the soldier just got in the way.'

Astrid's throat tightened. She swallowed hard, trying to get rid of a knot that had lodged there. 'I assumed the arrow was for Cressida. She's not that popular at the house, believe me.'

'I don't think so. Cressida said you were sitting to the left of her.'

'That's right.'

'I checked the angle of the arrow – it was meant for you.'

She shivered. Until now her investigation had been just a puzzle to solve. A curious game involving other people. Now it was all too real. Someone had deliberately damaged the engine of her boat – that was a warning. The crossbow? Now they were coming for her. 'Okay, Harper, let's hear it.'

He got his notepad out of his pocket and flicked through a dozen or so pages. 'Okay – let's go over the order of events. You first stumbled on DeVine's body in the icehouse, and you reported the death straight away.'

Astrid nodded.

'Eric Wainwright was poisoned next. Whoever did it followed you into the woods to get rid of you. You were supposed to have eaten those poisonous mushrooms too.'

'I was supposed to have eaten them?'

'Probably. The killer knew the forager tours always finished with Eric making a meal of his finds. They must have sneaked them into his bag at some point. Then...' he checked the notebook again '...having failed to kill you at the Arne they tried again at the battle reconstruction at Sherborne Hall.'

Astrid's mind worked furiously, putting all the information together just as Harper must have – and there was no other conclusion she could reach. 'You know, Harper, I think you're right.'

'Thanks.' He gave a smug smile. 'Not bad for a backwater cop.'

'We'll see.' She laughed, more out of nervousness. Anyone

could be watching her right now. Plotting their next move. Astrid looked around the square at the handful of people on benches. Up at the windows. She shivered again. 'Why would anyone want to kill me?'

'Because they believe or know you have discovered some incriminating evidence. Astrid…' He set the pen to one side. 'Is there anything you've not told me?' His serious tone was back now. 'And let me remind you, if you don't tell me the truth now it will be much worse for you later.'

Astrid hesitated. 'Okay – there are a few things.'

'Go on.' He reached for his pencil.

'You're going to need a new page for this.'

She told him everything she knew. How she climbed down into the icehouse and checked DeVine's wallet, then all about the exhibition, Lady Sherborne, the fake Constable, and how this morning the original painting had showed up in Cressida's office. He kept writing until she explained her theory that Stevie Greshingham might be the collector of the original.

'It's possible. I shall pay Mr Greshingham another visit.'

'Another visit?'

'Yes, Astrid.' He tapped his pen on his bottom lip. 'Are you going to ask me why I've already visited him?'

'No, because you're going to tell me anyway.'

'I am – it appears you were caught on his CCTV cameras nosing around his house. Remember?'

'Oh, yeah.' She shrugged.

'I told him you were harmless. Just a silly tourist looking at the expensive yachts. He said he thought that was the case and he wasn't going to take it any further.'

'I'm not.'

'Obviously.' He smirked. 'I assumed that. I was just getting you off the hook.'

'Thanks, Harper.'

'No problem. He's agreed not to press charges. In fact, he was flattered.'

Astrid carried on with the rest of the story. How the engine of her boat might have been deliberately damaged (she made a mental note to add 'boat skills' to the list of the killer's talents). How her husband had come down to London to give his judgement on the painting. How she'd been sacked this morning. Harper didn't interrupt her. When he'd finished writing it all down, he put his notebook and pen away and exhaled slowly.

'I'll be honest with you… I think your life is still in danger. But I can't put any round-the-clock protection on you, I'm afraid. My superiors wouldn't believe any of it at this stage. As you probably realised when you visited the station, they don't treat me seriously.'

'Yes, I'm sorry about that. Don't worry, I'm sure you'll get promoted soon.'

'Thank you.' He smiled. 'Now, is there anywhere you can go for a while?'

Astrid stretched her legs out, feeling the tiredness in them. She was tired of everything now. But she wasn't running away. No, she was sticking around. To prove her uncle right. To prove Simon wrong. She'd failed at her marriage. She wasn't failing at this. 'No, Harper – I'm not leaving. I'm going to see this through.'

She was expecting him to protest but he didn't. 'That's fine.'

'Not just a bored trophy wife after all then?'

'Apparently not.' He laughed. Then he stood up. 'Okay then – I'd recommend you put a strong padlock on your door. One over the engine well too. I'll chase up the things that you've told me about. See what I can find. And, Astrid…' He turned to leave. 'I wish you the best of luck.'

Astrid watched him cross the square, distilling what he'd said. Letting it sink in deeper. Someone was trying to kill her. But wasn't that progress, in a way? It meant she was right about the fake. Right about a lot of things. She was getting too close to the truth for someone. And now she was going to get a lot closer, however dangerous that was.

At the post office she bought a pack of plain notecards and three envelopes. Astrid paid for them along with a black marker pen and found a quiet spot by the packing area. She had to narrow down the number of suspects. This would be a way of ruling out three of them – or catching one of them.

On each note she wrote the same thing in block capitals:

I KNOW EVERYTHING – ICEHOUSE WEDNESDAY 2.45pm.

She researched the correct addresses for Lady Sherborne, Greshingham and Cressida – then slipped the notes into the envelopes and returned to the cashier to buy first-class stamps. The culprit had left a note for her, so maybe they couldn't resist rising to the bait. Then it dawned on her. All three of them could show up at the same time. And then what? Her hand hovered over the mouth of the post box.

No, she had to see this through whatever the risks. She posted the letters and set off to the hardware store.

On the way she texted Kath. She'd definitely want to be involved with finally cracking the case. Although, she'd have to make sure she wasn't in danger too.

I've laid a trap for the killer. Are you free on Wednesday afternoon?

Her phone pinged back with a message from her. A simple *YES!* followed by a long string of emojis that started with a 'thumbs up' and ended with a cat with red hearts for eyes. She sent another text back telling her not to mention it to anyone, not even Grub when they met in the pub. Another big 'thumbs up' was fired back.

She bought two big chrome padlocks and fitted them on the door and engine hatch. There was a wooden crate of tools on the decking. Cobb must have dropped them off. Something by the crate caught her eye – a flash of silver. She knelt down. It was Cobb's chain; it must have fallen from his neck. She picked it up, twisted it in her fingers, and put it in her pocket.

For a moment she thought about searching the whole boat for any more notes from Uncle Henry. Top to bottom. But then it dawned on her. She'd only found these notes after doing something to move on with her life. She was spring-cleaning the boat because she'd decided to make this her home. Checking the tide tables because she was going to take the boat out on her own. There would be no other message from Uncle Henry until she was ready to understand it.

There was no sign of Cobb in the boatyard. She went over to the work shed and noticed a light under the door. A sharp rap was answered with a faint 'Come in' from the other side. Pushing the door open she felt the warm air on her face. It smelt of wood smoke, pine sap and salt. Of him.

The room was panelled in light pine strips. There was a simple kitchen counter made out of a single piece of wood that hugged the line of the wonky wall. Cobb had no doubt made it himself. At the front was a long sliding glass door that looked out to a decked patio by the river. He was sitting in a leather chair, reading a boating magazine. 'Hey, Astrid.'

'Sorry to wander in. You busy?'

'No, no…' He put down the magazine and stretched. 'Let me get you a coffee.'

'I'm fine, thanks.'

'Okay, well I'm getting another one.' He went to an old range cooker and struck a match over the hob. Then he picked up a battered kettle and set it over the blue flame.

'You sure you don't want one?'

'Positive – I can't stay.' She looked round the room. It was maybe twice the size of the cabin – double-height ceiling, mostly. To the side of the door was a ladder that ran up to another level. She could just make out a bed up there. 'This is amazing, Cobb. Did you do the work yourself?'

'No. I employed some interior designers in Bournemouth.' He chuckled. 'They usually handle celebrities, but they made an exception for me.'

'Yeah, yeah.' She laughed. 'When are you going to stop teasing me, Cobb?'

'When you stop being ridiculous.' He smiled. 'So, listen, what can I do for you?'

'Well, actually… I wanted to apologise for yesterday. Blaming you for ruining the boat engine.'

'Forget about it.' He reached for a coffee can and prised the lid off. Shook out a good measure of granules into his mug.

'I fixed the fuel line when you were out. And I dropped off some tools at your boat.'

'Yes, I got them. Thanks.' She put her hand in her pocket and felt the silver chain. But she pushed it deeper in her pocket.

'So, will your husband be giving you a hand?'

Astrid took a deep breath. 'There is no husband.' There – she'd said it now. And it felt like taking out a splinter. 'Well, there is a husband – Simon. But we're not together now. It's a long story.'

He picked up the kettle and sluiced out some steaming water into his mug. 'I like long stories. Let's go outside.'

They sat in the chairs on the decking and she told him about how she'd discovered her marriage was over. He listened, sipping his coffee, occasionally brushing his knee with the back of his hand. When she finished speaking, he put his coffee cup down at his feet. 'I'm sorry,' he said. 'I know it hurts.'

'Less every day,' said Astrid, realising how true that was. And unexpected. 'Every day I feel a bit stronger.'

He crossed his arms, eyes straight ahead. 'In the end, we are all just humans… drunk on the idea that love, only love, can heal our brokenness.'

'That's good. Keats?'

'I dunno – it's from a fridge magnet I've got.'

'Oh.'

There was a gap in the reeds where you could see out into the estuary. A boat drifted past on its way out to the harbour bay. Astrid waited until it was out of sight. She was enjoying the silence. And the static that had built up between them – like a storm was moments away. Eventually she spoke. 'What about you, Cobb? What's your story?'

'I went through a rough divorce about three years back.' He pretended to shiver – as if it was all coming back to him. 'We were married for about ten years. I don't think it was ever right.'

'So why did you stay together?'

'Thing is…' He paused, as if considering how much he should tell her. 'Let's say, she had some emotional problems and I thought I could fix her. Because I could fix everything else.' He stretched out in the chair. 'Anyway. We have a son – Jason, who's nine. So I've to keep it together for him. Usual story.'

'It happens.'

She knew it was coming.

'What about you. Any kids?' There it was. Not that it bothered her. She didn't ever feel she'd missed out on having a family. It was something other people seemed to have a problem with.

'No, I was hoping for a dog first. But that didn't work out.'

He laughed hard. 'You're too funny.'

And you're too handsome for your own good, she thought. Right – it was definitely time to leave.

She got up and he followed her to the door. Then she remembered. 'You know, I was going to ask you about Henry. He left me a note and I can't work out what it meant.'

'Go on then.'

'It just said, "Astrid – you are where the ladders start".'

'Where the ladders start?'

'That's all it said.'

'Interesting.' He folded his arms. 'Maybe he wants you to try and be a better person.'

'A better person?'

'Yeah – I knew Henry well. He was always saying what a good kid you were – greatest thing since sliced bread. Then you show up.'

'Don't hold back then, Cobb.'

'You were rude. Snobbish. Butt tight like a barnacle. And I can't believe it's the same Astrid he went on about. First time I met you, you were…'

She held up her hand. 'I get the idea.'

'Okay. Sorry. But hey, now I've got to know you. You're pretty cool.'

'Thanks, Cobb. You too.' She stepped out into the sunshine and turned to him. 'Listen, I'm going to take the boat tomorrow, to prove something. And I don't want you rushing out to rescue me.'

'You sure? You made a right hash of things last time.'

'I did – and I can't promise I won't make a mess of things again. But it will be my mess, Cobb. Okay?'

'Got it.' He stared for a moment. As if he'd seen something else new in her. 'Then the best of luck to you, Astrid.'

26

Monday, Day 13

Astrid woke at just after ten, and spent another hour in bed. She would need to get as much rest as possible for what lay ahead today. She'd checked the tide tables the night before and worked out that the best time to set sail was five o'clock. Before then she'd have to learn about every reef and marker buoy she might meet along the way.

Thankfully Uncle Henry owned every guide and chart you might need to navigate a boat anywhere along the south coast. She took down a handful from the bookshelf and laid them on the table.

She applied herself as if it was an exam, only taking a break for lunch and an hour in the late afternoon for a bike ride. So, when she stepped behind the controls and pushed the throttle forwards, she knew she was as prepared as she could ever be. The rest was luck.

★

The chain ferry was docked up on the Sandbanks side – plenty of time to get out to sea. Spinning the wheel smoothly between her fingers she set a course to the west. It was quiet. Only a couple of speedboats zipped between her and the big channel marker.

Soon she was in open water, where the waves were knee-high. The boat shouldered each one, rolling slightly but staying true. Back in the harbour the water smelled of mud. Here the sea air was briny. Invigorating. She inhaled deeply. The engine thrummed steadily at the back of the boat. A cormorant flew low over the water in front of the prow, its wing tips almost touching the tops of the waves.

It took about an hour. First past a line of chalk pillars that stepped out into the sea – 'Old Harry Rocks', according to the chart clipped in front of her. Then on past sheer cliffs dotted with white birds. Coves and scalloped bays. Fields of wheat and meadows like a patchwork quilt thrown down to the water's edge.

She slowed the boat and studied the headland – trying to recognise the scene Constable had painted. The boat was too far out. She checked the chart – there were shallows ahead. She edged the boat forwards. A band of kelp, great belts of mustard-coloured weed, slapped against the hull. There was no turning back now.

Closer in towards the cliffs, about two hundred yards off, it began to feel more familiar. She lined up the view ahead of her in an imaginary frame. There was a winding path up the hill, slabs of rocks the size of houses at the base of the cliffs. She cut the engine and dropped the anchor. Yes – this was it. Constable must have taken a boat out to exactly this spot. But now what?

'Come on, Uncle Henry,' she whispered. 'I'm climbing the ladder for you here.' She closed her eyes and thought back to the last summer she'd seen him. They were painting in the garden. She could clearly see the canvas in front of them. Every detail. 'Detail' – that was it… add a final detail that will reveal the truth. So where is it then?

She opened her eyes again and stared ahead of her, studying every rock and fold on the headland. Where was it? Up the path to the ridge of the hill. The light was softening. There was a pinkish tint to the lowest clouds. Still nothing. Then right on the edge of the cliff… there it was – a white building. It was just a speck in the distance but she could make out what it was – a lighthouse.

Down in the cabin she went over to the far wall. Right in the middle was a framed chart of lighthouses of the south coast. So far she hadn't even looked at it. She traced her finger along the black and white coastline until she found the entrance to the harbour – then on another five miles or so west. On the edge of the cliff was a tiny drawing of a lighthouse – the 'Weymouth beacon'. Under it was the date it was built.

She gasped… *1956*. The lighthouse was built a hundred and twenty years *after* Constable's death.

So there was only one explanation. The forger had been out here on a boat, seen the lighthouse and added the detail to both the fake and the original.

She took down the framed chart and placed it face down on the table. On the back was Uncle Henry's writing again. The same black pen. The note this time said:

*Well done, Astrid. If you want to know EVERYTHING
– ask Sheepdip.*

The journey back seemed to take half as long. Her mind was racing so fast she barely noticed the landmarks in the failing light. Uncle Henry had to have been the forger. Didn't he? But there had been no sign of his own paintings on the boat. Nobody she'd spoken to had seen him painting either. And why would anyone add a modern lighthouse to both paintings, the copy and the masterpiece – they would be bound to be found out, whichever one an expert looked at.

If it was Uncle Henry, then all those months ago, years maybe, he'd put all his faith in her being that expert. One big gamble that she'd solve the riddle. And now she had to ask a dog for the answer. A dog.

By the time she got into the harbour it was dark. She picked her way between the blinking red and green lights of the harbour. The tide was receding fast. But she was sure she could make it back safely. And sure that tomorrow would be a very good day. Simon was about to be proven wrong this time.

27

Tuesday, Day 14

It felt strange to be lining up to buy a ticket at the English Trust visitors' entrance.

'Would you like to become a member today?' said a woman with a fawn bucket hat, thrusting a leaflet towards her.

'Maybe later.' She took a couple of steps, then stopped and turned back to the woman. 'You know, I might just do that.'

In the foyer was a sign on a stand that said: *'Press Event – 11.30 a.m.'.* A red arrow pointed down the corridor. She followed it and joined a short queue filing into the library. Inside the room had been almost filled with fold-out seats. Most were taken. At the front, just off to the side, were a handful of TV cameras on tripods. Smartly dressed reporters stood waiting behind them. Right at the front was a wooden lectern and an easel covered with a white cloth.

Astrid spotted a spare seat on the far end of the front row. She headed towards it. Out of the corner of her eye she saw Cressida get up from further down the row. Before she could sit down Cressida had blocked her way.

'Sorry, Astrid... it's invites only.'

'But I have this.' She took out a flimsy card. 'Apparently it's my "temporary membership" card. Surely you can't turn away a member?'

A frown cracked across Cressida's forehead. 'Please, this is not the time for a scene, Astrid.'

Astrid took one step forward. 'No, I think it's the perfect time for a scene.' She thumbed towards the reporters. 'The cameras can record it... That's not going to be good for footfall though, is it?'

Cressida glanced at the reporters. 'Okay, come on in then,' she said, shuffling back down the row.

Astrid found a seat and looked around. The audience seemed to be mostly visitors. There were a few other journalists on the front row clutching notepads and phones. Lady Sherborne was at the back, brushing dog hairs off her tweed skirt and impatiently checking her watch.

At eleven-thirty on the dot, Simon strode into the room and stood behind the lectern. He gave the audience an oily smile and arranged his notes. The reporters by the wall got behind their cameras and started adjusting buttons.

He waited for them to get ready then addressed the audience. 'Ladies and gentlemen, welcome to Sherborne Hall.' He paused. Obviously, he'd been expecting some applause. 'Anyway...' Another smile, a slow panorama from right to left this time, which quickly faded when he saw Astrid sitting on the end of the row. 'Right so...' He rustled his notes. 'My name is Simon Kisner. I'm head of conservation at the National Gallery in London. And this morning…' he turned to the painting under the cloth '…I'm going to reveal for the first time what I consider one of the greatest art discoveries in recent times.'

Lady Sherborne huffed loudly at the back. She'd clearly worked out that the painting under the sheet wasn't large enough to be her portrait.

Simon carried on with his presentation, explaining that the mystery painting would be the centrepiece of a later exhibition entitled 'the Treasures of Sherborne Hall'. Cressida gave him a little thumbs up, clearly loving the plug. He carried on, scattering in a few details about the restoration process and how he'd helped 'this marvellous painting see the light of day'. There was no mention of Astrid's involvement.

After a while the members began to shift in their seats. Simon noticed he was losing his audience. 'Right,' he said, sweeping his hand towards the easel, 'let me introduce the world to what I believe is one of John Constable's finest works.'

He stepped forward, gripped the corner of the cloth and slid it away from the painting. Lady Sherborne groaned at the back of the room.

'Painted in 1816, this is an exquisite landscape of nearby cliffs at Weymouth. The artist was on honeymoon at the time, as we can see from this figure climbing the path. I believe this is his new wife, Maria.'

Astrid squirmed – he'd got hold of her notes about Constable's honeymoon. Still, he was about to be publicly humiliated. Swings and roundabouts.

'We'll be providing a hand-out at the end,' Simon

continued, 'but does anyone have any questions at this stage?'

Astrid raised her hand in the air. Simon scanned the room, stopping well short of her corner of the front row.

A handful of reporters sitting down also had their hands up. He answered their questions quickly, which were all about Constable's early life and the possible value of the painting. Simon said it was impossible to say, but again stressed it was a 'major discovery'. Then he started to tidy his notes.

Astrid waved at him. He saw her out of the corner of his eye. 'So that's probably a good time to round things up,' he said, hurriedly packing away his notes into his briefcase.

Astrid got to her feet. 'Excuse me. I have a question.'

'Yes, I think we really should wrap it up there,' he said without making eye contact. 'We need to let the photographers take some pictures of the painting.'

'No, I had my hand up from the start.' She was a notch under shouting.

He checked the room. Everyone was staring at her. 'Of course, please... ask away.'

'Alright. This Constable. Are you sure it's not a fake?'

'What?' he snorted. There were a few other laughs, from the audience. 'No, of course it's not a fake.'

'And you'd stake your reputation on that?'

'Absolutely. I've spent time with the piece and all the tests confirm this is an original Constable.'

'So then...' She stood up and stepped forwards. The cameras in the corner swung round to follow her. 'Can you explain what the building on the cliffs is doing there?'

'Mmm?' He went over to the painting.

'On the headland. It's a lighthouse, isn't it?'

He slipped his reading glasses on and bent forward. 'It appears to be, yes.'

Astrid crossed her arms. 'In fact – I can tell you exactly what it is. It's the Weymouth beacon... and it was built in 1956.'

Simon had his back to her. But she knew there was no smile, because she'd just wiped it from his face. Right now he was wondering what would be the most dignified expression to make when he turned round. Then thinking about the nearest exit.

The audience began to chatter, the pitch building steeply.

'In 1956... but that's not possible.' Astrid pretended to be shocked. 'Because you said the original Constable was painted in 1816. He would have been dead for about a hundred and twenty years. Wouldn't he?'

He slowly spun round to face the audience, his lower lip slightly trembling. If she could frame that – it would be priceless.

'I'm sure there's an explanation,' he said.

'Go on then... let's hear it.' Astrid held her ground.

Simon picked up his briefcase and glanced towards the exit. A reporter to Astrid's right was on his feet. 'So, is it a fake or not?'

The truth was, it didn't matter. The painting on the easel could be the original or the fake – there was a lighthouse on both of them. That was the beauty of it.

The photographers pressed in to get a photo of Simon. Someone at the back shouted, 'Come on! Answer the question!'

Astrid sauntered down the aisle and left the room with a low roar of laughter ringing in her ears.

At the car park she leant with her back against the warm metalwork of the Mini, letting her triumph sink in. She'd dreamt that her revenge on Simon would be sweet. But this was so sweet it made her tongue fuzzy. Could it get any better? Well, maybe.

From around a tall hedge at the end of the car park, she saw Simon stumbling out into the sunshine. He checked behind him to see if he was being followed, then marched over towards her. He stopped in front of her, his face creased with anger. 'Are you happy now?'

'Yes… ecstatic.'

'But you know what you did back there, Astrid? You ruined my reputation.'

Astrid took out her key fob and opened the car. 'No, Simon, this one's on you.' She walked round the bonnet of the car to the driver's side.

'Bye, Simon. My solicitors will be in touch about the divorce.'

'Solicitors?'

'Dutton and Parker. They're expensive, but worth it.'

'Come on, Astrid. We need to talk about this.'

There was a shout from the corner of the car park. A couple of photographers were making a beeline for Simon, cameras in hand. Astrid got into the car, locked the doors and started the engine. Simon rattled the door handle of the passenger side. 'Astrid!' he pleaded, his face up against the window. She accelerated out of the car park, without even checking her rear-view mirror.

'Explain it again.' Kath was at the bar of The *Angler's Arms*, an elbow on the counter. 'There's two paintings out there, right?'

'Yes – the original and the fake.' Astrid took a mouthful of red wine. 'Whoever painted the forgery must have had access to the original. They painstakingly copied it, then added the detail of the lighthouse at the end to both paintings.'

Grub was playing darts. He was standing just behind a line of masking tape on the carpet. 'But the thing is...' he held up a dart '...they must have known that they were going to get caught?'

'Yeah,' Kath chuckled. 'Any idiot would see straight away that the lighthouse wasn't hundreds of years old.'

'Thanks, Kath.' Astrid laughed.

'Sorry, but you know what I mean. Why would they risk it when the rest of the painting was so convincing?'

'Because they wanted whoever bought the forgery to get caught?'

'That has to be it.' Kath nodded.

Grub threw a dart at the board. It hit the outer wire and bounced out. Sheepdip scuttled under the table.

'Hey, Grub.' Astrid waited for him to retrieve the dart. 'You were good friends with my uncle. Do you know if he was involved in all this?'

'Why do you say that?'

'Well, he's left me a trail of notes.'

'Notes?' said Grub.

'Yes – cards with messages on. Like he was guiding me to the truth.'

Grub rubbed his beard. 'You know, honestly… Henry was one of my best mates. He would have told me if he was forging art.' He threw another dart. It arced low, thunking into a double three. 'Getting there,' he sighed. He gathered himself for his final throw.

'So do most people fake art for the money?' said Kath.

'Not really. Most of them just want to try and show they're as good as the great masters. Or they want to embarrass the art establishment.'

'Yusss!' Grub shouted. The final dart was sticking out of the bullseye on the board. It hung there for a moment, drooped, and fell to the floor. 'Oh, come on!' Grub clapped his hands on both sides of his head.

'Never go for the bullseye,' said Kath 'it never stays in.'

Astrid waved over to Dolly, who was scouring away at something in the sink behind the bar. She trudged over. 'Same again for everybody?'

'Yes thanks, Dolly,' said Astrid, reaching for her wallet.

Grub gathered up the darts and turned to Dolly. 'What's the chances of getting a new dartboard, Dolly?'

She stared at him. 'What about a jacuzzi in the beer garden? Just for you, Grub.'

Grub shrugged and put the darts on a shelf below the chalkboard. Sheepdip watched him from under the table then hopped up onto the bench next to Astrid.

'I dunno, Sheepdip.' She rubbed gently behind his ears.

He sat upright and looked at her. A lopsided smile tipped across his muzzle. 'So what do you think?' Sheepdip stared at her, then started to lick her hand.

Grub came over. 'You two are thick as thieves.'

'He's a lovely dog.'

'You want to take him out some time?'

'For a walk?'

Sheepdip mewled and wheeled round in fast circles on the bench.

'Yeah – first rule of looking after a dog. Don't say the "W" word until you're ready to go.' He pointed to Sheepdip. 'Later, buddy?' Sheepdip settled back on the bench, his wiry chin on his paws.

'Yes, I'd love to,' said Astrid.

'Thursday? Five o'clock? I'll drop him over at the boat after work.'

'Thursday?' Astrid looked at Sheepdip. 'Yes, I think I'll be around.'

28

The next morning Astrid busied herself by working on the boat. First, she scraped at varnish on the deck to dislodge the bigger flakes. When that was done, she ran an extension lead up from the cabin and plugged in the circular sander that Cobb had lent her. It burred and hummed over the deck, throwing up a cloud of thin grey dust. Underneath, the wood was bright and smooth.

As she sanded, she began to think about Simon, and her marriage. Four years – and all of them happy. That's how it had seemed to her, anyway. If he felt the marriage hadn't been working, he should have told her. They could have tried to make it better. But no – he'd taken the easy route out, by having an affair. And she deserved a proper explanation.

She reached for her phone and typed in a text. If he wanted to see her then it was tomorrow or nothing: '*12.30 at the Haven Hotel.*' A minute later and he replied with a simple 'yes'. Good. She could get all the answers now. And then she could finally move on with her life.

She carried on sanding, not noticing the time slip past. When she next looked at her watch it was 1.05 p.m. Time to pack up the tools, make a couple of sandwiches and wait for Kath to arrive.

Just after one-thirty, Kath emerged from the reeds. She was wearing an off-white shawl over her head, which may have previously been part of a bed sheet.

'What do you think?' She wrapped the cloth over her face so only her nose was visible. 'I'm in cog-neat-toe.'

'I think you look like Lawrence of Arabia expecting a sandstorm.'

'Oh, right.' Kath pulled back the scarf. 'Too much?'

'Mmm… maybe, Kath. Listen, let me get you a sandwich and I'll tell you the plan in the car.'

On the drive over to Sherborne Hall, Astrid explained that she'd sent the same note to Cressida, Lady Sherborne and Stevie Greshingham, telling them to meet her in the icehouse. The guilty person would know the significance of the place and they'd have to show up to find out what she knew. She didn't tell Kath that it was possible that all three of them could turn up. Kath would only try and talk her out of it, and there was no way she was backing out now.

As soon as she stopped talking, Kath clapped her hands and rubbed them together. 'Ooh… this is going to be brilliant.' Then she noticed the One Direction notepad poking out of Astrid's bag in the footwell and pulled it out. 'Shall we write it up?'

'Ah… the notepad is full.'

Kath flicked through the pages. Every one of them was

packed with writing and arrows. 'Hey, ho.' She snapped it shut. 'You've done us proud, boys.' She kissed the cover and put the notepad away in the glove box.

Astrid giggled, trying to keep her eyes on the road. 'So, Kath, do you understand the plan?'

'Yup – it's a honey trap… and we are the big pot of honey.'

'I guess… but the thing is, Kath, I'm going on my own.'

'No, no… it's too risky.'

'If they see I'm not alone then they might panic and we'll have missed our chance.' Astrid slowed for a corner. 'I want you to organise the volunteers. You can be a rescue party if things get threatening.'

Kath stared at her. 'The volunteers?'

Denise and Harold were waiting for them by the scallop fountain as arranged. Denise was wearing a denim boiler suit, a torch in one hand, the walkie-talkie in the other. Harold was in full army camouflage gear. He stepped forwards and held up his hand. She could see there were two thick lines of burnt cork under his eyes. 'Who goes there? Friend or foe?' he said, even though it was broad daylight.

'Friend. It's me, Astrid.'

'Right – proceed.' He stepped back.

'Kath – this is Denise and Harold.'

'Good to meet you, guys,' said Kath.

Harold took Kath's hand and shook it vigorously. 'Ex-army… forty years' service.'

'Nice one – I had a brother who was in the army.'

'Bravo. How many tours did he put in?'

'None – he got chucked out after three months. Not his fault though – what happened was...'

'Sorry, Kath,' Astrid interrupted, 'can we concentrate?'

'No problem.'

Astrid looked around. 'Hey, where's Margaret?'

'I dunno,' said Denise. 'We last saw her in the boiler room.'

Astrid checked her watch. 'Don't worry, we've still got some time. I'll go and get her. You guys hang on here.'

Astrid slowly pushed the boiler room door open. She heard the quiet sobbing first, before she saw her. Margaret was sitting in a chair in front of the lockers, gently rocking.

'Margaret?' She didn't answer. Astrid moved closer and noticed that there was a letter in her hand, a torn envelope at her feet. 'Hey.' Astrid pulled up a chair and sat next to her. 'Are you alright?'

Margaret looked up, startled. 'Oh, it's you.'

Astrid rooted around in her bag and found a small pack of tissues. She peeled one out and gave it to Margaret, who dabbed at her eyes. 'Have you had some bad news?'

'Bad news? No, no. It's amazing.' She shuffled round to face Astrid. 'The job I applied for. The VIP tours thing. Well...' She looked down at the letter again, as if making sure. 'They've given me it. They didn't need an interview – apparently, I was the perfect candidate.'

'That's wonderful.' Astrid paused. 'Then why are you crying?'

'You know...' She let out a long sigh that rattled like the

pressure going down in a tractor tyre. 'Because this is the first job I've ever had. I'm seventy-six, Astrid, and I've never earned a penny.'

'Is that right?'

'You see, my late husband. He was a doctor.' She stopped.

'You don't have to tell me if you don't want to, Margaret.'

'No.' She looked up. Her eyes were pink from crying. 'No, I want to. I married young and had kids straight away. That was the deal – I looked after the kids, the house. He had his successful career and supported us all.'

'I guess it was the same for a lot of women back then.'

'Oh, it was. A different generation. You're lucky, Astrid, you have the choices now.'

'I guess I do.'

'The thing was – nobody was ever that interested in me. You know, at dinner parties – people, mostly men… they'd talk across me.'

Astrid reached out for her hand. Margaret slipped it into hers.

'Then he died and our friends… other couples, they melted away. I felt even more invisible. And that's why I came here to Sherborne Hall. So I could talk to people and they'd be interested in what I had to say.'

Astrid squeezed her hand. It was warm and rough. Except her thumbs, which were smooth. From sewing or cutting fabric, maybe. A life of working. None of it paid – until now. 'You're going to be incredible at this job.'

She held up the letter. 'And I'm going to get some money.' She laughed, as if that was the most ridiculous idea she'd ever heard.

'I'm so pleased for you, Margaret. You deserve it.'

'Thank you.' She squeezed Astrid's hand back.

'Listen, I'm sorry to hear about your husband.'

'Ah, forget it. He was a philanderer. Honestly, he'd jump on a crack in a plate. I don't miss him at all.'

They both roared with laughter. 'Come on, Margaret.' She helped her up. 'We've got another job for you. To catch a murderer.'

At the scallop fountain Astrid went over the plan with the volunteers. If they had any doubts about the riskiness of the operation, they kept it to themselves. All three of them became increasingly excited about the prospect of snaring a killer. Especially Margaret, who paced across the gravel, her hip now seemingly fully recovered.

'And Denise,' said Astrid, 'can we use the walkie-talkies?'

'Of course.' She took a handset out of her apron...

'That's good thinking, Astrid.' Harold stepped forwards. 'Good field communications are better than any weapon in battle.'

Denise handed over a walkie-talkie to Astrid. 'Right – I'll take this down to the icehouse at two-forty. You guys come along a few minutes later and hang back in the gardens. You can listen in from there.'

'Got it,' said Kath.

'Bet you it's Cressida,' said Margaret, grinding her stick into the gravel.

'We'll find out soon enough.' Astrid checked her watch. 'Now I'd better go.'

*

Astrid waited by the side of the yew hedge as the last of the visitors trailed back down the path from the woods. When they were out of sight, she clipped the chain across the gap and carried on to the icehouse.

She slowly took the stairs down, her eyes getting used to the gloom. There was nobody there. She checked the walkie-talkie light was still blinking green and tucked it into her bag. Then she slid the bag into the shadows by the wall.

The ice had melted a little more since the last time she was there. The black well of water had now spread out nearly to the edge of the walls. There was only a thin circle of ice up against the brickwork. Astrid shivered. It was a sheer twelve-foot drop into the darkness. DeVine wouldn't have stood much of a chance. He wouldn't have been expecting it – the push from behind.

She waited for about twenty minutes and was about to give up. But then she heard footsteps at the top of the stairs. They'd arrived. She stepped back from the rail.

Four...

Five...

Six... the firm tread of boot against stone was getting louder – there were another six to go. The footsteps slowed as they reached the corner.

She saw a hand on the rail. There was a cluster of heavy rings on the fingers that glowed under the wall light.

Astrid stared at the figure. 'Lady Sherborne?'

'Astrid?' Lady Sherborne leant her stick against the railings. 'Well, this better be good,' she growled. 'I've got better things to do than skulking around in icehouses.'

Astrid stepped out of the shadows. 'The note – do you know why I sent it?'

Lady Sherborne sighed. 'No idea. But if it's some sort of prank then I'll toddle off if you don't mind.'

'Prank?' Astrid studied her in the low light. Lady Sherborne was clearly irritated to be here. 'Yes, I may…' The relief was flooding away. 'I may have wasted your time. I'm sorry about that.'

Lady Sherborne went over to the railings and peered over. 'Oh, they've put some ice in there, haven't they?'

'Yes, and it doesn't seem to be melting too much.' Astrid stepped aside as Lady Sherborne walked past her.

'It's cold down here all year round.' She turned for the stairs, keeping up the conversation as she went. 'I remember them storing vast amounts of ice here when I was younger.' She didn't look back. It was clear that if she was talking, people were expected to follow. 'They used it for parties on the lawn.'

Astrid checked her watch. It was too late for anyone else to turn up. She hurried after Lady Sherborne. 'But there were fridges, right?'

'Yes dear, it wasn't that long ago.'

'I know,' mumbled Astrid. 'Sorry.'

They both emerged into the light and carried on down the path. 'You see,' said Lady Sherborne, 'they'd take the ice out of the lake in January or February. If you were skating you had to be careful not to fall into the gap. Then they'd store the ice for summer when there would be more outdoor entertaining.'

Astrid got to the hedge first and pulled back the rope for Lady Sherborne. 'They'd fill the fountain with ice for the champagne. There would be ice sculptures. It was a marvellous time. On a summer's night, the grounds back then...' She looked around the gardens. The last of the visitors had left. Everything was quiet and ordered.

'That must have been quite a childhood,' said Astrid.

'It was, yes,' she said, softly.

Astrid checked the paths. There was no sign of Kath or the volunteers. They'd obviously realised there was no reason to leap to her rescue and retreated to the boiler room. 'So, Lady Sherborne. I'm sorry again to have dragged you out.'

'Yes, what was that note all about?'

'It's to do with the fake painting. I thought...'

'I understand – you thought I might have tipped that antique dealer over the edge?'

Astrid shifted on the gravel. 'How did you know?'

'That young policeman interviewed me.'

'Harper?'

'Could be.' She puffed up. 'You thought I killed him?'

'You were on my shortlist, yes.'

'I'm flattered you think I'm capable of doing it.' She stuck out her hand. 'Well, I hope you find them.'

'Thanks.' Astrid took her hand and shook it. She felt the bones come together with a slight click. 'And if I could give you some advice.'

'Go on.' Lady Sherborne raised an eyebrow.

'The grounds are beautiful, don't you think?'

Lady Sherborne nodded. 'They are indeed.'

'If I were you, I'd make the most of them when the visitors have left. All those places you loved as a child are still here. They're just being looked after by someone else.'

She exhaled slowly, a hint of breathlessness from climbing the steps. 'Yes, I'd better... while there's still time.'

Astrid watched Lady Sherborne head back up the path

towards her part of the house. She could take her off her list of suspects. Everyone else, including the volunteers, would have to stay for now. The case was far from being solved.

Beyond the gardens the sun had dipped lower into the folds of the countryside. The light was perfect – golden hour – the grounds were bathed in a mellow glow. She took it all in for a minute or so. This was probably the last time she'd be here. There wasn't much reason to come back. She'd drop the walkie-talkie off with the volunteers and say goodbye to them.

As she rounded the corner of the hedge, she saw Emily ahead of her walking to the house. She caught her up just before the side door. 'Emily?'

Emily spun round. 'Oh hi, Astrid,' she said warmly. 'It's nice to see you again. Are you visiting the gardens?'

'Something like that. What about you?'

She held up a rolled-up poster. 'You know. Running some errands for Cressida – the assistant's job never ends. You mind if we keep moving?'

'Of course.' They went into the house and strode on down the corridor. Then Emily stopped. She tapped the side of her tortoiseshell Alice band. 'Silly me. I almost forgot. You left some art materials in the storeroom. I was going to get in touch.'

'Ah, yes, I probably did. I left in such a hurry.'

Emily checked her watch. 'You know, we could pick them up now if you'd like?'

'Sure, I mean, if you don't mind?'

'Not at all. Let's go.'

They went up a couple of flights of stairs to the second floor, then on through the house. As they passed through the rooms Astrid held back to take one last look. The gilded library, the long room with the panoramic view of the garden…

'Are you okay?' Emily was at the next door, holding it open.

'Yes, sorry.' Astrid turned and stepped into the hunting room.

Emily closed the door behind her. The curtains had been drawn, leaving only a thin gap. A bar of faint light reached out like a hand and climbed up the wood panels, searching for the missing hunting trophies.

Emily was by the window, pulling back the curtains so the last of the evening's light flooded in. She unlatched the window and pushed it open. 'Beautiful, don't you think?'

Astrid joined her by the window. 'Yes, it's as if the whole house is built around beautiful views.'

'I know. I probably shouldn't tell you, but if I'm working late I like to spend time here on my own. Sitting in the chairs.' She giggled. 'Even lying on the beds.'

Astrid remembered what Harold had told her. How he thought someone had been wandering around the house at night. Now it made sense.

'You're not going to tell anyone, are you?'

'Course not.'

Emily wandered to the next door. Astrid stood and took in the view. Her phone beeped in her bag. She turned it over without bringing it out. It was a message from Kath.

Just hanging out with the volunteers in the boiler room.
Meet us down here when you're ready.

She scrolled down.

And hey – I just heard from Pete, my photographer mate
who was there when the crossbow was fired. He spotted
someone in the back of the tent.

And down.

It was a woman with a ponytail.

'Is everything alright?' said Emily from the other side of
the room.

'Mmm... yeah.' She could barely get her words out. 'You
know, maybe it's getting too late. I could pick up the things
in the morning.'

'It won't take a minute.' Emily stared at her.

'No, why don't we head back down.'

Emily turned the key in the lock. 'I'm afraid we need to
get this sorted now.' She went over to the velvet rope that
divided the furniture from the rest of the room, unhooked
it and set it to one side.

Astrid walked to the other door... although she knew
before she twisted the handle – it was locked.

When she turned back, Emily was by the chairs in front
of the fireplace. There were armaments – crossed swords,
bayonets and rifles on the wall above the mantelpiece. She
reached up and took a bayonet from its hooks and leant it
against her chair.

'Come here,' she said, sitting down. 'Put your bag on the
table.'

Astrid checked the other walls. There was nothing that

she could defend herself with. She went and put the bag on the low table between them.

'That's it – grab a seat,' said Emily.

'Thanks,' said Astrid.

Emily opened Astrid's bag and tipped out the contents. Her phone, her wallet, her Chanel parfum spilled out over the table. Emily reached for the phone and checked it was off. Then she picked up the walkie-talkie and slowly brought her finger to her lips. She clicked the off button on the side. 'A bit clumsy, don't you think?'

Astrid shrugged. 'Must have just picked it up by mistake.'

'Of course you did.' She laid the bayonet across her lap. It was about a foot long – bright steel with a razor-sharp blade. 'Right. Let's get this over with, shall we?' she said with her usual tone of sunny efficiency. Whether delivering posters for Cressida or ordering new lanyards – Emily was always focused on doing the job. Astrid, it seemed, was her next task.

Astrid sat back in the leather chair. Using her peripheral vision she tried to work out which weapons were in reach. There was a poker by the fireplace in a metal bucket, halfway between them.

Emily caught her eye flickering towards it. Her hand shot out and grabbed the handle of the bucket. She pulled it closer with a disapproving shake of her head. 'I don't think so, Astrid,' she said, both hands back on the bayonet. 'Don't forget – I was raised on a farm. I'm used to handling tools and weapons.'

Astrid leant forwards. 'You mind if I put the rest of my things back in the bag?'

'Sure.'

Astrid packed her belongings back into the bag as Emily twirled the bayonet in her fingers. 'When I was a kid I had to use something like this to dock the lambs' tails.'

'Dock their tails?'

'Cut them off – it's a country thing.'

'Oh, right. A country thing?' Astrid sat back in the chair. 'So, is that what this is all about then, Emily?'

'No, no. I'm just helping Cressida. Making her life easier.' Emily put the bayonet on the table. 'Cressida got into a bit of a tangle with the fake Constable. She'd commissioned it from your uncle so she could sell off the original.'

'Why him?'

'She told me she'd seen his landscape work and it was brilliant. When she suggested copying a masterpiece he loved the idea – he just thought it was a game.'

'But Cressida told me she knows nothing about art.'

'No, no… she knows a lot about art. Especially the value of a Constable. There was a lot of money riding on that painting. And Cressida needed the money. All those lovely outfits of hers don't come cheap.'

'Sly old Cressida.'

'I know – I've been very lucky to have her as a boss. Don't you think?'

'You're a good match.'

Emily smiled. 'Thank you, Astrid.'

'So how was this great art theft going to work, then?'

'Simple. The fake was going to be part of the exhibition. Once it was up on the wall in front of the public, nobody would know. I mean, who would check that tiny white mark was a remote lighthouse built after Constable's death?'

'Me.'

Emily gripped her hands together. 'Yes, you had to ruin it, didn't you?' Astrid noticed that Emily's forearms were more muscular than she'd realised. There were lots of things that she now noticed about Emily. Her voice hid a slight West Country burr. Her clothes were deliberately plain – buttoned down and drab. She'd done a good job in not standing out.

'Well, that must have been annoying.'

'It was a bit. You were only supposed to give the paintings a quick clean and they could go up on the walls. Then Cressida was going to sell the original. She had a buyer lined up and the deal had to be done in the next few days. But then you noticed the fake and Cressida had to swap it back.'

'So she hadn't sold it yet… to Stevie Greshingham?'

'Stevie who? No, it's been locked up in her office. Waiting for the exhibition.'

Astrid leant forward – slightly nearer the bayonet. Emily's hand darted out and grabbed the weapon, placing it on her lap again.

'You're quick, aren't you, Emily?'

'I am.' She leant forward in her chair. 'Always one step ahead.'

'The perfect busy little assistant.'

Emily tipped her head to one side. 'That's so kind.'

So far, every one of Astrid's barbed comments had been taken as a compliment. Something had snapped in Emily's mind and there would be no way of getting through to her. Astrid might as well get all of the answers now, before… she swallowed, before Emily carried out the last part of her plan. 'So, you're saying that Cressida had nothing to do with the killings – you've done it all without her knowing?'

'Yes, my job is to clear up after her – on my own. I intercepted your invite to the icehouse this afternoon.'

'And this started with DeVine?'

'Correct. He supplied the frame for the Constable. It had to be authentic – the same date, roughly.'

'I think I've got it then.' Astrid raised her forefinger. 'The chalk on his sleeve came from the frame. They were auction marks, but you wiped them off.'

'I did, well done. Problem was, DeVine got greedy. After he found out the frame was going to be used to sell a valuable Constable he started asking for more. Fifty thousand – for an old bit of wood? Cressida refused and he threatened to blackmail her. That's when I decided to sort things out.'

'One step ahead.'

'Exactly. I sent him a note to collect the money at the icehouse and… he had his little accident.' She sighed. 'But then you showed up and started snooping around.'

Astrid looked into the bag again and brought out the first note telling her to meet at the Arne. 'This is your writing, isn't it?'

'Yes – I knew you'd never paid much attention to my writing before. Because I'm just the humble assistant, aren't I, Astrid?'

The room had got colder. A slight draught was blowing down the chimney. Emily was right – she'd overlooked her, as much as everyone else had. 'I guess I did, yes.'

'It's fine.' Emily brushed at her knee, as if the insult was there. 'So, I head down to the Arne. I was going to tell you there was something in the woods you needed to see, then when I was sure nobody was around, I'd finish you off.

And guess what? That old ranger turns up and you two go off to pick mushrooms.'

'Eric Wainwright.'

'Was that his name? Right, well thankfully I know a thing or two about mushrooms – I used to pick them on the farm. So, I put a couple of destroying angels in his bag when you were searching around in the undergrowth. I knew that he was going to offer to cook them up that evening. He's been doing it for years for the Trust.'

'But he could have spotted they were poisonous before cooking them?'

'I know. But he'd already identified everything in his bag as being edible, so I was hoping he'd just throw them in the pan. Which he did. I guess I got lucky. Apart from the fact that you didn't eat them, of course.'

'And that seemed reasonable to you? To kill him, an innocent man, if it meant getting rid of me.'

'Yes.' Emily appeared surprised that anyone would even ask that question.

'And the battle reconstruction – another innocent bystander got in the way?'

'The re-enactment guy? Yes, I had you in my sights and he stepped back and got caught in the crossfire.'

'And the boat? You scuppered the engine?'

'Right again. I know a bit about engines.'

Astrid had another flashback – in the corridor when Emily was helping carry her materials to the car. She'd asked if Astrid would be staying on her boat. Emily must have been snooping around.

'Damn... I should have worked it out when you

mentioned I had a boat. How would you have known that without spying on me?'

'I know,' said Emily, rolling her eyes. 'I was very angry with myself.'

'Nobody's perfect.'

'But you do know, at that stage I was only trying to scare you off. I thought you'd get the message and mind your own business. But no... here we are.'

'Sorry, I guess I'm a bit nosy.' Astrid put the note back in the bag. 'Well, you've got lots of skills; I guess I have to give you that.'

'Thank you. That's what Cressida said about my CV. "Versatile". That was her word – I was a "versatile" candidate.' She gripped the bayonet and stood up. 'Now then, let's go over to the window, shall we?'

'Window?'

'Yes, come on.' Emily flicked the bayonet in the direction of the garden.

Astrid got up and put her bag across her shoulder. The boards creaked as she crossed the room. The shadow of the antler chandelier spread out like cracks in ice on a pond.

She quickly glanced to the high corners of the room. There were no CCTV cameras in this room either – Emily would have made sure of that. 'This is going to take a bit of explaining isn't it, Emily? I mean... what story are you going to cook up now?'

'Mmm... yes.' Emily reached the window and unlatched a panel, pulling it towards her. 'I was getting to that.' She brought a card from her pocket and held it up. There was some writing on it. 'I've made up a list of things Cressida needs to say. A few bullet points so we're on the right page.'

'That's efficient of you.' Astrid stood by the window.

Emily looked at the card to jog her memory. 'A quick round-up then. You, your husband and your uncle organised the whole thing.' She carried on reading the list. 'He'd borrowed the original painting from his friend who ran the tests authenticating it. Uncle Henry painted a copy. You cleaned it up for us and were going to keep quiet and split the cash between the three of you. But then… whoops. Your husband had some falling-out and you decided to come down and shame him instead.'

'How did you know we'd split up?'

'I watched you – the sad crying woman on a boat.'

'Ooh… that stings. Still, not bad, Emily.' She looked out of the window. The gardens were empty. 'Then what?'

She put the card back in her pocket. 'Well, I was working late as usual and found you trying to steal the original Constable.' She pointed further down the wall. There was a frame under a cloth.

'That's it there?'

'Yes, I've copied the keys to Cressida's office and cupboard by the way. I told you, I've thought of everything.' She tapped her finger against her temple. 'Now back to the story – I locked both of the doors and challenged you. That's when you headed out onto the window ledge to escape.' She looked at her watch. 'You know, we'd better crack on. I should really have called the police about now.'

'Okay – so you want me to get up out of the window, on the ledge?'

'Yes, please.' She gripped the bayonet and held it out in front of her. 'If you want to fall off, that's entirely up to you.'

Astrid edged closer to the open window. There was a

stone ledge of around twelve inches. The drop beyond it was thirty feet down to the gravel path.

'Put your bag down then,' said Emily.

'Okay, but…' she unhooked it off her shoulder '…would you mind if I put on some perfume?'

'You have to?'

'I always promised myself that if I was going to die, I'd be wearing Chanel No. 5. You know what my mother used to say?'

Emily shrugged.

'My mother had lots of sayings. All of them were worth ignoring, except this one.' She reached into her bag and brought out the Chanel No. 5 bottle. 'A woman who doesn't wear perfume has no future.' Astrid loosened the stopper. 'You don't wear perfume, do you, Emily?'

'No – now hurry up.' Emily gripped the bayonet tighter.

'But this isn't regular perfume, it's parfum. Do you know the difference, Emily?'

'You can tell me on the ledge.'

Astrid climbed up into the open window, one hand on the edge of the window frame, the other gripping the bottle. She could feel the draught from inside the house pushing against her. 'The difference is the oil content. Parfum is much more concentrated – up to forty per cent.'

Emily put her hands on her hips. 'How fascinating.'

In a single movement, Astrid jumped back into the room and sprayed the bottle into Emily's eyes. She winced in pain and brought both hands up to her face, the bayonet falling from her grasp.

'And it's also £200 more an ounce.' Astrid kicked the blade across the room. It clattered across the boards.

Emily got on all fours, still blinded, and began searching with her hands for the bayonet – like a cat chasing a bell in a ball.

There was a rattle of a key in the lock by the door. A moment later it swung open and Kath strode in, her fists balled up. 'Where is she?'

'Don't worry, I think I've got this,' said Astrid. 'Just pull down that tapestry – we'll wrap her up.'

Emily was still scrambling around on the floor, groaning in pain. Kath reached up to the corner of a tapestry. Harold and Denise swung into the room and quickly measured the situation. Denise seemed more shocked at Kath.

'No, no – stop!' she shouted. 'It's seventeenth century, Flemish.'

Kath let go of the tapestry. Emily rubbed her eyes and got to her knees.

'Quick – let's use something else.' Astrid went over to the fireplace and pulled the rug over from between the two chairs. 'This alright, Denise?'

'Absolutely,' she said, 'it's actually IKEA. Another of the Trust's dirty little secrets.'

Astrid swung the rug over Emily in a cloud of dust. Harold ran forwards and sat on top of it, compressing Emily down among its folds. Kath joined him, sitting on what may well have been Emily's head. 'Well done, Astrid,' said Kath. 'We heard everything on the walkie-talkie. It never switches off, apparently.'

'I know. Thanks for the back-up, everybody.' She looked to Harold and Denise, who were beaming with pride.

Margaret appeared at the doorway. She was breathing heavily. 'Sorry I'm late, the stair-lift was out. I've complained to management about that until I'm blue in the face.' She shuffled forwards and poked the carpet with the stick. 'You under there then, Emily?'

There was a muffled moan from under the rug.

Margaret scanned the room, her eyes stopping at the velvet rope that had been unclipped by the fireplace. 'Oh, no...' she gasped. 'Of all the things you've done, Emily, and now this.' She went over to the rope and clipped it back into place, then came back to the rug. 'Nobody is allowed to go behind the rope. Nobody!' Margaret landed a sharp strike on the most protruding lump in the fabric. Emily gave a sharp howl. It was obviously her head.

'Well then,' said Astrid. 'Who wants to call the police?'

29

Thursday, Day 16

The private mooring for the Haven Hotel was tucked behind a breakwater of concrete blocks that jutted out into the channel. She tied the boat up and set off down the boardwalk. There were a number of red and white *'Mooring for Patrons Only'* signs. She'd just point them out if anyone asked. Nobody did. It was a hot day. Too hot for an argument. Although, there was a good chance she was about to have a blazing one with Simon.

He'd texted ten minutes ago to say he was sitting in the open-air section. A table right at the front. She walked straight into the restaurant and headed down a line of tables arranged along a whitewashed wall. The silk of her Stella McCartney cocktail dress felt warm against her skin. She was glad she wore it. A couple of male diners seemed to agree. A middle-aged man tipped his baseball cap back and tracked her down the aisle. The woman he was with hissed something. 'Huh… no I wasn't…' he muttered. He was.

Simon was at the end table, right in the corner. He

carefully took out his AirPods, tucked them into the top pocket of his white linen shirt and got up slowly, his arms held out in front of him. 'Astrid...'

'Let's not, Simon,' she said, sliding into her seat.

'Okay. I get it. That's cool.' He sat back down and stared at her, his head tipped slightly to the side. 'The dress... I don't remember you buying that?'

'I can't remember either.'

'Well, you look sensational,' he said, flicking his fringe back. 'Just sensational.'

Astrid slipped her bag from her shoulder. 'You look good too, Simon.' It was true. He'd picked up a tan this week, and it suited him. It made him seem much younger, more athletic. 'You promise you'll tell me the truth this time?'

'Promise,' he said, crossing his thumb over his heart.

'Right, well let's start with the Constable. Then we'll get on to us.'

'Fire away.'

'You had nothing to do with it, right?'

'Astrid... of course I wasn't involved.' There was a bottle of mineral water on the table. He poured some into her glass, then filled his own. 'You know that whole spectacle was pretty embarrassing for me, right?'

'I'm glad – that was the idea.' She sipped the water. Good start, Astrid. 'So did the police interview you?'

'Yes, I was given quite a grilling. That young sergeant...'

'Harper.'

'That's him, Harper. He even put me in a cell for a few hours.'

'Oh, poor you, Simon.' She looked out across the bay.

The water glittered in the midday sun. It was time for the *us* questions. A shadow passed over the table.

'How you guys doing?' A waiter in a black polo shirt with 'The Point Restaurant' embroidered near the shoulder was standing over them. 'Can I get you some drinks?'

Simon raised his hand. 'I think we're okay with the mineral water, thanks.'

'Excellent. And do you need more time with the menus?'

'Yes.' Astrid breathed in. 'The thing is, my husband has been cheating on me with my best friend. Well, former best friend. So I'm just going to try and wring out some kind of apology before I have anything to eat.'

'Rrright...' The waiter smiled. 'Ten minutes?'

'Perfect.' Astrid smiled back.

Simon waited until he was out of earshot. 'Astrid... you are going to stay calm?'

'Don't worry – I'll be calm, as long as you answer my questions.'

'Fine... so what do you want to know?' He sunk back in his chair.

'You and Gina – how long?'

'Three months. It's over now.'

'Who started it?'

'Both of us, I suppose. It just sort of happened.'

'So why did you do it?'

'That's a question I ask myself every day, Astrid. I deeply regret what I did, and I am so sorry.' He held out his hand. 'Please.'

'No.' She pushed it out of the way.

'Everyone makes mistakes. And that's what this was – the

worst mistake I've ever made. But I can make it right. I desperately want you back, Astrid.'

'Hah! How can you say that after you got me sacked? Then you march down here and ruin my next job.' She leant forwards. 'And you even took credit for my work. Unbelievable.'

'Astrid, Astrid,' he said, a hangdog expression on his face. 'I was confused and hurt that you'd left. I guess I lashed out...' He reached out slowly and took her hand.

'Simon... Don't.'

He rubbed her finger where her wedding ring used to be. There was only the slightest mark now. 'Let's not throw our marriage away for one mistake. We had everything. A beautiful flat, friends... the job you always dreamed of is still there for you.' He leant forward and she caught a waft of his cologne. It smelt of juniper and vanilla, and she adored it – and he knew that. That's why he'd worn it today. He wasn't playing fair.

She wrenched her hand away. 'No, Simon. What you did was unforgivable.' Her voice trembled. 'You caused me so much pain.'

'I know, but we can get through this. Listen, Astrid – all relationships have their ups and downs.' He drew his chair closer. 'You see, you spend so much time with classical paintings. Those swooning images of romantic love – Venus and Mars, Paris and Helen. But the reality is, relationships aren't like that. There are always rocky patches. You have to just forgive and move on.'

'But I've worked so hard to forget you. So hard.' She closed her eyes and caught another trace of his cologne, and with it that memory. Five years ago. When they first met in that crowded bar. When he whispered to her. She opened her eyes and tried to say something, but the words never came.

'Let's start again, Astrid. A fresh start.' He reached into his pocket and brought out her wedding ring. He put it down on the table between them. 'We'll be an even stronger team than before.'

She slowly reached out and slid the ring towards her.

'Put it on, Astrid.'

She took the ring between her thumb and forefinger and turned it in the light. It felt warm to her touch. The most familiar object she owned.

'That's it. Then we can have a lovely day. I'll order your food, and choose a wine you'll like.' He picked up the menu and opened it.

'Order the food?' She paused. 'You always order my food, don't you?'

'I know what you like.'

'No. No, Simon.' She put the ring down on the table. 'That's not why you do it.'

'Yes, it is. It's because I love you.'

'But it's everything. Tracking me down by my phone. The texts asking me where I am when you're on business. And this dress.' She pinched a fold of silk at her hip. 'I had to hide it from you because you'd disapprove. It's not love, Simon, it's control.'

'That's unfair.'

'No, it's not.' She snorted. 'I don't want Venus and Mars, I just want to order my own bloody food.' She took her sunglasses off and put them in her bag. Because she wanted to see him clearly. For the last time. 'And I can't believe it's taken me this long to realise it. Right under my nose was the biggest fake of all – you, Simon.' She stood up.

'Where are you going?' He was on his feet.

'I'm getting on my boat and I'm leaving.'

'Boat? I didn't know you could sail a boat.'

'Neither did I. And who knows what else I can do without you.' And she left, without looking back. She'd have preferred the fake line to be the one ringing in his ears. She was proud of that. The boat line was pretty good, though. Still, other than that, the whole thing had gone perfectly.

Grub arrived at the boat with Sheepdip just after five. He handed over a small cloth bag of bits and pieces – a small lead, chewed tennis ball, bone-shaped treats. 'Bribes' he called them.

She told him all about the evening before and he listened without saying a word, until the point Emily was trussed up under the rug and the game was up. He put his hand on her shoulder. 'You did it then. I'm proud of you.'

'Thanks,' she said.

'And your boss, Cressida? Have they arrested her yet?'

'Yes – I got a call from Harper. He said she agreed to meet him in her office. She was all packed and ready to go when he arrived.'

'She sounds organised.'

'You've no idea, Grub.' She laughed. 'Only thing I'm annoyed about is it looks like my soon-to-be ex-husband is in the clear.'

'Your ex-husband is involved?'

'He's an art conservator too. He came down from London

to assess the Constable. Seems he didn't have anything to do with the fake though.'

'So that's it? You have all the answers.'

'Almost.' She looked at Sheepdip who was sitting obediently on the deck. 'Almost.'

He wished them luck and set off back down the path. Sheepdip watched him go then came trotting over to Astrid. He sat by her feet, waiting for orders.

'Right then, Sheepdip. Where shall we go?' Sheepdip stared at her.

Maybe you had to stress it a bit more? Like those British tourists on holiday when they ask locals for directions. Even when the person tells them they don't speak English, they repeat themselves a little louder. Then start miming.

Astrid got down on all fours in front of him. 'Where. Do. You. Want. To. Go?' she said loudly, her hand sweeping out to the countryside.

Sheepdip tipped his head to one side. Astrid reached into the bag and brought out the lead. Sheepdip saw it, dodged over the rail of the boat and pattered off down the boardwalk. 'Not a fan of the lead then, Sheepdip?' she muttered.

She caught him up on the path. He stayed ahead of her by a few yards, checking behind him until she'd put the lead back in the bag. Then he sped up, zig-zagging from one side of the path to the other and ferreting about in the undergrowth – so all you could see were the tops of the cow parsley rattling and swaying like umbrellas in a storm. He popped out again, and chased off down the path.

They followed the same route past the bridge that she had taken a couple of days ago – with a few detours. Everything seemed to be worthy of inspection to Sheepdip – clumps of bracken, fallen trees and cow pats were all given a good sniff. He did give the farm a wide berth, scuttling cautiously past on the other side of the path. Maybe this was where he'd fallen into the sheep dip?

In an hour or so they reached high fields that looked back down on the valley, with Hanbury tucked away in a bend in the river. Astrid sat down and brought out the bag that Grub had given them. Inside she found a greasy strip of something dried and meaty. He held it down on the grass with both paws as if it was going to get away. As he chewed at it, she stroked the soft top of his head. How did she feel so close to him, when they'd spent so little time together?

When Sheepdip finished snaffling down the last gristly strands of the treat, he got up and wandered back down the hill. They took the same route back through a wood and along the path. At the boat, he hopped over the rail and sprawled on the warm smooth wood and slowly got his breath back.

She went downstairs to the cabin and ran a glass of cold water for herself. A cereal bowl half-full of water for him. If their walk together had been about finding the last pieces of the jigsaw, it had been a failure. A silly idea. There were still lots of unanswered questions about her uncle. But it had been worth it to spend time with him. It was time to give him back now. Then she realised that she didn't have Grub's address. They'd only ever met at the Angler's Arms.

She waited for Sheepdip to stop drinking from the bowl and reached for the brass medal that hung from his collar.

On the front was his name – *'Sheepdip'*. She turned the medal in her fingers. There was an address. *'Curlew's Rest. Hanbury. Care of Henry Swift.'*

She breathed out sharply. 'Henry!' She crossed her arms and looked down at him. 'Sheepdip?' He began drinking the water again. 'Are you Henry's dog?'

Sheepdip looked up from his bowl, water dripping from the whiskers on his chin. His eyes twinkling. The name Henry had jogged a thousand memories – all of them good, it seemed. He stood up and glanced about the boat.

'No... don't worry. It's fine, sweetheart.' She got out another treat from the bag and set it on the boards. He pounced on it and settled into chewing.

Then she checked the back of the medal again, studying it carefully. There in the corner was a smear of paint. White – cloud white. She hurried downstairs again and brought up her work briefcase. Had the paint been used on the boat? A fence? A painting?

She reached for a small bottle that said *'Silver Chromate'* on the label. Tipping a drop of clear liquid onto her thumb she rubbed the white mark on the medal. Her thumb came back bright red – as if it had been pricked by a needle. There was zinc oxide in the paint – there had to be. The paint was Zinc White, an essential oil paint for any serious artist. Uncle Henry must have used it to paint the waves and clouds. And the lighthouse. He had created the fake Constable. Emily was at least telling the truth about that.

Sheepdip rolled on his side and scratched his pink tummy with a back paw. 'Sheepdip?' She applied her sweetest, most authoritative voice. 'Where's Uncle Henry?' It reminded her of the TV show *Lassie* that she used to watch as a child.

Lassie would always rush off to find a burning barn or a child down a well. It was ridiculous. But hey, that's all she had right now. Sheepdip rolled back onto his feet. He shook himself, then trotted off down the boardwalk.

Astrid followed him as he turned left onto the path. She caught up with him when he was almost at the boatyard. This time he ignored the verges and carried straight on, crossing the concrete slipway and over to the side of the big shed. There was a door there, which she hadn't noticed before. He sat down on the step and peered up at her.

'You sure?'

Sheepdip scratched at the bottom of the door. Astrid knocked a couple of times then stood back and waited. Eventually Cobb opened the door. He looked at her, then down to Sheepdip.

'Okay.' He nodded. 'You better come in.'

When she was inside Cobb went over to a flight of bare wooden steps that ran up to the upper level. He indicated that Astrid should go first. She started to climb, Sheepdip hopping up the steps ahead of her.

At the top level there was a cord that hung from the ceiling. She pulled it and there was a clicking and humming. A row of three overhead lamps lit up the space. She stepped forward to the centre of the room, turned slowly to take it in. It had been an artist's studio. There were a few canvases, landscapes mostly, propped against the wall. In the corner was a simple wooden stool placed in front of an easel. The floor was speckled with different-coloured paint.

'I get it now,' said Astrid. She went over to a painting of the river. There was a bend she recognised further upstream. 'This is where he painted?'

'Yeah, I let him have the space. There was no room on the boat.'

She brushed some dust off the painting. 'He was great, wasn't he?'

'Incredible. He could have made a lot of money. But he didn't care. He'd just give these paintings away to everyone he met.'

'So you knew he'd faked the Constable?'

'Yes, he told me all about it.' Cobb went over to the window and drew back the curtains. There was a view up to the hills above the village. 'It was his master plan. You know…' He paused.

'I need the whole truth today, Cobb.'

He nodded. 'Okay then. He'd had some heart problems. So just in case, he wanted to leave everything to the person he cared most about. He said he didn't get on with your father – they'd argued about something he couldn't tell me.'

'That sounds right.'

'So, that left you – his favourite niece. Henry wrote his will with you as the sole benefactor. Then when this marketing woman at the Trust…'

'Cressida?'

'That's it – Cressida. She offered him a deal to copy a Constable, and he agreed straight away. But he said he'd add something to it that would give it away. It was a game. Everything was a game to Henry. Like the notes he gave you.'

'The first rung of the ladder?'

'Yeah – it's on the fridge magnet. Let me get it.'

'Honestly, Cobb, there's no need.' But he was already up and on his way down the steps. When he came back, he had a book in his hand. 'It might be in here.' He showed her the cover. It was an anthology of poems.

'I thought you said it was on a fridge magnet? I didn't...'

'Didn't have me down as a big reader, did you?'

'I guess...' she said sheepishly.

He found what he was looking for in the index, then rifled back through the pages. 'Here we are – William Yeats.' He handed the book over.

She was about to read the poem, but he was ahead of her. 'Now that my ladder's gone.' He spoke gently. The words flowing in a slow stream. 'I must lie down where all the ladders start. In the foul rag-and-bone shop of the heart.' His voice trailed off, and she felt sad. Not because of the poem, but because he had stopped talking. He did have the most beautiful voice.

'That's lovely, Cobb,' she said.

'Yeats wrote the poem when he'd run out of ideas – he was stuck. At the bottom of the ladders.'

'Starting from scratch again?'

'Exactly. Just like you. Henry told me you had this amazing talent for art, but you gave it up. You'd got this big job at a gallery. Married the boss. Fancy flat by the river.'

'It's true.' She went and sat in the chair by the easel. Ran her finger along the ledge that held the canvas. 'Everything I've done since I've been here. It's felt like he's been watching over me. Cleaning the boat, taking it out, discovering the view of the Constable out at sea. Not the murders – he couldn't have predicted those. But the rest... he'd left a puzzle for me?'

'Yes – but it wasn't about you discovering a fake. It was about you rediscovering who you used to be. That's what

Henry said. He wanted you to be that happy, brilliant kid he knew all those summers ago.'

Astrid sat there in silence for a moment. 'I get it now.' She turned to him. He had his back to her, staring at the view. 'And you knew all along, right?'

'Yeah. I'm really sorry.' He faced her. 'I felt bad not telling you. Grub too. We were the only ones Henry told. He insisted we keep it secret.'

'Don't worry, Cobb. And I'm sorry to have underestimated you.'

'That's okay – everyone does.' He shrugged. 'Hey, there's something else he left you.'

'Really?'

'Actually. It's *someone* else.' Cobb walked over to the far wall. Sheepdip was lying under an old radiator. Cobb picked him up and pulled him to his chest. Sheepdip gazed at Astrid. 'He's your dog now. If you want him?'

'I thought he was Grub's dog?'

'Grub's been looking after him for you – until now.' Cobb put Sheepdip down on the floor. He padded over to her. 'If you want him, that is?'

Astrid knelt down in front of him and rubbed him under the chin. Sheepdip closed his eyes in pleasure. 'Of course I do.'

They all wandered to the door, and when it was opened, Sheepdip rushed off across the yard back to the boat. Astrid stepped out into the sunshine and spun round to face Cobb. He was leaning against the doorframe. Hands planted in his pockets. Too handsome for his own good. But that wasn't all of it. He was the most honest person she'd met. Someone who knew exactly who he was. Someone you could trust.

'Hey, Cobb – you fancy getting a drink some time?'

'Just me and you?'

'Me and you.'

'Let me see…' He rubbed his chin. 'I'll have to check my diary. But yeah… why not?' He grinned that annoying grin, and shut the door behind him.

She stood there for a moment. Not ready to walk away. That nagging feeling you have when you've left something behind. Except this was something she hadn't said. She'd wanted to tell him what she really thought of him. That he was amazing. She wanted to grip his shoulders and kiss him hard. And not let go. But she hadn't said it, and that was okay. Because there was time. There was lots of time now.

One Week Later

The weather had been fine and sunny over the previous seven days. It was shaping up to be one of the warmest summers for a long while. People said she'd 'brought the weather with her'. It wasn't something she'd ever been told before – that she was responsible for much sunshine in others' lives. Until now, maybe. Now that she was happy. It was as if someone had turned up her brightness setting.

She greeted strangers who passed by the boat with a wave. She stopped to talk to other dog walkers, rather than hurrying past. Sheepdip was pleased to meet any old dog. He'd run circles around anything with fur, whatever the size.

Astrid had worked hard on the boat and it was cleaning up nicely. She'd had plenty of time now she wasn't employed by the English Trust. Head Office had offered her the job back but she'd said no. Sherborne Hall was in her past. They agreed to pay up for the full contract so she had enough money for a while. In return, she did one favour for them: she carefully removed the lighthouse from the original Constable. It had been an easy job as Uncle Henry had used a watercolour. The Constable was now returned to its former glory.

She'd also finally got round to writing to her father. She told him all about Uncle Henry and how he'd left her *Curlew's Rest*. Inside the letter she slipped a sketch of the boat she'd done in watercolour and ink. And she sent a postcard to Clare. A simple message saying sorry for not staying in touch. It was a start.

Sergeant Harper was in a fine mood too. He dropped round to see her on the Saturday morning. He was in shorts – navy blue with a crease that aimed at pale knees.

Everyone, he told her, was singing his praises down at the station. These had been the biggest crimes they'd seen for a long time, and Harper's involvement hadn't gone unnoticed. There was talk of him being fast-tracked to the Bournemouth branch.

Harper admitted that he may have downplayed Astrid's involvement in the case, but was sure she wouldn't mind. In fact, he'd told his bosses he'd been keeping an eye on both Cressida and Emily for some time. 'Ready to pounce,' he said, making a clawing gesture in the air that sent Sheepdip diving under Astrid's foldaway chair.

Astrid told him she was more than happy for him to take the credit, which was true. Her career as a gallery conservator was over – which she was more than happy with. So it was nice to think that she'd given Harper's career a boost. Anyway, it was best that the case was closed now. Especially as the police still had no idea who forged the Constable. 'If only we knew?' she'd said with a smile.

'If only,' he replied and he closed his notebook with a shrug, as if this was his gift to her – not to ask any more questions.

He left about half an hour before her guests started

to arrive. Muraki was first, squeezing through the reeds, a suitcase pressed to his chest. He looked around in astonishment. 'What is this, Astrid?' he said, stumbling aboard.

'It's a houseboat, Muraki, not the lost city of Atlantis.'

'Yeah, but you're living on it.' He put his suitcase down. 'I mean, you're the last person I'd think would live on a boat.'

'It's good to see you,' she said, embracing him.

Next was Kath, who was wearing a wide-brimmed hat and a smart black dress – the first item of clothing she'd seen on her that didn't have marker pen or logos for local companies on it. 'It's going to be posh, right?'

'I guess, yes.'

Kath spotted Muraki, who was inspecting the front of the boat. She smacked her lips. 'Now then, Astrid. Where have you been hiding that one?'

'Oh, that's a friend of mine from the gallery – Muraki. Go and introduce yourself.'

Kath brushed down her skirt and set off.

The volunteers were next. Margaret bagged the last folding chair and asked for a cup of tea with three sugars before even saying hello.

'Hey, Astrid – you know that she got the VIP tours job?' said Harold.

'Yes, she told me. Isn't it great?'

'Brilliant,' Denise said. 'I'm much happier that she got the job than me. They're giving me more shifts in the gift shop... so, it's all good.'

Grub arrived a minute later, in cargo shorts and a blue Hawaiian shirt. Sheepdip rubbed against his ankles.

Astrid looked at them both. 'Thanks for letting me have him, Grub. I hope you don't miss him too much?'

'Hey. He'll be much happier with you, Astrid. I can't really give him the exercise.' Sheepdip went back under Astrid's chair. 'I can always pop in and say hi.'

'Any time.'

'And you know...' he wrung his hands '...I'm sorry I couldn't explain what was going on before. Henry made us swear to keep it quiet.'

'Hey, don't worry about it. Cobb explained everything.'

'You did great by the way. I knew you'd get there,' he said, squeezing past towards the front of the boat.

Next was Anthony Dutton, who climbed on board and immediately noticed the box of tools laid out on the deck. 'Hey, Astrid,' he said, pointing at them. 'If you're carrying out any renovations on the boat yourself, you can offset them against your self-assessment tax return. I'd be happy to look after the paperwork.'

'That's good to know,' Astrid said.

Finally, Cobb arrived wearing smart black trousers and a pressed light blue shirt. He studied the newly varnished deck, muttered 'good job' and went round the boat to examine the rest of her handiwork. Then he slipped the rope from the prow and joined her beside the dashboard. They didn't speak until they were near the first marker buoys.

'You look stylish,' she said to him.

'Thought I'd make an effort.' He scruffed up his hair with his fingers. 'I was thinking about brushing my hair as well. But then, you know... life is too short.'

'It is.' She looked around the boat. Everyone was seated

on the deck watching the islands glide past. 'Life is too short to be with people who make every day seem long.'

He nodded, letting the words sink in. 'Is that from a poem?'

'No, Cobb, that one's from a fridge magnet.'

He laughed, then ran his hand over his neck.

'Wait.' She put her hand in her pocket and brought out the silver chain. 'I found this on the boat a couple of weeks ago.'

'A couple of weeks?' There was a slight smile at the corner of his mouth.

She unclipped the clasp, and put it around his neck. 'Yeah.' She felt herself blushing. 'But hey, it looks too good on you.' Her thumb brushed his neck. His hand darted up and took hers. Then he gently kissed the backs of her fingers.

'Astrid,' he said.

'Yes?'

'I'm not going anywhere.'

She turned away from him to hide the huge idiotic grin that had spread across her face. He took the wheel and centred the prow between the markers. 'Let's get her out on the water, shall we?'

They all strode up the boardwalk to the Haven Hotel. Astrid spoke to a waitress, who counted the rest of the party over her shoulder with a confused expression. Perhaps she was trying to figure out how such an unusual mix of people all knew each other. She eventually smiled and escorted them to a line of small tables that had been pushed together. Then she went off to get a bowl of water for Sheepdip.

Everyone took their seats. Kath and Muraki were on either side of Astrid. Muraki gazed out over the channel. A flotilla of boats, jet skis and yachts jostled forwards through the choppy water. 'This is wicked, Astrid. I had no idea it was so close to London.'

'I know, you'll have to come down more often.'

'I will,' said Muraki. 'And out there, on the horizon. What's that?'

Astrid squinted into the sunshine. Far out at sea was a sliver of land. 'You know. I've never noticed that. Kath, you know?'

'Course,' said Kath. 'That's the Isle of Wight. Never been, but it's supposed to be beautiful.'

'Maybe I'll get over there some time.' She turned back to the group. A few of them had opened the menus and were frowning at the prices. Margaret was shaking her head as she ran her thumb down the list. Astrid tapped the side of her glass with a knife. Everyone turned to her. 'Listen, guys. I'm getting this – it's my treat.'

There were some murmurs of protest. 'Seriously, and I'll be annoyed if you don't have whatever you want.' Seconds later and they were all reading the menus again. Kath had already reached the *House Specialities*. 'Brilliant!' She cracked her knuckles. 'They've got lobster.'

'Do you like lobster?' said Astrid.

'Dunno. Never had it before. But I was rock-pooling as a kid, and one pinched me.'

'In a rock-pool?'

'Yeah, well it was probably a lobster. Anyway – it's payback time.'

The waitress came and took the drinks order. When she

returned and handed them out, Harold waved over from the other end of the table. 'What about a toast then, Astrid?'

'Oh, well, yes. We should.' Astrid held her glass of wine by the stem. She stood up and faced them. 'There's someone who's not here today. And is greatly missed by those who knew him.' She caught Cobb and Grub look at each other and nod. 'Someone who saw life as a game. And enjoyed playing it every day.' She raised her glass. 'To Uncle Henry.'

'To Uncle Henry,' they all chimed, clinking their glasses.

Then they started chatting again, the conversation bubbling over the sound of the waves on the rocks below them.

The waitress, who'd been standing by the low wall, came over to Astrid. 'Madam. How would you like to pay for this? Cash or card?'

'Card please.' She reached into her bag and brought out a credit card from her purse. 'Actually,' she held it back. 'Could you charge it to my room please? I'm staying with my husband – he'll settle our final bill.'

'Of course. And what's the name?'

She held up her credit card. 'It's Astrid – Mrs Astrid Kisner.'

'No problem, madam.' She backed away.

Muraki and Kath stared at her.

'And that, my friends,' said Astrid, 'is the last time I ever use that name.'

Acknowledgements

This is my first book. It was written over the lockdowns of 2020/2021, when escaping London and living on a boat in Poole seemed like a good idea. I never thought it would get published – and it wouldn't have, if it hadn't been for the following people.

My superstar agent Thérèse Coen at Hardman & Swainson for her sage advice and being an all-round good egg.

Thorne Ryan at Head of Zeus for her irresistible enthusiasm for this story and her brilliant work on the edits.

Stuart White, the founder of WriteMentor, who's done more to support aspiring writers than anyone I know.

My wise and wonderful writer friends Jules in Edinburgh and Caroline in Newcastle.

Lisa Cumming for casting a keen conservator's eye over the first draft.

Rana Das-Gupta, who I bumped into on the Isle of Wight ferry and kindly invited me for a weekend's sailing on his Fisher 37.

All the volunteers and staff I met at the English Trust's Osterley House in West London. Of course, none of the characters in the book are based on any of them.

WhatsApp buddies Damian, Ken, Jon, Hag and Joe 'Smooth' Kennedy for the high-quality lockdown banter. Plus, Phil 'Dog' Delahunty whose feedback that 'it wasn't as bad as I thought it was going to be' inspires me to continue writing.

And my family – always my family... the greatest bunch of pugs on the planet.

About the Author

M.H. ECCLESTON has had a fairly meandering career – starting out as a radio presenter for the BBC, then staying at the Beeb as a journalist and producer for six years. After that, it's a bit of a blur – he spent a couple of decades, at least, freelancing as a foreign correspondent, TV presenter, voice-over artist and film critic. For the last few years he's been a full-time screenwriter and now novelist, with some wildlife gardening in the summer to keep himself sane and pay the bills.